Bob Fiddaman is a two-time human rights awardee and creator of The Fiddaman Blog, a popular research project highlighting the nefarious activities of the pharmaceutical industry and global medicine regulators. He is also the former poetry slam champion of Birmingham, UK (1999). In 2011, his first book, 'The Evidence, However, is Clear: The Seroxat Scandal', was published by Chipmunka Publishing.

Growing up, he wrote many short stories and poems for family, friends, and, in later years, work colleagues.

He has always had a keen interest in religion, the paranormal, and ufology.

Born in London, but living most of his life in Birmingham, Bob now lives in Boquete, Panama with the love of his life, Kristina. He has three grown children, Danny, Marc, and Gary.

From a very early age, I started seeing repeating numbers. Now, it appears, I am in the midst of connecting to repeating letters.

This is for KK.

Bob Fiddaman

# No Other Man

AUSTIN MACAULEY PUBLISHERS™

LONDON • CAMBRIDGE • NEW YORK • SHARJAH

A CIP catalogue record for this title is available from the British Library.

ISBN 9781035806201 (Paperback)
ISBN 9781035806218 (ePub e-book)

www.austinmacauley.com

First Published 2023
Austin Macauley Publishers Ltd®
1 Canada Square
Canary Wharf
London
E14 5AA

I'd like to acknowledge those spiritual beings who guided me throughout this whole writing process. I cannot prove they were around me, I just felt they were. Their guidance unlocked this story that was held captive inside my head. This, along with a musical soundtrack and imaginary silver screen provided me with an insight, my own movie premiere, if you will. It was a silent movie until I made the characters come alive. Musical composers Hans Zimmer, James Horner, Danny Elfman, to name but a few, provided me the music, via Spotify, to accompany the scenes.

I'd also like to acknowledge an old school teacher (who shall remain nameless). "Fiddaman", he once said, "You'll never make anything of yourself."

Thank you for being the driving force of my imagination, sir.

A very special thank you to my publishing team, Austin Macauley. From the editing to art departments, they have been a superb professional outfit that I hope to be associated with for the second, and possibly third instalment, of this story you are about to read.

# Prologue

Don Williamson was born in Birmingham on 31 July 1964.

Teresa O'Brien and Sara Louise Conway were present at his birth, even though they had been murdered some years previous, Sara in 1948 and Teresa in 1957.

Karen Crawford was born in Idaho on 21 April 1974.

Sebastian Chantel and his brother, Anthony, were present at her birth. They, just like Teresa O'Brien and Sara Louise Conway, had been murdered some years previous. Both had died on 19 March 1969.

Teresa, Sara, Sebastian and Anthony all had wings.

**For Dad
The Gentleman**

# Chapter One
# The Poem

## God's Thumbprint in the Sky

*God's thumbprint in the sky Alongside stationary pinpricks of light*
*Some blinking, twinkling.*
*A black duvet with countless holes Hiding the light beyond infinity. There's a*
*question mark tilted Maybe it holds all the answers?*
*When the sun sleeps*
*The sky explodes with dot-to-dot images.*
*Tonight they are clearly visible.*
*The cotton wool balls are somewhere else, Sprinkling their waters, putting up*
*blinds.*
*Someone, somewhere, shoots bullets across the sky, I see them flash by.*
*There's only one colour beyond the duvet*
*Where there is no night, no darkness.*
*Light beyond the realms of understanding, The holes giving us hope.*
*God's thumbprint a constant reminder of what we are.*
*And where we are going.*

Don Williamson, 2001

# Chapter Two
# 13 Years Later

Katy Johansson had been out when it happened. She felt the pang of pain, it was a pain associated with loss, that feeling of a sudden emptiness, that gut-wrenching feeling that you are alone and that you seriously fucked up with your decision making abilities. The pangs of pain were new to her, she had never experienced them before and she found them increasingly difficult to deal with.

In the past, she had finished with boyfriends, she felt no guilt or shame but her relationship with Don was different; she felt pain and, at times, it was intense.

Going behind Don's back and sleeping with another man, at the time, didn't bother her in the slightest but every now and again, since the split with Don, it would come back to niggle her. The other voices inside her head tried to keep the guilt and shame at bay, those voices were successful for the most part but the guilt and shame kept knocking on the door of Katy's mind.

She'd had a one night stand with Hjalmar while she was with him and after she'd told Don that she couldn't see any future for them, she met with Hjalmar again. In total they had three dates. A meal, a bouquet of flowers and two romps in the bed with Hjalmar, who had a body that every woman dreamed of. Sadly he was just an in-and-out type of man when it came to sex.

No foreplay, no exploration, no dirty talking or role playing; he was nowhere near as exciting as Don. It was the infidelity that excited Katy.

She finished with Hjalmar on their third date, she told him that she just wasn't ready yet for another relationship. She had told him about Don, in fact Hjalmar grew tiresome of Katy's insistence to talk about her ex-lover from England. Hjalmar took it on the chin, paid the restaurant bill then phoned a fuck buddy called Viktoria.

Katy felt deeply ashamed of fucking Hjalmar behind Don's back, her shame somewhat lifted when she remembered how Viktoria, Hjalmar's fuck buddy, only had him for one night. She'd never see him again. Men like that need their balls cut off, she thought. Katy smiled at that thought, at the memory.

*** 

The Kraken was busier than usual tonight. An all-male stag party was visible by their tee-shirts emblazoned with *BRIDEGROOM SECURITY*. One single male from their party, presumably the husband-to-be, was wearing a tee shirt that said, *THE END IS NEAR, BUY ME A BEER*.

The all-male party was loud, brash and drunk. They were all from England. She wasn't physically attracted to any of them, to be honest she found it difficult to understand what they were saying because of their regional English accents. She wasn't looking for sex, not tonight, at least not penetration. Sex, to Katy at least, was much more than penetration.

"Hello, is it true what they say about Swedish women?" One of the all- male party had asked. Another, "My cock died earlier, can I bury it in you?" was apparently an attempt at humour. She smiled at the comments even though she found them lewd and disgusting. It was an act that she had perfected, an Oscar winning performance yet again from Katy Johansson. Meryl Streep, eat your heart out, she thought, as she continued to engage in the flirting.

A man called Luke, was from the stag party. He latched on to her when his friends had approached her, he was basically playing the shining knight in armour in the hope that he may get lucky with Katy. Katy knew this, she could read men quite easily, especially drunken men, they were basically pigs on heat, she thought. He spoke with a different accent to the one that his friends were speaking, one she could understand better, one she was familiar with.

He sounded just like Don but the similarities ended there. He stood over six-feet tall and had bulbous eyes that enlarged to an even bigger size each time he looked at Katy's cleavage, deciding to wear a low-cut top earlier that evening she knew she would draw the attention she wanted, she needed. Her brief conversation with him ended when he asked her if she liked anal sex. She wasn't offended at the question, she was offended at how the bulbous giant had thought that she was that type of woman.

In truth, Katy wasn't scared to experiment when it came to sex but she didn't want to let the lanky lech know. She took a last sip of her drink then whispered in his ear, "Watch me." She left him standing at the bar. He could do nothing more

15

than to look at the half empty glass Katy had left behind, the only evidence of her being a pink lipstick mark around the rim of her glass.

She turned to look back and saw him pick up the glass and then look towards her direction. She headed slowly towards the exit, for a brief moment her eyes met his. She motioned him towards her then exited the fire safety door. She knew he would follow her. The bulbous buffoon couldn't resist her, most men couldn't when she was in a playful, teasing mood.

Once through the exit door, the Stockholm icy air hit her face. She reached into the pocket of her jeans and pulled out her car keys, she then rummaged through her bag feeling for a box of cigarettes and a lighter. She lit her Marlboro Red, carefully cupping her left hand over the flame to stop the intrusion of the icy wind. She inhaled then exhaled before hearing the exit door behind her open.

"Just like fucking clockwork, so fucking predictable," she muttered under her breath.

"Follow me, my car is over by the food-truck," she told him. He jogged to her like an excited schoolboy then asked if they were going far as he hadn't told his friends inside that he was leaving.

She stopped mid-stride and grabbed the back of his neck, pushing it and his head towards her open mouth. She slipped her tongue inside his mouth and kissed him hard for at least 20 seconds. She then pulled away, knowing that her tongue inside his mouth had the desired effect in arousing him.

"We're going as far as you want too, baby," she told him before asking, "Just tell me how far you want to go?"

He let out a childish scream of excitement and moved in for another kiss. Katy turned her cheek and prompted him to follow her to the car, taking the same route to it that she had always done, out of sight of prying eyes, and more importantly, security cameras.

He walked with her and tried to make more conversation; she found him tedious, she found most men tedious. He was weak, he'd be easy prey.

***

The accent was the trigger of her emotions. She went home that evening with Don on her mind. She'd had fun with the bulbous lech. She'd given him what he wanted then gave herself what she wanted.

She was now approaching her apartment door and she recollected how Don had carried her into her apartment one night, *Just carrying you over the threshold sweetheart*, he had told her. One recollection led to another. Filling her kettle to make herself a cup of tea brought back memories of Don standing there, in her kitchen, filling the kettle, making her dinner, emptying her washing machine, pampering her with his sweetness.

Nothing else was important, the evening at The Kraken was all but a distant memory, as was the drive home from the wooded area north of The Kraken

Katy slipped out of her clothes and threw them into the washing machine.

She'd managed to stain them that night. "Fucking red wine," she said as she slammed shut the washing machine door and then sat for a while staring as water filled her machine. It was trance-like. She watched her washing machine fill, the water soon turned pink. Each rotation of the washing tumbler would wipe away the evidence like an artist would erase a poorly sketched pair of hands.

15 minutes later, she showered before getting into bed. Being in bed triggered the memory of Don holding on to her as if she was the most important person in the world, never once letting go of her whilst they slept until morning. She missed hearing his breathing, and she missed feeling the heat of his body next to her. She rearranged the spare pillow, tonight it would be Don. She put her arm over it and brought it close to her before wrapping her leg over it.

She missed Don. She was in love with him.

Earlier tonight, at The Kraken, had brought back her love for Don, it had never really gone away, not properly anyhow. She had merely buried it in an effort to move on in her life, a decision she deeply regretted. Katy was the master of burying memories, when she wanted to, that is.

It had been a while since they had last made contact. She had written him a 'reasons why' email; he had responded but she never made any effort to respond back. She needed closure and just didn't want to keep up the correspondence because she knew that he was hurting and prolonging the email thread would have prolonged his hurt.

She knew that in the long run, by not replying it did both her and Don big favours. It didn't mean she loved him less per se, or that she didn't care, she just didn't want to hold Don back and more importantly, didn't want to hold herself back.

Don had been different to her past boyfriends. He was a gentleman, he believed in the art of seduction and foreplay that to Don wasn't just about the body, it was about the mind. He treated her well, helped her around her apartment, even washed sheets which Katy found unusual as she had never met a man who would wash sheets once every week as Don did. What a fool she had been to let him go.

She felt no guilt in sleeping with Hjalmar while Don had been back at her apartment carrying out household chores. She didn't even feel the guilt when she returned home that night to a candlelit dinner prepared with love by Don. She didn't even feel any guilt when Don had made love to her that night. She never showered after returning home from Hjalmar's place, she still had traces of him inside her.

Katy had a unique ability to not feel guilt, at times she did, anyhow.

Tonight she felt differently. She did feel guilt at cheating on Don all those months ago. She also felt guilt at finishing with him and cutting off ties about a week ago; a week in which she had found lust and carried out what the voices in her head told her too. Yes, she wanted to move forward but she wanted Don to be part of that new journey.

Maybe it was the guilt or because a new year was approaching, maybe it was the thought of being alone as 2014 slipped into 2015, or maybe, she thought, they were meant to be. It all stemmed from the English pig who had been ogling her earlier that evening in The Kraken. Earlier he was breathing hard and fast. She had aroused him to the point of no return, that's all she could remember, the rest was a blur

She recalled beckoning him whilst standing at the exit door in The Kraken, she even remembered Silvana Imam's *Ta Av Dig* playing in the background as part of DJ Pappa Jay's set. The kids loved him, they loved his choice of music, they gyrated in unison, each making lewd dance moves to the lines, *Du är så sexig, gör mig så girig,du är så lättklädd, så ivrig.*

That's all she could remember, the events were like a jig-saw puzzle, only Katy couldn't care less if she could piece them together or not. She couldn't even recall how she had spilled red wine down her top, she didn't even like red wine but was partial to white.

*** 

Luke, the English tourist, was now deep in the woods, his head bludgeoned. The second blow was the fatal one, the first merely made him incoherent.

18

It came out of nowhere while she leaned forward so he could suck on her erect nipples.

He was excited as was Katy, but both had different reasons.

He didn't see the hammer Katy had placed on the back seat earlier that evening.

*** 

She reached for the glass of water on her night stand along with it the boxes of Haloperidol and Aripiprazole, both marked with the stamp of 'Valkyries University Hospital'. She swallowed her pills then replaced them back on the night stand along with the empty glass. She switched off the lamp and became encompassed in darkness.

Bringing the pillow, and the memory of Don Williamson closer to her, Katy drifted off to sleep; her psychotic actions from earlier that evening buried deep in her mind, as was the abuse she suffered at the hands of her uncle when she was a little girl.

# Chapter Three

Don Williamson was 50; he was divorced and at a point where his life had reached a crossroads. That's matters of the heart for you. His shower had been slowly trickling water for the past 5 minutes, the slow trickle was neither too hot nor too cold, and it wasn't even in between, being more cold than hot. His landlord had made umpteen promises to fix the flow.

Don had just about given up any hope of feeling warmth whilst taking a shower; pissing on yourself would bring more satisfaction, he thought. It often did.

He worked from home, a two-bedroom apartment, via his laptop, performing searches for a Swedish law firm who specialised in fighting for compensation for those injured by medical devices. The work was long but paid the bills and gave Don a comfortable lifestyle. At times, he'd had to work through the night, researching devices and manning the firm's email account for potential clients.

The workload increased on the back of the firm's press releases in various media outlets. More awareness about potential claims meant more people inquiring if they had a case or not. He afforded the luxury of working wherever he wanted, all he needed was his laptop and an internet connection, and of course, an ability to speak fluent Swedish.

Since his divorce, back in 2001, he'd had a string of one night stands, some out of boredom, some out of pure wanton lust, some because female friends had, overnight, turned into insatiable fuck buddies. He still remained friends with the fuck buddies but didn't really forge any strong relationships with his one-nighters.

Janine Preston had been a friend of his since his childhood. She was married at just 17, divorced at 23. Don had been out drinking one night at his local; he'd saw Janine and they reacquainted themselves, talking all night about their childhood days over Kings Norton Park. They had always had a good friendship growing up.

He'd even helped her through her divorce by arranging a get-together of old friends, just to cheer her up. Janine had felt amorous after she and her friends had bumped into Don one night. He had popped in to a bar in Birmingham city centre, he'd only gone in to kill the time before his train arrived for his short trip home.

He ended up back at Janine's place that night. They had both consented but they both didn't really enjoy the experience of the aftermath. It was kind of awkward to face one another after that, but they still kept in touch, albeit via Facebook.

Ruth Hope was another fuck buddy. Don had worked with Ruth during the early 2000's. He knew more about her life than she did. They ended up fucking down an alleyway one cold December night. They both knew the score, both knew they had to face one another at work the next day, both knew that it was for one night only.

Their work relationship continued after that fling. They even had sex on other occasions, detaching themselves from love whilst attaching themselves to lust.

Bridgette Gillespie had been Don's neighbour for almost 3 years; when his wife left him he had been offered support from Bridgette. He didn't really fancy her much. She had red hair and he wasn't really a fan of red heads, something that was always in his repartee when telling jokes to complete strangers in bars whilst under the influence of alcohol, "I went out with a red head once, no hair but a big fucking red head."

Bridgette Gillespie and Don ended up in bed together after she had knocked on his door brandishing a cake she had baked for him. It was just one night, neither wanted more.

All three were now married and although, he still kept in touch with them, he would never see them in the fuck buddy light again, unless of course they divorced. Messing around with married women wasn't Don's thing. His wife, Trudy, of 6 years had shit on him from a great height with a man whom she worked with at the local bakery and he knew the pain of infidelity; a pain that he would never inflict on another human.

The one night stands, who he never remained in contact with, were women he'd met at various bars, all had different backgrounds—secretaries, barmaids, hairdressers, factory workers, a couple of strippers, the unemployed, nae unemployable, and even a police officer. She'd used her handcuffs on him back at her place; she also left severe bite marks on his shoulders and his buttocks.

The only three serious relationships he had experienced since his divorce were Claudia, a woman 3 years his senior from Scotland; she had kids who never really liked Don. The distance between Scotland and Birmingham was difficult but, because the luxury his job afforded him, Don spent more time in Scotland during those 6 months than he did in Birmingham. His relationship with Claudia lasted just 6 months.

Zoe, from Weymouth, was a woman 2 years his junior, she criticised almost everything Don did. That lasted 3 months, to be fair to Zoe, Don manipulated the situation so she would dump him.

Then there was Katy, a woman he had been in a long-distance relationship with for the past year or so.

Katy lived in Östermalm, a large wealthy district in central Stockholm. She liked the close proximity of the nightclubs that it had to offer. Katy liked to party, even at the age of 35. She just liked the thrill of it all—the dancing, the drinking, and the amorous attention she drew from both men and women.

Her apartment was rented, typically small but appropriate for the rent she was paying each month. She and Don had met in The Kraken, a Swedish nightclub, when he had travelled there for on-the-job training from his employer. She liked the look of him, he liked the look of her. They slept with one another and continued their relationship when he returned home to the UK, albeit via emails and *Skype*.

His job took him back to Sweden twice a year, so it seemed that this was a long-distance relationship that could actually work where so many fail because travelling great distances is rarely an option for both parties. Katy travelled to see him once, she spent a week with him. It was that week where they both agreed that he should spend time out in Sweden with her, to test the water, so to speak.

His plan went pear-shaped when Katy had told him that she no longer wanted him in her life. She was 15 years younger than Don and they had spent the last year in that bubble of love where coincidences become fate and talking about sex online seemed far easier than talking about it face to face. In truth, they learned more about one another in those 1.5 months of living together than they did for the 13 months that they had been speaking online to one another.

She'd promised to be his dirty girl in the bedroom when he arrived there, of course that never happened. It was great sex, fantastic actually. He got to satisfy her with his mouth, something he was good at, she got to satisfy him with hers, something she was good at, but the deep fantasies that they had spoken of previously online were never carried out; they rarely are.

It ended abruptly when she didn't want him in her life anymore, citing that she could see no future in a man from England. In truth, the attraction had gone. She no longer found him attractive, not in the sense of his looks, in the sense of excitement, at least that's how Don took the news. Don knew he was a bit of a stick in the mud.

He knew he could satisfy in bed but outside of the sexual arena, he was a pretty boring guy. He called her his 'princess'. To be fair, she was stunningly attractive on the outside but he had, on a few occasions, witnessed a more darker side to Katy. She felt insecure around other women, particularly if they were good looking. She called them 'cunt whores', something that Don didn't particularly like.

He balanced her insecurities with his own feelings for her, he loved her and felt proud to be with her. He knew all along that he was punching well above his weight. A woman 15 years his junior, your stereotypical Swedish blonde with looks akin to Emma Bunton from the Spice Girls.

Yes, he thought, as the water trickled pathetically, he was punching well above his weight, which, incidentally, had plummeted since his return to the UK just over a week ago. He still had his pot belly though.

He returned home a broken man and here he was now underneath a broken shower trying to lather the soap in his hands whilst keeping his chest moderately warm with the slow flow of water that trickled pathetically from the shower hose.

Life sucked.

Towel drying himself, whilst trying desperately hard not to look at his pot belly, Don made the decision to forget about her. He'd spent hours online watching videos and the one common denominator regarding relationship break-ups was the 'no contact' rule. Do not contact your ex, just have nothing to do with them. In times of heartache, think about the very moment when they dumped you and how worthless they made you feel.

Of course, the whole 'love yourself' bollocks was also advice given via the medium of the internet. The 'love yourself' thing seemed too new-age for Don, it was out of his comfort zone; besides, he couldn't really love himself under the current circumstances. It's hard to love yourself, he thought, when two of the three serious relationships since his divorce had ended up with him being dumped. If that didn't tell him something was wrong with him then what would?

He purposely looked at his pot belly. Disgusting, he thought. No wonder Katy dumped him.

It was 6 am on the dot and it was still dark outside; dark, wet and miserable; hardly weather to lift the current mood but if Don wanted to make changes, he knew that the weather was the least of his concerns.

He looked in the mirror. A shave was the order of the day, he'd leave his goatee intact, he'd had it since he didn't know when. Besides, women liked it; at least that's what Claudia, Katy and Zoe had told him. Then again they had once told him how much they loved him so their goatee rating skills meant nothing to him today.

'Tis the single life for me, Don thought, as he pulled a tee-shirt over his head. The old school playground male motto came to him, the two L's—Love 'em and leave 'em.

Deep down he knew his problem had always been forgetting. Deep down he knew that his problem was forging relationships with women who lived far away from him, far enough for him, and to be honest, for them, not to fully commit to a relationship. Maybe it was his safety net, maybe the fun was in the travel, the anticipation upon his arrival by train, coach or plane? He didn't know the answer but there was a pattern.

Claudia—Edinburgh; roughly 300 miles, roughly 5 hours by train.

Zoe—Weymouth; roughly 200 miles, roughly 5 hours by coach.

Katy—Östermalm; over 1,000 miles, roughly 5 hours by plane then transit.

These were his journeys.

Don didn't know it yet but he was in the midst of a journey that would change his life forever. His journey had started back in 2001, although he didn't know it. Forces around him did, they had planned it and he was about to embark on it. It all centred on a poem Don had wrote.

A poem that he had inadvertently encrypted with a code. That code had been sought after by many, particularly the Catholic Church.

If the emptiness he felt today would have known what laid in store, then it would have lifted and Don would have eaten, something he hadn't done in a week, at least nothing of any sustenance. The odd bar snack with alcohol kept him going.

Don Williamson's life was about to change on a dramatic scale. It was all part of the *plan*.

# Chapter Four

Karen Crawford had just finished her photo shoot. She was bound by contract to shoot four times a year with the *Orange Model Agency*. A strange name but quite apt given that more than half the models, in an attempt to look tanned, actually looked orange.

Karen had it all—stunning good looks, natural curly light brown hair that reached halfway down her back, surgically enhanced breasts, an hour-glass figure and money, lots of money. She had the charisma too. Her American accent and mannerisms enchanted her to the British public.

She was 40 and still turning heads. Her topless shots, back in the late 90's, had appeared in various magazines; she was loved and lusted by millions yet she felt lonely. She, like most beautiful women, wanted to be loved inside, or at the very least, wanted men to recognise all she had and not just her body and good looks.

She knew that this would prove difficult the longer she chose to pose for the camera in tight clothing, but she had the body that magazines loved and it was money in the bank for Karen's future.

The shoot today saw her pose in a bikini range. It was, as usual, with the *Orange Model Agency,* shot in the best possible taste in front of a green screen which would later become a backdrop of Copacabana Beach once the photos went to print. Air fans, strategically placed and gently blowing, would simulate a gentle breeze and show Karen's curly light brown hair in great detail. The photo set would be paid, in part, by Lacombe Hair products—a French company, who would also carry a full page spread next to the photos of Karen.

She was off soon, a break she needed and intended to thoroughly enjoy, a five week vacation starting with a week at Snow Ridge Ski Resort in Turin, NY with her American psychic friend, Angie; after which she would fly into Paris for a week then head down to explore the delights of what Italy had to offer. Portugal and Spain were next, finally finishing in London for a few days of pampering and girly shopping before heading home.

She'd hit the shops after the hullabaloo of Christmas, a time of year that she never really enjoyed. In her eyes, Christmas had become commercialised and had put unwanted pressure on too many people. Sure, she had no financial worries but she felt for those that were less fortunate than her. Karen did, however, enjoy the New Year celebrations and she looked forward to spending that time in her new adopted home, England.

Home was an hour or so away from central London, in Cobham, Surrey.

Karen's career had started at an early age. She was just 16 when her parents were approached by a local child modelling agency. She was the face of *Crackle Corn*, a nutty based corn breakfast cereal, before moving on to being the body that graced TV screens in the *Sheer Nylon* commercials, the brand of stockings that gave most men an instant erection and most women an inferiority complex that such a carved beauty as Karen could exist.

Her big break came when she appeared as a presenter on an adult based late night show, *Celebrity Celibacy*, on British TV. It was a panel show that featured the latest news items regarding celebrities. The two teams, each consisting of three celebrities, would make jokes about the relevant news articles, jokes that were scripted behind the scenes. The show ran for 5 years and made Karen a household name.

Her body clinging dresses had been the major reason for the viewing figures to soar. She knew how to flaunt it, she knew how to get the attention, and she knew she could make most men grow, and that gave her a sense of power and she enjoyed the thrill. Men were weak when they met her, often stuttering or unable to avert their eyes from her curvaceous body. Again, she knew this. Again, she enjoyed it. Again, she felt in control.

She moved to London from Idaho shortly after her stint on British TV had bought her national fame. Years later, fame and fortune afforded her the luxury of purchasing property in both London and Idaho, a huge ranch that she rarely visited.

Hollywood had approached Karen when she hit her 30s. They saw her playing a 'girl next door' type role but it was something she shunned, opting instead to pursue her modelling career. She wasn't particularly fond of the glitzy life-style that Hollywood had to offer in any case, preferring instead to spend her days relaxing at her mansion in Surrey and her nights in the centre of London where the paparazzi and, more importantly, free publicity were never too far away.

Photos of her in the national press meant more visits to her website, which meant more downloads of her videos, basically videos of her taken during her modelling sessions. They were the biggest cash cow. Posters were next; they were advertised at £10 each or £25 if you wanted them signed. Her website was popular, three and a half million hits or so and over 630, 000 downloads of her videos, all at £6 a pop.

There wasn't a magazine that didn't feature photos of her. She was the apple of the public eye, the fantasy of most boys hitting puberty and most men who chose to ogle photos of her rather than make their own relationships work. Women liked her too, well some did. They liked her fashion sense, and they liked the power she had over men.

Lesbians and homosexuals saw her as their role model. Karen was not a lesbian but had often fantasised about sharing her bed with another woman. The closest she had got was a drunken kiss (tongues inside mouth) with Bella, another model, who had unfeasibly large breasts.

She'd had a series of relationships that never really panned out. Hollywood heartthrob Lincoln Lewis was the longest. He and Karen had an on-off relationship and the media lapped it up. She finally called it a day when she caught him sniffing cocaine in his trailer on the set of his last movie, *Stun Guns*.

Flings with other celebrities didn't last as long as the 2.5 year relationship she had with Lincoln. Actor/comedian Ricky Sherry lasted just over 6 months. Karen confronted him about photographs that had appeared in the tabloids. Turned out he was sleeping with Rachel Rude, a porn star.

She'd been single now for almost 5 years. She missed the intimacy and companionship but had given up on finding her soulmate. She knew that he would never be anyone from her circles though. When two famous people unite, it's basically a clash of egos, she thought.

If there was a 'Mr Right', he'd have to be your average Joe. Millions of male hearts everywhere lived in hope that it would be them after reading in *Time* magazine that she would consider a relationship with someone outside of the celebrity circle. The forum on her website went into overload shortly after *Time* magazine hit the streets.

She looked at her watch as she approached Gracie's Emporium, it was 2.22.

She was unfashionably early. She'd order food for herself and Bella and then sit outside so both she and her large breasted friend could smoke and watch life pass them by. Bella was loud and dining anywhere with her usually drew attention.

Being recognised was okay but there were just times when they each liked their privacy. Eating was one of those times.

A bizarre chain of events was around the corner for Karen, events that would be the beginning of something that had been in the pipeline for a number of years. She had been told by her American psychic friend, Angie, some years ago that something was on the horizon. Upon her return from Europe, she would finally meet that horizon.

Bella Thornton had just finished her photo shoot for the latest edition of *Bra Busters*. She was meeting her friend, Karen, for lunch at a quaint bistro which was just a just ten minute walk from the studio.

She had been on the front cover of many top shelf magazines a record 106 times. She had the kind of breasts that, whether you were male or female, you just couldn't stop yourself from staring at. She had looks to go with them too. A brunette, with penetrating blue eyes and a body that had filth written all over it, who enjoyed nothing more than spending time with her girlfriends.

She'd had a string of lovers, none of which could put up with the ogling and drooling of other men when they saw her, none of which could deal with Bella's history as a porn star.

Now, she just chose to live the single life. A vibrator that she nicknamed 'Boris' gave her the desired orgasms she needed. Men, to Bella at least, were just too complicated, clingy and immature. Yes, she still enjoyed the attention, she even enjoyed the uncomplicated relationships, those quick one night stands where she would get what she wanted then ask whoever was in her company to leave.

She, like Karen, had work done on her breasts too, no reduction or enlargement, just a firmness added. It was a cut-throat business and a career that was short, making her breasts more firm meant they wouldn't be travelling south for a while which, in turn, meant Bella could earn more money selling herself to *Bra Busters, Massive Mams, Bap Bazookas* and other magazines of that ilk.

Bella was born in the east end of London and had carried the accent with her throughout the years, often using cockney rhyming slang when shopping at the local market. Her parents still lived in Whitechapel; Bella, herself, opting to buy a plush apartment on Canary Wharf.

She'd gone straight into the modelling business at the age of 16. Her oversize breasts were, throughout her school days, the constant butt of jokes. Two weeks after her 16th birthday, she appeared topless in a national newspaper.

From that point those that had made fun of her at school had started to tell all and sundry how they and Bella were really close friends. Bella turned her back on the back-stabbers and took a journey down the path where her assets provided her financial security and fame.

At 27, she appeared in a number of soft porn movies where suggestion was the key. No close up shots just bobbing heads and shadows carefully directed and shot that would leave the viewer knowing exactly what her character was doing without actually seeing it up close.

At 32, she stepped it up a notch by appearing in a series of hardcore porn movies, the type where anything goes and the word taboo just did not exist. She made a pretty penny from those five movies then threw the towel in on it all. Those five movies alone had paid three quarters of her mortgage off for her apartment in Canary Wharf.

She was popular amongst the working class. She was the local girl who, because of her threepenny bits, had put Whitechapel on the map for reasons other than Jack the Ripper. The older generation admired her, the younger generation misunderstood her. Bella was purely in this business for the money, nothing more, and nothing less.

Lad's magazine, *Bullhorn*, had, in 2013, voted her the second most desirable woman in the UK, losing out to the top spot by just 3,000 or so votes. The number one spot had been awarded, for the past 8 years, to Karen Crawford.

***

Karen was already sitting outside Gracie's Emporium, a posh bistro, when Bella arrived. As promised, Karen had ordered a pot of English tea and two plates of tuna fish pasta with a side salad. Both were wearing pink joggers, both were without make-up, and both were wearing sunglasses in an effort to keep away fans and the press. There was a winter chill in the air.

"Hey, Jugzy," Karen mused as Bella approached the table.

"Hey, mama," Bella replied.

They spoke of the morning's events. Karen telling Bella of the shoot with her orange friends whilst Bella told Karen how much oil they used on her tits just so the light would reflect off them a certain way.

"You looking forward to the ski slopes?" Bella asked.

"You betcha, I'm packed already and I don't leave for a fortnight."

Bella had never really asked Karen if she was an accomplished skier. To be honest, Bella didn't really know the first thing about skiing apart from what she had seen on TV as a youngster. She, like most kids back then, liked watching the ski accidents, the compilation of skiers falling down steep hills whilst trying to manoeuvre around slaloms, all was set to music of some varying hilarity.

Bella wasn't really a sporty type of person, although she did like watching football and rugby. She'd slept with three Premiership footballers but had yet to bed a rugby player.

"I don't know how you could see skiing as a holiday, too much fucking hard work, if you ask me." Bella, as usual, was loud and to the point.

"Well, Bel, it's only because you have enormous breasts that you would find it hard. Jesus, I think anyone would have difficulty skiing downhill with jugs that size."

Bella wasn't offended in the slightest. She never really liked skiing that much anyhow but did like ski clothes.

"So, you're gonna be meeting you old friend, the psychic woman, right?"

"Yes, Angie. We go back years, Bel."

Bella was about to give Karen a lecture on cold reading, a set of techniques used by apparent psychics whereby it would give them the ability to gain information about someone without that person realising. She knew she'd be wasting her breath though as the bond between Karen and Angie was strong.

"Then across to Europe after that, huh? All those Italian men will be drooling in the streets when they see you." Bella wasn't wrong, Karen was simply stunning.

"Oh, I'll be dressing down, Bel, you know what it's like. Men see me and immediately think I'm the same person who wears slinky dresses whilst brushing my teeth." Karen was referring to a recent series of photographs that had appeared in the national press, all for a toothpaste manufacturer that had paid Karen handsomely for a photo-shoot to advertise their toothpaste.

"Yeh, but don't dress down too much, babes. You need to meet one of those Italian stallions and get rid of that pent-up frustration. How long has it been now since you had a game of hide the salami?" Bella had such a way with words.

"Oh, I don't miss the sex, Bel, your body kind of gets used to it after a while. It's been 5 years since I last slept with someone. I'm waiting for Mr Right."

Bella sighed and asked, "The '1111' guy, right?"

"Got it in one, sister," Karen told her.

# Chapter Five

"My gran phoned to tell me she's had a chairlift installed. I didn't know skiing was so popular in Cornwall."

Don often felt that the way to a woman's heart was through humour. He wasn't trying to impress the women stood at the bar so he could get them into bed, he just liked telling jokes, he liked the response, the attention; it made him feel worthy again.

To be honest, he was trying desperately hard to forget about Katy, desperately hard to try to rid the knotted feeling in his stomach, desperately hard to try and rid himself of the emptiness he felt, and of the worthlessness he felt and of the images of her in bed with another man. Being the joker gave him a new identity; he was someone else for a while, attention-seeking because he needed attention.

"My friend asked me to walk down a hill with him. I declined."

That was enough for Suzy and Julie to leave the bar, or at least leave the area where Don was standing, or more to the point, swaying. He'd been drinking for 2 hours, Jack Daniel's and Coke. It reminded him of Katy, although it bought back hurtful memories. He'd been drinking with her a month or so ago in Sweden when she popped outside for a cigarette.

She'd been gone a while so he went looking for her. From a distance he saw her flirting with a younger guy, then saw them exchange phone numbers. He said nothing, he didn't want her to think he was the jealous type. He didn't even say anything when he saw her return a smile, as he and Katy left the bar that night, to the same young guy.

A lingering smile that showed the young man how interested in him she was, as he and Katy left the bar that night. He wished now that he had told her he saw her.

His state of mind put her and the young guy together. He didn't know it, he just thought it as a consequence of the way Katy had told him she saw no future for them. In truth, Katy had taken the young man's phone number. She was flattered and it was always a nice feeling to 'have one in the bank' should things ever go pear-shaped between her and Don. She orchestrated the pear-shaped symphony when she slept with Hjalmar one afternoon while Don was back at her place.

She was surprised Don never asked her about the rash on her neck, a rash that always appeared whenever her skin met stubble. Three days later, she dumped Don.

Don was unaware of her infidelity at the time, he still was but the movie playing out in his head showed nothing but infidelity.

The more he drank, the more he could blank out the images of Katy. He'd gone without food now for four days straight, the alcohol wasn't being soaked up by anything but he didn't care; he just wanted to stop feeling miserable, wanted to stop thinking of his girl having sex with another guy. Let's face it, it's images of a sexual nature that are the hardest to deal with when love has been shattered, even if they aren't actually true.

Eventually, you know the inevitable will happen and by some cruel twist of fate, you'll more than likely find out that the woman you still love is either in love with someone else or is fucking someone else by overhearing it in a conversation or reading it on their Facebook wall.

Don caught the attention of the buxom pint puller, Annette, and waved his glass to signal that he wanted another Jack Daniel's and coke. She obliged and Don rewarded her with "Keep the change," after handing her a fresh £5 note from his wallet. He liked Annette, he'd once had a blowjob from her in the beer cellar.

He was sat on a barrel with his trousers around his ankles whilst she was bent over him, performing the art of fellatio. She was the only one night stand that he kept in touch with, if ordering alcohol can be deemed as keeping in touch, that is. It was the only woman that he'd ever had sex with that he had ever handed money to, albeit to buy alcohol.

Fate was having some twisted fun with Don as Coldplay's *The Scientist* was played. The Lyndon Poacher pub had a covers band on in the lounge. Don had decided to leave music to one side until he could get over Katy, but music being music, it always manages to find you, even if he was only next door in the bar.

Tonight was no exception. *The Scientist* was 'their' song and he now wondered if she was saying that to another man.

Jake, his long-time friend, saw the sadness in his eyes. He knew how much Don was hurting, he knew how much he loved her. *The big hearted guys get hit the hardest,* he had told Don upon his return to the UK. Jake had never understood why Don had never settled with a woman that was closer to home, someone that actually lived in Birmingham would have been a start but Don just didn't want to settle with anyone; he just wanted Katy, *his* Katy.

Jake had sat Don down just one day after he returned from Sweden. A lot of what he said made sense but Don was in the irrational phase of a break up and any form of logic offered was initially accepted then brushed aside by the demons of suspicion. He had every right to feel suspicious. His marriage had ended because his wife sought solace in someone else.

It was baggage that he thought he had left on the carousel of his subconscious mind but Katy ending things meant he was unlocking the baggage once more— a suitcase of insecurities, heartache and worthlessness. If only she knew the wounds that she had reopened. In truth, she did but she didn't really care; those were, after all, Don's issues and not hers. It was just her way of justifying the manner in which she ended things with Don.

The song and the memories it stirred had tipped Don over the edge and he began sobbing, his head falling to meet his hands, his legs weak through no sustenance. Jake grabbed him.

"The moment she told me will be forever etched in my mind. My vision tunnelled as I listened to her tell me the words I never thought I'd hear come out of her mouth. My heart sank into my stomach. I wanted to drop to the floor to cry and vomit. She made me feel worthless," Don told Jake through uncontrollable sobbing.

"Look, Don, I know you don't want to hear this but you've got to start by ridding yourself of anything that reminds you of her. You don't have to throw the things away, but get it out of sight. Maybe then you can rearrange your room so you can live in a new, clean environment. You are in an emotional storm. You will cry without warning because some sort of trigger reminds you of her, and you will want nothing more than to see her again.
"But the first rule of a break up is the no contact rule. No contact means you do not see pictures of her. You do not check up on how she's doing on Facebook or email her either. It has to end so you can heal."

Don knew Jake was right. It was all logical but he couldn't let her go just yet, not tonight, not after hearing their song. In any event, what if she saw his silence as a green light to move on and forget about him?

Jake was happily married. Don wanted what Jake had, he wanted to go home to a wife, he wanted to travel with a wife; he wanted to love a wife and have that love reciprocated. He couldn't envisage ever having that, neither could his friend of 25 years.

"C'mon, Don, let's get you home," Jake said as he slipped his hand under Don's armpit to help him lift his long-time friend to a standing position.

His heart bleeding, his stomach with that endless knotted feeling, Don knew that there was only one thing he could do. He would, when he got home, look on the internet for methods of suicide.

Teresa and Sara would make sure the methods were not carried out.

# Chapter Six

*Teresa O'Brien Born 3 Jan 1946*
*Thomondgate, Limerick, County Clare, Ireland*
*Died 17 April 1957*

*Sara Louise Conway Born 20 Jan 1931*
*Fremont, Nebraska*
*Died 2 August 1948*

It was just like any other day in Limerick, County Clare, save for the shops being open. It was a Wednesday, which meant half-day closing for a lot of the shops around the Thomondgate area where Teresa O'Brien lived and played. She'd been walking home from school when they saw her.

Tommy McGinty was 15 and was playing with his brother, Brendan, who was the same age as Teresa, 11. Tommy had a thing for the 'Queen of Pin-Ups', Bettie Page. He'd become infatuated with her when, in 1955, when Tommy was just 13, she won the title 'Miss Pinup Girl of the World'; the same year Bettie appeared naked as a centrefold in *Playboy* magazine.

Tommy had managed to obtain a copy and had also managed to smuggle it in to his parents' house where he hid it beneath a loose floorboard in his bedroom that he shared with his younger brother. It was his most prized possession. He'd lost count at how many times he had masturbated whilst looking at the full colour glossy centrefold of Bettie. Those private moments were hard to come by.

He'd always have to read to his brother, Brendan, first. A fairy-tale story of some kind that Tommy would often make up as he went along; he was good at storytelling and would always leave Brendan wanting more. Tommy knew that it was a productive cliff-hanger in as much that he could blackmail his brother. *If you don't go to sleep then I won't tell you what happens tomorrow night,* he would tell him.

It worked too. The sooner Brendan slept, the sooner Tommy could lift the loose floorboard to the right of the dressing table in the bedroom. That's when he and Bettie Page could be alone, under his bed sheets mostly.

11-year-old Teresa had the same jet black colour hair as Bettie, it was almost the same length too, and just like Bettie's, it shined.

Tommy called to Teresa, "Come over here, Teresa, myself and Brendan want to show you something we found earlier."

"What is it Tommy McGinty?" She asked.

"You'll have to come over and see for yourself, me and Brendan have hid it in the shed just over there." Tommy was pointing at an old shed some 25 yards away on an allotment.

It was 3.30 in the afternoon and neither Tommy nor Brendan had been to school that day, their mother had slept in; a bottle of Gin the night before knocked her out for the count, as it often did. Teresa had walked the mile and a half to St Joseph's Roman Catholic School earlier that morning, she was now heading home and was just 10 minutes from her front doorstep in Killeen Road.

Teresa liked school; she liked most of the lessons and teachers. She loved listening to the nuns, even though at times she found it difficult to understand their teachings. Most of all, Teresa loved Jesus.

"Okay, Tommy McGinty I'll go home and change first," she told him.

"No, Teresa, you have to come now because it might escape." Tommy knew that Teresa had an interest in animals. Every weekend he had watched her from his parents' house in 32 Killeen Road, opposite to where Teresa lived. She and her mother always walked to the nearby stables to feed the horses, then the ducks that paddled majestically on the River Shannon that was just minutes away from Killeen Road.

Every Saturday morning at 9 am, without fail, Tommy would peek out of the bedroom curtains to catch a glimpse of Teresa O'Brien, just enough of a glimpse that he could memorise and bring into his lustful fantasy when he and a copy of *Playboy*, specifically the centre page spread, when he and Bettie Page were alone.

Curiosity got the better of Teresa that day, that fateful day.

Tommy had told his brother to wait outside while he took Teresa inside.

Brendan had protested but Tommy had used the same blackmail trick he used every night with his younger brother.

36

"Do as you're told, Brendan, or I won't tell you what happened to Hansel and Gretel later," he had told him.

Once inside, Teresa was on her journey to the other side. It was the beginning of the end for her life on earth but the beginning of her life as an angel.

Her body was found three days later. She'd been strangled to death with a belt.

It was the belt of Tommy McGinty's.

Teresa O'Brien was present at her own funeral. Nobody could see her.

Nobody except Sara Conway, who had an arm around her and who was explaining about life on the other side. Teresa and Sara would remain side by side forever. That was the *plan*.

Sara's fate had been similar. Born Sara Louise Conway in 1931, she was 6 years older than Teresa. At 17, her earth age, she could show Teresa the light, the love, and the other side where everything was so different and so much more beautiful.

In the summer of 1948, Sara Conway, known as 'Conners' to all those who knew her well, was kidnapped, raped, and then killed by Haskin Bruette. She too attended her own funeral in Fremont, Nebraska; she too was comforted by an angel. She'd been told of the *plan* and about Teresa, whom she would meet in 9 years' time.

It would all begin on Wednesday, 17 April 1957. Bruette went on to kill four more teenagers in the space of 6 months before he was caught. He was handed down the death penalty and spent 11 years on death row at the Nebraska State Penitentiary before eventually being fried on 12 October 1959.

Two girls, two brutal murders.

Two angels. Both chosen by Archangel Gabriel.

# Chapter Seven

Two weeks had passed. Bella had bared all during her various photo shoots; Karen was on a ski slope somewhere in New York and Don was still alive.

Don had gone home from the pub two weeks ago and passed out in front of his laptop. He'd looked at noose tying methods, but he had no rope. He looked at how quick death would be if he placed a hose over a car exhaust and then fed the hose through a gap in a car window, but he didn't own a car; come to think of it, he didn't even own a hose.

He would have put his head in the oven and gassed himself, had his oven had not been electric. Jumping off a bridge wasn't an option as it may have not resulted in death and he could have been left paralyzed for the rest of his life, stuck in a body with no way out.

On the bright side, his shower had been fixed.

He'd broken the 'no contact' rule a couple of times, pleading with Katy to reply to him, trying everything to get a response, to keep that fading connection alive.

She finally responded. She never addressed his questions, his insecurities; her email just finalised things on her terms. Her email to him read:

*Dearest Don,*

*I know you are hurting and I am sorry for causing you that hurt. I realised when you were here that I was not ready to live with another man again. You know about the abuse I suffered as a child and you really helped me come to terms with it all.*

*Yes, we had fun, you are a fantastic lover but living alone for as long as I have and to have that solitude and freedom meant that I found it difficult to have you around. I would find it difficult to have anyone around, Don. To lead you on would have been wrong. I'm just the type of person that could never do something like that and, rightly or wrongly, I decided to tell you before we both got in too deep.*

*We must now try to move on with our respective lives. It's hard, I'm crying as I write this but we both have to be strong and think with our heads rather than our hearts. I will cherish the moments we shared together and want you to start loving yourself. You are a good man, Don, and I just know that you will find peace and happiness soon.*

*I wish you well and hope that one day we will both reach a stage of emotional stability and should we ever cross paths we can embrace and give thanks to one another for the happiness and love we shared together.*

*You have enriched my life and I will forever be thankful that I met you.*

*Be good to yourself Don. Goodbye*

*Katy*

\*\*\*

Katy was in the midst of more one-night stands. Men were rich-pickings at The Kraken. and various other bars in and around where Katy lived. The Kraken was used, in the main, by the younger generation but quite often middle-aged men would frequent the quieter area of the bar in the hope of picking up girls young enough to be their daughter.

Katy despised those type of men and also despised the young girls who fell for their charms. It sickened her. It enraged her.

At times, she could not stomach the older guys at The Kraken so would choose, instead, to visit quieter bars, sometimes with work colleagues, sometimes with friends, but mostly alone. It was easier to pick-up when alone and nobody would ever know about her disguises and identity changes.

She'd read Don's emails and probably would have responded to them differently had she have received them two weeks prior, a time when she yearned to have him back in her life. That's how it was with Katy—sadness and loss one minute, excitement and fun the next. One return email was enough; she had work to do, men to meet, fantasies to live out and new identities to create.

\*\*\*

Don had read Katy's email over and over. He even replied but she did not answer. Finally, after checking his email almost every 5 minutes for the best part of two days, he decided to delete her email address. It was a symbolic gesture, he was cutting the ties that bind, he was turning the page, and he was starting a new chapter, or at the very least he was trying to. He also deleted his Google news update.

He had previously set up updates on all things happening in Östermalm. It had put him there when he read about certain events, car crashes, neighbour feuds, and other meaningless news feeds.

Katy's actions had caused self-loathing in Don. He didn't want to be who he was—unloved, unappreciated, used and spat out as if he were burdensome. He never felt unconditional acceptance with his former wife and, when looking back, he never felt it with Katy either. He felt the four Ds—Defeated, Defective, Deserted, and Deprived. He also felt like he was a coward, he couldn't even carry out his own suicide.

He'd been for long walks alone, exercise, even if it was just walking, was good, at least that's what the internet experts had said. Apparently, he'd read, exercise increases brain serotonin function in humans which, in turn, improves mood.

One particular walk through a local cemetery had been peculiar, to say the least. Don had been walking around the cemetery for about half an hour and had decided to exit the gates. He heard the caw of a crow, a caw that followed him.

Every now and again, the crow would swoop down to where Don was walking. It would get so low that Don felt himself ducking as it approached. After each swoop, the crow would find a tree along the path, watching Don and offering another caw. The crow followed Don down the path, flying from tree to tree and belting out a caw of approval as Don neared the exit. Don thought that the crow was protecting a nest of eggs and just wanted to make sure that he wasn't a poacher.

There was more to it though. Only Don didn't know. The crow was, in fact, protecting Don, guiding him, just as he had been since 2001.

Drastic changes were needed. He'd considered going to see his doctor for a course of antidepressant therapy but he knew this would just merely paper over the cracks. Besides, word on the law circuit was that those pills just push people over the edge; they make you numb and also make you do stupid things without fear of consequence.

He didn't really like pharmaceutical companies, much of his work for his employer 'Cederquist & Linklaters Associates' had saw pharmaceutical companies deny that their medical devices were the cause of patients being injured. If they could lie about devices, then they were probably less than truthful with the products they marketed as 'antidepressants'.

In any event, Don didn't see depression as an illness; he saw it more of a state of mind, a set of circumstances that had to get worse before they could get better. He didn't see, or indeed believe, that the names for mental illnesses, such as Obsessive Compulsive Disorder, Bipolar I, Bipolar II, for example, held any scientific merit. They were just disorders made up by people who voted them in, via a show of hands, to the Diagnostic Statistical Manual of Mental Disorders; a manual, that over the years, that had even been ridiculed by most of the profession it was aimed at.

Depression, albeit circumstantial, was taking hold of Don. He was sleeping longer, drinking more, had lost his appetite, and stuck in a bubble of sadness. He wanted to push himself harder but something, he felt, was holding him back. He needed a new direction, something to distract him from the loss and end of a relationship. He needed change.

A concert was looming, he'd have to travel to London and meet friends whom he'd met over the years. They all had one love, *The Blinkers*—a popular rock band they had all been following from the early 70's. Maybe meeting with them and seeing his favourite band would help Don's mind switch gears, Don thought.

Maybe it would bring about the change that he was searching for and hopefully kick start a new journey, a new road to travel down, one less painful than the one he was currently on.

The get-together had been planned shortly after *The Blinkers* announced a set of dates across the UK while Don was in Sweden. Tickets were like gold but his close-knit friends always came up trumps, some of them knew the band members personally and would never fail in getting a spare ticket. They always sold at face-value, anything more was unheard of amongst the hardcore fans.

Don was in luck; Cameron, his Scottish friend, had ordered him a ticket via *TicketMaster* and text messaged him the good news. *We're lucky, Don, fuckers sold out in 4 minutes but I grabbed two, one for me, one for you. Block fucking C, brother!*

Don hadn't really thought about the concert and meet-up with his old friends until now, it lifted his spirits somewhat.

He checked his phone again, just in case there was a message from Katy.

There wasn't.

He'd focus on the London trip for now, he told himself. He fired up his MP3 app on his phone and played his favourite *Blinkers* tune, *Rock Until Dawn*. This excited him and for 3 minutes and 5 seconds, he was momentarily lost from the present and thinking about the immediate future and rockin' out with Cameron and his fellow comrades in London.

The crow was already on his way to London. It needed to survey the area and memorise it. Don, it thought, would be okay for now.

# Chapter Eight

Karen flew first class everywhere, Barcelona to London Heathrow was no exception. Such a short flight, however, just meant a larger seat and that she'd be served first with the airline snacks on offer. She could afford travelling first class, it was a perk of the job. Her agent had made all the holiday arrangements.

Flights, hotels and chauffeurs to greet her as she arrived at her various destinations across Europe. She had the sun, sea and Sangria, was hit on by the amorous male Italians, but was now in London, where there was no sun or sea. The sun would, however, make an appearance later; it wouldn't offer much heat in the December sky though.

Her chauffeur, who held up the standard Crawford' sign at Heathrow arrivals, was Luigi, an Italian. He never hit on her though, it would be unprofessional to do so; besides, he was like a father-figure to her. Her agent had made all the plans and Luigi was soon heading towards Claridge's in Mayfair.

Karen had checked-in to her suite; a suite that overlooked the streets of surrounding Mayfair. The suite was bathed in iconic art deco interior that boasted a huge bedroom, it even had an impressive entrance hall. Karen was used to the five star lifestyle. She showered and changed then headed downstairs.

*Hey, Bel, give me a call when you get this message. I'm stopping Claridge's in Mayfair, I have a suite and was wondering if you fancied hitting the shops with me. Let me know.* Karen slipped her android back into her handbag and caught the eye of the waiter. She motioned her head and beckoned him to her table. "Could I see the breakfast menu, please?" She asked him.

*** 

Bella had been in the shower when Karen rang; she was washing off the smell of sex, a one night stand with children's TV presenter, Tony Turner, real name Rasputin Witschke. The children's TV department thought it best to give the newcomer an easier name for the kids to pronounce. He'd been sniffing powder all night and his appetite for sex meant that Bella would actually have an orgasm.

She came on him seconds after he came in her. She came again when she continued to ride him. He, unlike most men, continued to stay hard after he had ejaculated.

She could just not pass up on such an opportunity. There was no emotional ties, it was just sex.

They were both single so no partners would be damaged. At around midnight last night, they had slipped out of the back entrance of 'The Cuckoo Club' to avoid the waiting paparazzi who were congregated outside the front in the hope that they may catch a celebrity on their way out, worse for wear and abusive.

Those types of photos exchanged hands for far more than any celebrity behaving themselves.

They caught a black cab back to Bella's apartment in Canary Wharf. They each did a few lines of coke then they partied hard, on Bella's bed. Bella took the lead, mostly. She was a strong woman and had held Tony's wrists flat against the mattress while she straddled him.

He was quite skinny and had ginger hair but Bella had heard through the grapevine that he was pretty good in bed, so looks weren't overly important, at least not for her. They partied all night, almost every position imaginable, and some not so imaginable. They eventually drifted off to sleep around 3.30 am.

Tony was scrambling eggs when she returned from the shower clad only in a bath towel.

"None for me, thanks. I'm heading into Mayfair to meet a friend. I'll call you a cab," she told Tony.

"So, we should hook up again eh, Bel?" He asked, more out of politeness than anything else. He knew Bella was a one-night type of girl but was unprepared for what came next.

"Why?" She asked, before adding, "You're pretty new to this game. Here's how it works, we meet, we fuck, and we leave. You go home and tell your friends that you fucked me and they give you a big slap on the back for nailing the bird with big tits. If we meet again we say hi to one another then we continue walking in opposite directions. It's simple."

He never replied. He slipped the toast into his mouth and threw his shirt on.

He felt bruising around his nipple where Bella had sucked him last night. It was a notch on both their bed posts.

Bella had slept with more celebrities than she could remember. Tony had just slept with three, Bella being by far the dirtiest.

20 minutes later, Bella was in a cab heading towards Mayfair. It was a lifestyle she, just like Karen, had become accustomed to. She'd hugged Tony as he left, she felt a slight tingle between her legs. Tony certainly lived up to the trouser snake rumour that was already circulating among the celebrity circles.

***

Bella's cab pulled up outside Claridge's where she was greeted by the concierge. "No luggage," she told him. She knew her way around most of the classier hotels London had to offer, so made her way up to Karen's suite as if she'd been doing it on a daily basis for the past year or so. Reception had, as instructed by Bella, phoned ahead to Karen.

"Here she is, Jugzy Malone." Bella laughed as she saw Karen standing in the doorway with her arms held outward. They embraced and exchanged niceties before Bella asked, "So, tell me all about those Italians, did you meet anyone special?"

Karen faked a sigh, then added, "Unfortunately not, Bel, but I did have a great time."

Karen led Bella into the bedroom; a line of bags was on the dressing table. "Yours is the blue one," she told Bella. Karen always bought gifts for Bella. Today's was a bag within a bag. The blue gift bag was quickly discarded by Bella.

She removed the trace paper from the bulk to reveal a Chiarugi vegetable-tanned leather satchel.

"Oh, Karen, you shouldn't have," Bella told her.

"Never mind that, tell me more about you and Tony Turner," Karen asked.

Bella had briefly told Karen about last night's notch in the bed post when she called her back after listening to Karen's message when she towel dried in her bathroom back at Canary Wharf.

"Well, what can I say, Kaz, he certainly lives up to his reputation. Not only is he well endowed, he stays erect for a good 10 minutes after."

They laughed.

"He's quite sweet. He even asked if we should see one another again," Bella told her.

"And what did you tell him?" Karen asked, already knowing the answer.

"I just asked him why," Bella told her. Again, they both laughed.

"Okay, let's hit those shops, Bel, we can eat back here later. I have nothing else planned, unless of course you do?" Karen asked.

"Nope, not unless Brad gives me a call because Angelina's broken his heart," she joked.

"I thought maybe we could take a girly shopping trip to Knightsbridge, blitz Harrods then head into the West End for the serious stuff," Karen told her.

The 'serious stuff' was shoes. Both had a penchant for them. Between them, they owned over 2,000 pairs, most of which were never worn.

"Sounds like Heaven, Kaz," Bella replied.

Karen grabbed the back of her hair and moulded it into a bun effortlessly before pushing two hair grips into place. She'd done it hundreds of times, it was second nature to her now. She picked up her Burberry scarf, purchased in Rome, and wrapped it once around her neck before slipping into her double breasted black *Emilio Pucci* blazer, complete with gold-tone crest buttons.

It was the perfect accompaniment for her black *Paul Smith* pleated trousers. Her mother's pocket watch, left to her when her mom had died, was slipped into her trouser pocket.

Finally, her Gucci shoulder bag was opened so she could slip her android inside. Neither Karen nor Bella went anywhere without their mobile phones. Missed phone calls could have potentially meant missed revenue, not that either were short of money but both would never turn down easy money either. What they spent in the shops today could be recouped in just an hour of sitting posing for the camera.

Bella grabbed her Michael Kors mini brown cross-body bag and placed it inside the bigger Chiarugi satchel that Karen had bought her.

A taxi was waiting for them at the hotel entrance.

"Why the taxi, Kaz?" Bella inquired.

"Oh, Luigi needs to rest, besides the limo will just draw attention to us. The walk will do us good, Bel."

Bella held the back door open for Karen. "Your carriage awaits, Ma'am," she purposely stretched out the word ma'am.

"You sound like a lamb," Karen quipped before climbing in the back of the cab. Bella slid next to her and shut the passenger door.

"Haaaaaaaaaaarods, please, driver," Bella blurted out. They both laughed.

The cab driver shook his head at the middle-aged juveniles and pulled away from the Claridge's forecourt.

"So, Karen and Bella, you off shopping then?" Terry Laverty, a cab driver of 32 years, asked them whilst looking in his rear-view mirror. He knew it was a dumb question given Bella had somewhat told him in a lamb voice. He knew who his passengers were, most men did. They were instantly recognisable and, according to other drivers who worked for Hackney Carriages, they tipped well.

"Yes, just a quick shopping trip…" Bella replied before Terry told her his name.

"It's Terry, Bella, named after my old man; he lived in Whitechapel and knew your parents."

Bella looked surprised and asked how his father knew them.

"He worked on the docks with your father, Bella, Terry Laverty; unmissable, he was six feet two and had hands like shovels. Did your folks ever talk about him?"

"Sadly, no, so how long you been driving black cabs, Terry?"

"Over 30 years, Bella. Ooh I could tell you some stories about some of the celebrities I've picked up, none as nice as you two though."

Karen whispered in Bella's ear, "He wants a good tip, be nice to him."

"Well," said Bella, "we'll be even nicer to you if you take the back streets and get us to Harrods quickly, Terry. How about taking a left here to avoid the traffic ahead. I'm sure you know where to go once you hit the end of the side street."

"There's no flies on you, eh, Miss Thornton," he joked before making a left-turn.

Karen and Bella laughed. There were, indeed, no flies on Bella; she knew the streets of London as well as she knew the back of her hand.

# Chapter Nine

Don's train pulled into Euston station. He'd paid the cheaper fare which meant stopping at almost every train station to pick up passengers who had also opted for the cheaper alternative. The more expensive train travelled direct, no stops. He'd paid over the odds for the faster train but had missed it earlier.

He'd been drinking coffee in Starbucks close to where he lived and the waitress accidentally knocked his latte into his lap. He made no fuss but it meant he had to return home and change his trousers. He missed his train and had to wait another hour for the next one.

He mentally cussed himself at paying the price of a fast train only to have to endure a slower one stopping at almost everywhere before making the slow crawl into London. It didn't really mess up his plans. He was travelling early just to do some sightseeing of his own. It was going to be retail therapy without actually making any purchases. Window shopping through the eyes of a pauper because, Don thought, London was so fucking expensive.

Euston station was, as usual, busy. His favourite rock band was in town, a concert that had sold out in just under 4 minutes, making the 80,000 or so extremely happy, and the ticket touts even happier.

He'd been a fan of *The Blinkers* since he first heard them back in '78. *Blazer Brigade* was their 1978 release and it wasn't long before Don purchased their back catalogue, five albums, the first being a 1974 recording. He'd always managed to see them each time they toured. They were playing Wembley Stadium later that night and he'd planned to meet some old friends that he'd met down the years at various shows.

Germans, Argentinians, Swedish and Scots had all planned to meet outside the gates of Buckingham Palace. They wanted a group photo with the royal home behind them. Don wasn't really keen on the royal family, he didn't like the way they handled Princess Diana's death.

He'd thought about Katy on the way down from Birmingham; it was the fact that he was meeting the Swedes later today that made him think of her. The passing weeks had, as everybody had told him, eased the pain somewhat. He still wasn't ready to enter into another relationship, part of him still clung on to hope that Katy would contact him to tell him how wrong she had been and how she couldn't live without him in her life.

He took a deep breath each time he heard his phone bleep with a text message; he let out that breath when he realised by looking at the sender's number that it wasn't her. He'd often thought about texting her but he just couldn't put himself through the frustration and heartache of her not replying.

He had some spare time before the 4 pm meet-up outside Buckingham Palace.

He'd planned what he'd do the night before. He'd always wanted to walk around Harrods; he just wanted to see what he couldn't afford and what others could. In any event, they may just have something affordable for him to purchase, most shops did after Christmas. Anyone else would feel down at not being able to have what others could, but Don had already experienced that, he still was.

A small twinge in his stomach appeared at the thought and he quickly focused his thoughts elsewhere, anywhere where he could block out the pain. He hummed a *Blinkers* tune to himself.

He descended down the escalator oblivious to the tourists riding the stairs with him. The smell of the London underground always reminded him of his childhood. He'd been to London on a school trip and he'd never forgotten the smell of the underground rail system and the memory that it always seemed to bring up whenever Don smelt it. It was a distinct and unique smell—a mix of dust, grease and something vaguely metallic.

Within 10 minutes, he was walking out of Knightsbridge tube station. He was thankful that there were no long waits on the underground. Euston to Green Park, 4 minutes, a 2 minute wait before boarding the tube to Knightsbridge, a short 2 minute journey.

Knightsbridge was busy as he walked out of the station. The London red buses reminding him that he wasn't in Birmingham any more. A Japanese tourist stopped and asked for directions but Don didn't know the directions to Brent. He did know, however, that the tourist was a good distance from Brent but didn't wish to explain to him, he'd already been held up earlier.

Instead, he pointed the Japanese man to the clerk selling tickets at Knightsbridge tube station after which he headed towards Harrods, hands in his

Crombie coat and head held up to make sure he crossed the road when he was supposed to.

The street was busy as shoppers were out in force snapping up items that were not sold at Christmas. Items that had been marked down in price that enticed those with money or, as the case may be, those with a good credit rating. He observed modern day Britain.

The majority of pedestrians speaking into their mobile phones or looking at maps on hand held devices. London, to Don at least, reeked of money yet; at the same time, the stench of poverty was all too apparent.

Street beggars and doorway tramps, with their sole belongings in black bin bags or stolen trolley's from supermarket car parks, were to the left and right of Don as he approached a set of pedestrian lights where the more fortunate were waiting to cross.

He pulled out his phone. He wanted the street beggars to believe that he was busy. Nine times out of ten if beggars, in the past, had seen Don texting (pretending) or talking (pretending) on his phone, then they had left him alone. He felt for them but didn't really feel safe pulling his wallet out. It was one of those conundrums that faced him from time to time.

As a human, he felt humanity towards his fellow man yet, even though he was in a position to help them, he rarely did because he brushed their plight to the side with so much ease, often thinking of himself and not those in need. He knew he needed to work on this.

He was pretending to text at the pedestrian lights; he even typed in a few letters, none of which made up a word. He quickly looked up and saw that he was huddled with shoppers, those that had money. Those that probably wouldn't beg him for his money. They may even have been pretending to talk into their phones as well. A slight twinge of guilt washed over him.

He put his phone back in his pocket and waited for the pedestrian lights to change.

That's when he smelt it.

The Holygrace scent was unmistakable. Katy had a bottle. He loved her wearing it. He recalled reading the bottle one day to see what contributed to the wonderful aroma. Jasmine, pink pepper and bergamot all combined into one, an aroma that was etched in to his nasal passages.

He was close to the scent, it was finding him, making his nostrils come alive.

He looked around at the pedestrians waiting for the walk sign to flash. He wanted to reach across and move his nose close to the flesh under each of the female chins. He counted them. There were fifteen females within smelling distance, it could have been any one of them that was wearing the Holygrace.

An Asian woman was aware that Don was looking in her direction, she moved her eyes uncomfortably as not to catch his. Don looked around once more, he didn't know why, he had nothing to gain by doing so. So, some woman was wearing the same scent as Katy once did, it was bound to happen sooner or later.

In any event, what would he do if he did manage to track down the scent? Chances are it would be one of the fifteen women he had mentally counted who were stood next to a male companion, he could hardly approach them and ask if they were wearing Holygrace, he already knew the answer anyway. He glanced across the waiting pedestrians once more, somewhat dejected at not seeing Katy.

Just another pathetic attempt at hope, he thought. His hopes yet again dashed by not seeing what he wanted to see—his Katy, smiling and apologetic.

One final look around.

That's when he saw her. She looked as beautiful as she did on the TV screens and magazines, even though she appeared to be dressed-down. The woman she was standing next to looked familiar too.

Karen Crawford's eyes met his.

# Chapter Ten
# 3 Years Ago

*From: Angie <angiejakobs@ajpsychicservices.com>*
*To: Karen <karencrawfordodelia@crawfordodelia.com>*
*Subject : Follow up from the reading yesterday.*
*Date: Wed, 9 March 2011 11:11:11*

*Karen, I just want to follow-on from the reading I gave you yesterday. You remember I told you about love and why it hadn't come to you yet? Well, I slept, or tried to sleep, last night and the question kept popping in to my head. Eventually, I drifted and had a visitor in my dreams.*

*He was a male figure yet very feminine; it could mean that it was a female presence coming to me in the form of a male. I'll explain this to you next time we meet.*

*Anyway, here's how I perceived the message.*

*There will be just one man that you fall in love with. He will be your soul mate, you will know when your eyes meet his that he is the one. You will meet him when you're least expecting it. It may be across a crowded room, it may be a glance across a restaurant or just what you may think is a chance meeting, but you will meet him.*

*He would have recently had his heart broken and it will be your mission to mend this tortured soul. The angels are telling me that this man has good intentions, he will fix you and you will fix him. Joining you two together has already been put into place. You cannot fight it, you will not be able to ignore it. It will be your serendipity, it will be the making of you.*

*You will both meet because you are both broken. You will both connect immediately, your hearts, your mind and your spirit. You will remain together forever, both here and when you both cross over to the other side. There is a reason for this man coming into your life, Karen. I'm not sure what that reason is but this* will not be a chance meeting. It's been planned by forces of a great love, the angels of love.

Don't take this lightly, Karen, it <u>WILL</u> happen. I don't know when and I don't know how but I do know that it will happen. Grab him if you have to, he's a keeper. His heart is so full of love, I can feel it, and I know what he can offer you. If you have to, kidnap him and never let this guy go. He is a man of great integrity.

Now, here's the confusing bit. The spirit in my dream was holding a question mark. This has been baffling me and I still don't know what it symbolises? I am 100% certain that you will meet this man, and you will know instantly that he is your one true love, of that there is no question. I also know for certainty that he will be a Leo, born towards the end of July. You can use this for confirmation when you eventually meet him.

For you, Karen, there is no other man.
A.

**Angie Jakobs. Psychic—ajpsychicservices.com**

# Chapter Eleven

Karen met his gaze, she saw the heartache in his eyes immediately. She didn't know how she saw his sadness, she just did, she felt it; the feeling reached inside her and squeezed the most gentlest of squeezes around her heart, and at the same time, she somehow heard Angie's voice, *He will be your soul mate, you will know when your eyes meet his that he is the one.* He was looking at her intensely, his deep brown eyes melting her, washing her with an experience of love that she had never, *ever*, felt before.

She pulled out her mother's pocket watch, still keeping her eyes fixed on the handsome stranger. Her eyes briefly left his as she looked at the time on the watch. It was 11.11. She returned her gaze and he offered a smile, unbeknownst to Karen, it was his first sober smile since his separation with Katy.

Karen returned his smile with one of her own. They had connected. Angie Jakobs was so fucking amazing, she thought.

She wondered what to do next. She ran the email Angie had sent her through her head. It was sketchy as it had been 3 years since it landed in her inbox. Were there any instructions, what if he just walks away? Angie had sent her a return email shortly after her prediction. It was short and, at the time, confirmed how brilliant Angie was. Angie had wrote:

*Oh my God, LOL. Check the time on the last email I sent you.*

*** 

She was the most amazing woman he'd ever laid eyes on. He knew who she was straight away, even without her make-up he knew it was Karen Crawford, the famous American who had moved to Britain many years ago. She wore a Burberry scarf around her neck and her hair looked different than usual, it was tied up in a bun, hiding her famous curls.

She was truly beautiful in real life more so than she was in the glossy photos in magazines that he had seen of her and her TV appearances on game shows, interviews and adverts. She was of good stock, he thought, standing perfectly straight, looking so calm and peaceful. It was an instant attraction and the feeling was mutual.

Time stood still. Neither of them could hear the sounds of the busy London traffic or the conversations of pedestrians waiting at the lights to cross over the road. The only sound both of them heard was the sound of their own heartbeat, a rhythm that was quicker than normal, a rhythm of excitement, of anticipation, of love. Their eyes unknowingly surveyed one another's facial features.

He noticed the blue intensity of her eyes, the quaint nose, and the luscious lips while her eyes were directed to his goatee beard and lips that she desperately wanted on hers. He had short, cropped hair, slightly grey and receding at the front. She was drawn back to his eyes; they were loving her as much as she was loving them.

Bella hadn't noticed the love being conceived. She was busy talking into her mobile phone. It was the police; her Canary Wharf apartment had been broken into.

Time continued to stand still for Karen and Don. His brown eyes were reaching inside her, her grace and beauty were mesmerising him. They were locked in a moment; one of those clichéd moments that, however brief, seemed to last forever. She heard Angie's voice again, *You cannot fight it, and you will not be able to ignore it. It will be your serendipity.*

The sound of his heartbeat faded, allowing those outside his moment to intrude. The noise of the traffic slowly faded back again as did the noise of the chitter-chatter around him. Karen felt the noise levels increase too, her and his moment invaded. Don was unsure what to do next, was he mistaken, was the famous model really gazing at him or was it someone next to him or over his shoulder?

He didn't want to break his gaze so continued looking for more confirmation that she really was looking at him. The increasing feeling of wanting, loving was overwhelming.

The large-breasted woman standing next to Karen had started to cry and Don knew this was an opportunity to introduce himself. Karen turned her attention to Bella who, at this point, was swearing down the phone at the police officer who had been given the task to inform her that her apartment had not only been burgled, it had also been trashed.

The pedestrian lights signalled to all those waiting so that they could cross the street, the obligatory 'bleep bleep' accompanied the green light, they swarmed across en-masse, ignoring and manoeuvring themselves around a frantic Bella and a consoling Karen, and an approaching Don.

"Is everything okay?" Don asked. Bella ignored him whilst Karen turned to him. She felt her heart speed and a strange tingling sensation grew in the pit of her stomach. Once again she heard Angie, *Grab him if you have to, he's a keeper. His heart is so full of love.* Fuck, she felt like she was 16 again.

"We need to get out of here," Karen told Don, adding, "Do you live close by?"

"Sadly no," he told her.

She turned to Bella who was now in a fit of rage and shouting more obscenities into her phone.

"It's fucking supposed to be burglar proof you complete and utter moron of course I have insurance but that's not the point, you fucking idiot. Calm down? Calm fucking down? Let me speak to your superior."

"Please, Bella, stop making a scene," Karen told her whilst Don made a mental note of the large-breasted woman's name.

Crowds were beginning to gather. Karen had already sensed that they would. She and Bella had dressed down for their shopping trip, they always did. Recognition brought on way too many fans who always wanted photographs and kisses. Saying no to some of their admirers had, in the past, put Karen in fear of her life.

A man and woman had approached her last year, she was in a rush and had, politely she thought, refused to have her photo taken with them. The woman had flew into a rage, calling Karen a slut. The man had grabbed Karen by her throat.

She saw rage in his eyes. Luckily for Karen, a group of council workers had intervened.

"Can you help us get somewhere safe please?" She asked Don. She didn't need to use her puppy dog eyes, he was already smitten with her, as she was with him.

"Come with me," he said. He knew there was a hotel close by as he had seen it when mapping out his trip last night. He was meticulous like that, almost military-like. Karen grabbed Bella by the arm and they followed Don. He found the hotel within 3 minutes or so and signalled a concierge standing outside the *Levin* Hotel.

He walked over and Don asked him to call a taxi. He explained who the two women were and Don saw the recognition in the eyes of the concierge. "Right away, Sir," he told Don before breaking into a slow run to the entrance.

Don put his arms around both women. Karen felt his touch, so warming, so inviting. Bella, Don noticed, flinched.

"Walk with me," he prompted. He ushered them to the hotel entrance, a taxi had already pulled up and the concierge had already opened the door.

"Thank you so much," Karen said to Don. She held him by the side of both arms and kissed his cheek. He caught a whiff of her scent. It was, indeed, Holygrace. Her hands on his arms were straight out of a dream or Hollywood movie, *Notting Hill* where Julia Roberts played a famous American actress and Hugh Grant played a down on his luck bookseller, sprung to Don's mind.

Karen wanted so desperately to ask him to jump in the taxi with her. She wanted to sit next to him, to talk to him, to watch him as he spoke, to imagine putting her lips on his mouth and have him run his fingers through her hair. She felt an overpowering impatience; she felt a strong desire and excitement to learn more about this man just as an avid reader of a thriller novel would be excited to turn the next page so they could read a twist unfold.

She had never wanted anyone so much as she wanted this complete stranger. He was surely the one her psychic friend, Angie had spoke of. Don, on the other hand, was still trying to deal with the fact that the famous Karen Crawford had just touched him. Moreover, she had just kissed him.

"Meet me in the lobby of Claridge's Mayfair at 7 tonight," she whispered.

In an instant, she turned and was inside the taxi telling the driver the same address she had just whispered in Don's ear. Before the driver could push his foot on the accelerator, Karen turned to look out of the rear passenger window. Just one final look at the stranger before, hopefully, she thought, seeing him again later that night.

He was looking back at her, smiling. She offered a smile back and gently bit her lips sending out a subconscious message to Don that she was interested in him. Very interested.

The taxi pulled away and Don wondered what the fuck had just happened.

# Chapter Twelve
# 3 Years Previously

*From: Angie <angiejakobs@ajpsychicservices.com>*
*To: Karen <karencrawfordodelia@crawfordodelia.com>*
*Subject: Angel Number 1111*
*Date: Wed, 9 March 2011 11:58:17*

*Karen,*

*1111 is so significant. I'll explain.*

*Number 1111 is created by the influences of the number 1. Number 1 aligns with the vibrations of developing beginnings and also means starting afresh. The repeating number 1 is often the first sequence that appears to many people, as it has been with you. That's why I stress to you that it applies to you as my message was sent to you at this time. (11.11)*

*You, my dear, are going to experience a major spiritual wake-up call or an epiphany and I honestly believe it will transpire when you meet this man. I can't tell you when but I can tell you that it is going to happen and you will know instantly when it does.*

*Use the positive energy of the Universe to bring to fruition your deepest desires, hopes and dreams. Reach out to the Universe, Karen, and it will reach out to you.*

*A gateway has opened up for you, Karen, and it will all happen very quickly. Within hours of meeting this man, you will not be able to forget him, you are not supposed to. You are meeting for a reason and it's not just about love and fate.*

*There's a far bigger reason, I just don't know what it is yet but it is something bigger than you and I could ever imagine. It's of biblical proportions, Karen, and has all the blessings of those that surround you.*

*More will come to me as the time nears, or maybe you will just tell me when it happens.*

*You* WILL *Know.*

*Create your reality.*

**A.**

**Angie Jakobs. Psychic—ajpsychicservices.com**

# Chapter Thirteen

Bella had returned to her carnage. The burglar, the police had told her, hadn't broken in at all. CCTV footage had shown Bella leaving her apartment earlier with Tony Turner. She had left her keys in the door. They showed her the footage and asked if she knew who was entering.

A hooded male was seen on the CCTV footage wearing a scarf over his mouth. Her response was typical Bella. "I haven't got special powers you know, I mean, it's not like I can see through fucking clothing."

The burglar had taken items of jewellery and a laptop, Bella told the investigating team, that consisted of two Police Community Support Officers, one male, one female. She was told to make a note of everything that had been stolen and to contact her insurance company. She'd already made a mental note that the 30 or so grams of cocaine was missing from the top of her bedside cabinet.

She was thankful to the burglar for taking it as the police swarmed her room. She quickly estimated the loss of the white powder; it was good gear, coming in at £50 per gram. Fifteen grand gone in the blink of an eye, all because she'd left the fucking keys in the door. The jewellery and laptop could be replaced via her insurance company. She could never make such a claim for her missing coke.

A pillow case had been used to carry the goods and, judging by the CCTV footage, the intruder was in and out of Bella's apartment in under 4 minutes. The female Community Support Officer showed her the footage of the intruder leaving, her pink pillow case in his hand, loaded with her laptop, jewellery. The officer told her that many burglar's used the same method to carry away goods.

Bella thought, 'Fucking fifteen grand worth of goods.'

The male Community Support Officer was busy looking at Bella whilst making notes. A look of recognition appeared on his face. Bella was used to it but, nonetheless, found it unprofessional.

"Don't forget to lube that dick of yours when you watch one of my porn movies later," she told him. His face turned crimson and he put his notebook away in his top pocket before telling his partner that they should leave and file the burglary back at the station.

Both officers left and Bella looked around her apartment. She didn't want to be alone and thought about giving Karen a call. She opted instead to call Tony Turner, she felt that she had been harsh with him earlier. Besides, sex, for Bella at least, relieved stress, plus Tony could get his hands on some more coke.

She picked up her phone and entered the first two letters of his name, he was listed as 'Trouser Snake Tony', she then hit the call button.

\*\*\*

Karen had returned to her suite at Claridge's and logged in to her email account where she had read the series of emails Angie Jakobs had sent her 3 years ago. She'd put them in a special folder marked 'Him'. For the second time that day, she thought that her best friend was 'fucking amazing'.

She pulled up Angie's email address then hovered her cursor over the compose button. She put a smiley in the subject box, in the body she wrote:

*It's happened, 1111.*

She then headed for the en-suite bathroom. She needed to shower. She needed time with the handsome man, the shining knight who had come to her rescue earlier. She needed to remember every minor detail about him; he would, in her fantasy, be taking a shower with her.

Her hands, her fingers would become his. She could not wait any longer. She opened the shower door and turned the circular shower knob. She closed the door to encase the heat.

She removed her clothes and felt herself quiver in anticipation. Goosebumps spread down her back as if prompted by invisible fingertips running down her spine. What was it he said when he put his hands on her? She couldn't remember so she made it up, *I am very attracted to you Karen, would you mind if I kissed your lips?*

Her nipples stiffened at her mini fantasy. She was already moist between her legs as the images turned into her own mini porn movie; a movie that featured just her and the handsome stranger. She, in her fantasy, was holding his hand, leading him in to the shower.

She opened the shower door, steam bellowed out. She stepped inside and slid the door shut behind her. She was already halfway to having an orgasm before the water touched her hair, before the mind role-play had even started. The water felt good. Her fantasy felt better.

She was in the moment. A moment that belonged to just her and the stranger she had met earlier, the 1111 guy.

# Chapter Fourteen

Don never went to Harrods as he'd previously planned. He, instead, found a pub as he needed a strong drink to numb the sensation running through him. He'd walked into the pub without reading the sign above the window, the name of the bar was 'The Crow's Nest'.

He had just had an encounter with Karen Crawford, she had just kissed him for fuck sake. What was that all about? And giving out her hotel address to him? He couldn't make heads nor tails of it all. His hands were shaking as he lifted the straight Jameson's whiskey to his mouth.

He normally drank it with a shot of Coca Cola but right now, he needed the sharp hit in an effort to make sense of it all. That moment before the signal sound of the traffic lights, it was more than a moment. One of the most desired women on the planet had took an interest in him, a paralegal who had only recently had a shit shower fixed. It was all totally bizarre.

*The Blinkers* or Karen Crawford? It was a no-brainer. He looked at his watch, it was fast approaching 1.50. He needed to call Cameron, his Scottish friend, to tell him that he wouldn't be able to make it to Buckingham Palace for the group photo of *Blinkers'* fans but what excuse could he possibly give? 'Oh hi Cam, sorry I can't make the show tonight, Karen Crawford has invited me back to her hotel'— that would have sent his bearded friend into a state of complete apoplexy.

Don thought about just sending him a text message but that would have just raised more questions and, to be honest, Don's hands were not able to hold the phone, let alone draft a text message to his bearded friend. He could always head over to Buckingham Palace to meet the Europeans, he thought, but how would he leave them when they all headed to Wembley Stadium? He opted not to call them at all. He'd explain it all another time, when he actually knew how.

He looked at his watch again. It was 1.51. He'd have to kill some time and he couldn't do it propping up a bar and knocking back stiff drinks all day. He was going to meet Karen Crawford at her fucking hotel. The same Karen Crawford who had smiled at him, the same Karen Crawford that had kissed his cheek and invited him to her hotel.

He downed the whiskey in one gulp and ordered another. She had reached in and touched his heart. Any previous remnants of pain that he felt over Katy had all but disappeared.

Amazing, he thought, how one chance encounter can take away pain. If only he had met her 5 weeks ago, then he would never have had to endure all that pain and suffering. He didn't know that the pain of loss was all part of the *plan*; a *plan* that had been under preparation for some time. The train times, the latte being knocked over, the Japanese tourist, and the smell of Holygrace—all *planned*.

He finished his second whiskey and headed out the door into the bright sunshine and cold breeze. He didn't feel the cold. He had no idea how he was going to kill the time. His time was still standing still after his chance encounter and it was all he could think about.

He headed to McDonald's, the big yellow M drawing him in subconsciously, as Karen biting her lips had earlier, and was soon ordering a double cheeseburger without cheese. He didn't like cheese. He, as a kid, had once been given a 'new cheese' to taste by an older boy who lived on the same street. Turns out it wasn't cheese at all, it was a 3 week old dog turd. He had never eaten cheese again.

Thankfully, there was a newspaper on the table he sat at. The full page advertisements caught his attention. Multiplex cinemas had, it appeared, paid handsomely for the print space. He'd kill time by going to the movies (*that was the plan*). He, having made his mind up, turned the page.

A photo of Karen Crawford greeted him. She was advertising a toothpaste but marketing being marketing they just had to have a full body shot of Karen. The photo was black and white, the dress she was wearing was a light colour. She was perched over a bathroom sink brushing her teeth, her body arched perfectly to show off those famous curves of hers. The ad had the slogan,

*The One Good Minty Taste That You Want In Your Mouth, Scoober's Minty Toothpaste.*

Fuck, she had just kissed him and invited him back to her hotel. His heart raced at what just might happen between them later. He brushed aside any romance quickly, she probably just wanted to thank him for helping her earlier. He didn't care, he was just excited at the prospect of meeting with her again, the thought of which sent his heart racing.

He looked at the toothpaste advertisement again, his eyes following Karen's sexy curves and provocative pose. Maybe, he thought, she may be interested in him, after all she was looking at him, she did smile at him, she did bite her lip to draw attention to her mouth. Maybe, just maybe?, he thought, he hoped.

He closed the newspaper then picked up his half-eaten double hamburger, minus the cheese, and left via the front door. The London air was getting colder as the afternoon wore on. He slid down a few side-streets to avoid the heavy traffic on the main roads. Google Maps showing him the quickest route to the cinema.

Whilst walking, he removed the hamburger from its bun and in an instant it was consumed. He threw the bun, complete with salad, pickle and dressing, towards a nearby bin that was already overflowing. The bun landed on top of the pile and Don gave himself a mental high five.

It fell off the pile seconds after he turned and continued to walk down the street.

A crow swooped to pick up the discarded bun. It cawed.

Don never saw it. Don never heard it.

# Chapter Fifteen

Angie Jakobs was a psychic medium. She had her own prime time TV slot on network television and had been endorsed by many Hollywood stars. She had been given an ability at a very early age, she preferred not to call it a gift. She had helped the police find missing persons on countless occasions and had even led them straight to the front door of four high profile killers.

More recently, she had helped them find a sniper. Brett Myer's had shot and killed three adult pedestrians, he'd left his rifle at the scene of his last victim. Angie had held it and led police to his front door. When holding items from crime scenes, she did not see the killer but she saw through their eyes. She also felt emotion and the whole experience could, at times, leave her in a state of mourning.

It was hard to let go at first but, over the years, she was able to gain comfort by seeing what the killer could see. The images were gruesome but she knew that the victims were showing her how their killer had left them. At times, she witnessed the crime; they were harrowing for Angie particularly as they were from the point of view from the killer.

With Myers, it was the barrel of flowers outside his home that gave him away.

In her visions, Angie became Myers and saw the overgrown weeds next to the barrel. She saw his hand move the weeds and reach inside the barrel for a set of keys, presumably his front door keys. On the barrel was a single plaque with the street address of Myers—'2501 Carlson Av'.

Child killers, Ray Pontin, Greg Hanson, and William Cappens, had all evaded the sleuthing of Idaho's finest detectives that was until Angie Jakobs became involved. The child killers were always top of Angie's priority list though and she worked tirelessly with investigation officers on three cold cases.

Ray Pontin, she had told the Idaho State Police, lived close to the Canadian border. He, she had told detectives, often made trips to Canada. There were four children that came to her, each had told Angie about the Silver GMC pickup truck with Idaho license plates. All four children, Angie felt, had fallen prey to the driver of the vehicle.

Each of the children showed the name of a construction company, 'Hunter Moon Construction'. Turned out the owner of HMC drove a silver GMC pickup. Forensics did the rest.

Kaylin Westwood and Jessica Richardson were both found with fibres under their fingernails. The fibres, forensics found, came from the custom moulded carpet in the back of Ray Pontin's silver GMC pickup truck. It wasn't enough for a conviction but it was enough for a warrant to search his home.

That's when investigating officers found items of clothing belonging to 15 year-old Kaylin Westwood, 17 year-old Jessica Richardson, 12 year-old Pauline Carter-Lewis, and 14 year-old Annie Sommers. They also found items of other children's clothing.

Pontin later confessed that he had killed four others. He drew circles around their burial places on a map for the officers that had interviewed him.

Greg Hanson had killed two boys from the Bonners Ferry neighbourhood.

He lived alone and was a regular church goer. Angie tuned in to both boys. They told her he worked with children and that they were in black bags at the bottom of Kootenay River, their killer had taken their socks off and painted their toenails. It was commonly known that the two boys were found in black bags in the river but the Idaho State Police had never allowed the toenails being painted information out into the public domain, so they knew Angie was on to something.

He lives in rented accommodation, she had told them. He is a school teacher and knew the boys and their families. Shortly after, the Idaho State Police arrested Greg Hanson, he had been the History teacher for Charlie Pickering and Nathan Armstrong at a private Church of Jesus Christ of Latter-day Saints school in Bonners Ferry.

Finally, she led them to William Cappens. On Angie's advice, police had staked out his four bedroomed house in Rexburg. Angie had told them that he took photographs after he had murdered 10 year-old Justin Stevens. Justin had showed Angie a Polaroid. She woke in the early hours after a particularly bad dream and 10 year-old Justin was standing at the foot of her bed. He held a Polaroid camera in one hand and a bunch of photos in the other.

When the police finally entered Cappens' home, they found a biscuit tin open on his dining table. Cappens had invited the two officers in after they had knocked on his porch door. He'd had an unpaid parking ticket and, they told him, they just happened to be in the area. He was wearing a vest stained with barbecue sauce, evidenced by the chicken leg hanging from his mouth.

He'd hoped that the police would be on their way after he offered them a cold lemonade. Unfortunately, for Cappens at least, he'd left the lid of the biscuit tin off and Detective Romanski noticed the square framed photographs sprawled across the dining table. On each of them was a thumbprint of barbecue sauce; the same barbecue sauce he and Detective Simmondson had noticed on his vest when he had answered the door.

Cappens had been looking at the photos whilst eating his chicken. The photos revealed a bound and gagged 10 year-old Justin Stevens.

Only the most ardent of sceptics would put the ability of Angie Jakobs down to 'luck' or 'good old-fashioned detective work'.

When she wasn't doing her psychic work, she would be on the ski slopes somewhere in the world or would be in some field perfecting her archery skills. She could have been a professional archer. She'd even been told that by the archery school instructor. *Angie, you're a natural. With hard work and plenty of practice, you may one day make the Olympic Archery team for the USA.*

Deep down she knew that her mediumship was given to her and it was a path that she could just not ignore.

Archery was just a hobby. Mediumship was her life and helped others.

She worked, as most psychics tell us they do, with visions that appeared to her. Sometimes, she would see dead people, sometimes she would see something from her childhood that was associated with the person she was reading. She'd often hear music that others couldn't hear, again this was always associated with the person she happened to be reading.

At an early age Angie had honed her skills by using her powers of perception, an ability to gather facts and translate them into prediction of the short-term future. Her ability to do this became second nature to her by the time she was 13. She had an ability that allowed her to tap into her intuitive, inspired, and subconscious mind.

It enabled her to access information on a deeper level. She perfected the art of not over-analysing as she knew that it could build blockages, traps and more often than not could lead to limited repeated thought processes. She surrounded herself with love when the visits came, almost like a force-field of love enshrouded her to protect her from negativity. She trusted her gut and her instincts, and that brought her more spirits from the after world and more peace to those she was reading.

Her *gift* was her interpretation of it all.

"Most of us can tune in to spirit," she once told viewers on her weekly TV show. "Where people go wrong is through their interpretation of what they see or hear, they are often distracted by outside influences," she added.

She gave an example.

"I was contacted by a student of mine who has an incredible talent, she had, for about a year, being seeing signs, symbols, she'd also been having dreams. Everything she saw related to the present, in particular a relationship that was unfolding. She, eventually, allowed it all to unfold and love blossomed.

"Sadly, outside influences distorted her way of thinking and the relationship failed because she listened to these outside influences rather than spirit. The signs and symbols she had previously seen became less frequent because she wasn't tuned in to spirit anymore. If you don't listen to what you hear or act upon what you see then spirit will pull away.

"If you listen to the advice of family and friends rather than your spirit guides then you will miss out on some pretty amazing life experiences. She dumped the man that spirit had guided her to. She believed that spirit had told her to do this but during her own readings she allowed the thoughts of others to invade spirit world. The messages she received were a mixture of spirit messages and 'advice' given to her by living friends, she could not distinguish between the two."

Angie then told how the student entered in to another relationship, she did so because her friends had told her he was the 'better option'. A dancing instructor who, on the outside, appealed to her student. On the inside, however, his heart was full of himself and not others, unlike the heart of her student's previous boyfriend.

"Spirit pulled away because she did not listen to the advice. The symbols and signs they offered became associated with the new man in her life because her friends had planted the seed. She failed to understand what spirit was telling her. Lust took over love and we must never allow that to happen.

"We must never allow our hearts to be ruled by our heads. Remember, we are born with love embedded into us. Our thinking is our own creation, we adjust to the opinions of others and we forget that we should listen to what our hearts tell us. It's all about love.

"Sometime later," Angie said, "she learned that the new man in her life had a string of women that he was seeing behind her back. Devastated, she contacted the guy she had dumped. He had moved on and found love elsewhere. She lives alone now and tells me she is happy but I can see her heart, I can see her aura, I can see it in her eyes.

"She is happy with her decision and also at peace with it but her head ruled her heart and when we work with spirit we have to learn to listen and feel with our hearts and not our heads. Spirit doesn't punish us but it does sigh in desperation when we miss signs of when we allow outside influences to interfere with what is meant to be."

She opened her email and read the message from Karen.

*It's happened, 1111.*

She smiled and connected with her spirit guide. She felt their nod of approval, then responded to Karen's email with three words and a smiley.

*No other man. :-)*

# Chapter Sixteen

What should she wear, should it be informal wear or sexy? Should she pull out all the stops and wear something revealing, something seductive? She knew that she didn't need to, she could wear a potato sack and still look ravishing. She thought that something that clung to her slender body would suffice. She, at that moment, opted for the body clinging white *Gucci* dress.

No man could resist her curves and bumps when she had worn it before. She had turned many heads, had felt and seen the lust in the eyes of many men, most of whom had to disguise their ogling as they were with partners at the time. She would wear a full length coat upon his arrival, making sure that her hair was worn down in all its natural curled beauty.

He wouldn't know about the dress until she led him back to her suite for 'coffee'. Once there she'd take off her coat and walk away from him, just so he could see enough of her, just so he could imagine the things that he wanted to do with her. She would beckon him to sit with her, her dress would ride slightly up her silky thighs.

He would be powerless. She would be in control. She wanted that control tonight, well, for the first session of love making at least. She would fuck him then he would fuck her. She felt like a harlot—*his* harlot, a harlot for no other man.

She was in the shower; the water was of impeccable temperature and emerged with force. She lathered the complimentary coconut oil into her neck and breasts, moving her hands across her shoulders where stood a single tattoo, '1111', that was inked in black on to her skin. She placed her head under the water and fantasised that he was with her, behind her, inching his hardness closer to her. She felt his hands touch her, just as they had physically touched her earlier in the day.

Closing her eyes, she brought him deeper into her fantasy. His arms grasping her shoulders as she backed into him. She imagined his hot breath on her neck and then imagined his lips kissing her shoulders as his hands reached around to cup her breasts before massaging the sweet smelling coconut oil into them. Her right hand slid off her shoulder and brushed over her erect nipples.

First one finger, then two found their way into her opening. She was wet with a thicker substance than the coconut lava that coated her body, she was wet for him. Her fingers became his and she briefly heard herself moan with gratification. The thought of his fingers inside her made her shudder with exhilaration.

Karen was close.

She wanted his mouth upon her, on her neck, on her breasts, on her wetness.

She pushed down on her fingers then slid them out again, making sure she rubbed them across her clitoris, making sure to keep the image of him in her mind's eye. She laid her hand flat on the glass door and arched her body in such a way that would make penetration with her fingers more comfortable. Sliding her fingers in then rubbing her clit, she built up speed as the movie of the stranger pressing against her ass while he sucked on her neck played inside her head.

She repeated these five times.

She let out a gentle moan each time she slid her fingers inside. She fantasised that she could hear him moan in delight and also had him bite her shoulders, just hard enough to leave his mark.

She envisaged his smile again and those deep brown eyes, his reluctance to approach her earlier, his hand around her as he ushered her and Bella to the taxi, and his voice, that sweet English accent. She sucked it all in to her fantasy.

His voice. His smile. His eyes. His touch. She tingled.

Then finally, the vaginal contraction that brought on the rapid pleasurable release.

# Chapter Seventeen

Don was heading out of the cinema; the movie, he thought, was mediocre. An action thriller called *Scorned*, that didn't really have much action at all and was about as thrilling as a visit to the dentist. He missed much of the plot, his mind was elsewhere, it was with Karen Crawford, or rather it was playing out possible scenarios. Did she just want to thank him for hauling her ass into a taxi earlier or was she genuinely attracted to him?

He replayed their moment and felt his heart pound against his chest. She had broken her gaze twice, once to check her watch, once to attend to the frantic woman she was with, a woman she called Bella. Why did she look at her watch, why, after she looked at it, did she return her eyes to his, why did she offer a smile, why did he feel her in his heart, why him? So many questions with no obvious answers.

He headed towards the pedestrian lights, again the image of the famous American woman foremost on his mind. Quite a coincidence that she was wearing Holygrace, the one scent that he really liked. Had it not been for him smelling it he would never had met her gaze, nor hers his, he thought. (the *plan*)

He crossed the pedestrian lights with the busy shoppers, glancing at his watch to make sure that the two hour movie he had just sat through wasn't in fact a 4 hour movie (it felt like it). He headed west, he'd find a bar that served hot meals. He wouldn't order too much as he didn't know if Karen Crawford had plans for them to eat at Claridge's. Fucking Claridge's, he thought.

He'd only previously seen it on TV; it was where the rich and famous stayed. He doubted very much if paralegals could even afford the starters on the menu. This thought made him uncomfortable. How could he afford to take Karen Crawford out for a meal? He didn't even know if a Liebfraumilch was a wine that rich and famous people drank.

Come to think of it he didn't even know if a Liebfraumilch was a brand name or if it was a place name? He knew it was German and he'd once read somewhere that translated it meant 'Beloved lady's milk'. All well and good for pub quizzes but he didn't really see Karen Crawford as a woman who would enjoy a good old knees up in a cockney bar where pies and pub quizzes were the order of the night. He doubted that Karen Crawford had ever been into a pub.

A hooded man was handing out leaflets yards ahead, Don looked at his watch in an effort to not make eye contact with the outstretched arm. For the second time that day, he went into his acting role. If he looked busy the beggars wouldn't hassle him. Don moved to his right to further distance himself from the outstretched hand (*that was the plan*).

He stepped into the cycle lane and felt the crunch immediately. The front tyre rammed into his right leg, the cyclist fell forward, his head decorated with his crash helmet, hurtling towards Don's rib cage. In an instant, he felt his ribs crack, this was followed by a burning sensation in his shin, one pain cancelling out the other. The cyclist landed on him knocking him fully into the cycling lane.

He'd heard the hooded guy shout, "Look out," but his reaction and insistence to not make any contact with the leaflet guy meant he was now lying in a crumpled heap. A couple of cracked ribs and bruised tibia his penance for not being observant to the time on his watch when he had looked at it seconds ago in an effort to avoid the hooded guy. The time had been 5.17 (1717).

The hooded guy, Andrew 'AJ' Simmons, was just trying to make a living.

He was a former drug user and just trying to make ends meet. Handing out leaflets wasn't what he wanted to do, he wanted to be back in the office phoning potential clients again. He knew that the chances of that were slim; the drugs had taken their toll, addiction was his world and, as a result, he lost his job.

He'd turned to crime to feed his addiction, petty theft at first then moving on to street mugging, knowing it was wrong but also knowing that he needed to feed his addiction. He'd lost his wife and kids too. They'd moved as far away from him as possible, to Aberdeen. He'd pleaded, he'd cried and begged for forgiveness. He'd made promises that he would get himself clean but deep down he knew that he wasn't ready to kick the heroin. Heroin, at that time, was his life.

Don, feeling the excruciating pain, felt the hooded guy's hand on his shoulder. "Don't move, brother, just sit still." Mr Hoody pulled out his phone and within seconds uttered, "Ambulance please."

"Thank you for your help," Don managed to say through gritted teeth. The pain was fresh.

"No problem at all, brother, just stay still and the ambulance will be here soon, best to get you checked out." Mr Hoody's hand touched Don's shoulder.

Don asked, "What is your name?"

"It's Andrew, but most folk call me AJ."

Don looked up at AJ, one of the leaflets Don had been trying to avoid fell in front of him. He reached to pick it up. AJ saw he was struggling and handed him a leaflet from the pile he was holding.

Keeping his hand on Don's shoulder, he said, "I don't think you'll be going here tonight."

Don looked at the a-4 sized leaflet and learned about a new show in town. A west end theatre was premiering the stage production of *Gabriel*. It was about Archangel Gabriel. An unknown actor was the lead role. He looked handsome with his tanned skin and well-trimmed beard. He had wings and his palms were pressed together.

A lone crow looked down from the scaffolding high above where Don was sprawled. Its caw lost in the noise of the London traffic. He flew off the scaffolding then headed west.

# Chapter Eighteen

Angie's message to Karen read:

*Loving others in their own chosen path is setting the energy you want in your world.*

*The only Gabriel message that should concern people is the one above, Karen. It is a golden rule.*

*We know that it is imperative that we treat others as we would wish to be treated. Archangel Gabriel is verbally expressing that when we do this it sets energy into universe that pours through our lives so we obtain what we give. We reap what we sow, however small.*

*A loving personality not only makes the mind more placid and tranquil, but it affects our body in an affirmative way additionally. On the other hand, abhorrence, jealousy and fear worry our placidity of mind, make us restless and destroys our body. Even our body needs the tranquillity of mind and is not suited to restlessness.*

*This shows that a gratefulness for tranquillity of mind is in our blood. Hatred, jealousy and fear are not with us when we enter this world, the only emotion we are born with is love. Hatred, jealousy and fear are all taught us. Love is born the day we are.*

*These are the fundamental guiding reasons to love others as they are and sanction them to choose their own path in life, no matter how erroneous we think they are. The majority of us have a number of stories to tell about those we have tried to change to our way of thinking. But it seldom works, it has not deterred us from still endeavouring to change them.*

*We don't need to change them, Karen. Yes, we can offer an opinion but we don't need to convince anyone that our opinion is better than theirs.*

*The most kind and loving way we can relate to others is by allowing them to be who they are while valuing and acknowledging their choices in life. We may not concur with them but we should value their choices even if those choices are ones that we wouldn't make ourselves.*

*We are being reminded that what we do for ourselves and for others affects all God's creatures. So, Karen, for the sake of the world and for our own contentment, we should remind ourselves that loving and kindness is the rule that advances our health and well-being and guides the being of the glorious conditions of reverence, care and harmony into the world.*

*I'm not suggesting for one minute that the actions of Hitler should be applauded or anything like that. I'm suggesting that our actions cannot change the actions of others. It's their path and we have to revere that path because evil has to be respected; it's potent and if we fail to respect it then we will fear it when it enters our lives. Combat the actions of others with love, not with anything else. Trust me on this, Karen.*

*Gabriel is around you, Karen. Gabriel is an archangel of action. Things are about to change for you and you will need to embrace what is coming your way. Do it with love, don't be fearful of it.*

The email was dated 31 July 2013.

Karen had emailed Angie last year, a day after she had been attacked in the street, both verbally and physically. The message Angie was trying to relay was simple. If Karen had stopped and given the man and woman time then the outcome would have been different. If she had ignored what she wanted and held compassion for what others wanted then she would not have experienced what she did.

\*\*\*

The same rule applied to Don. He showed a lack of compassion to AJ, he thought about nobody but himself and now, here he was, waiting to be discharged from Chelsea & Westminster Hospital.

Others referred to this rule as Karma.

It was 6.45 pm.

# Chapter Nineteen

She hadn't even slipped into her dress when the call came. She was wearing just a bra and panties, one stay-up stocking was proudly shimmering on her left leg, and the other was on the bed. She'd applied red lipstick to accentuate her lips, not too deep, it was more of a pink than a red.

She picked up the phone.

"Call from Don Williamson, Miss Crawford, do you want me to transfer?"

She paused for a moment, who was Don Williamson; was he a reporter, was he an acquaintance that she had met, if so, how did he know she was stopping at Claridge's? She then remembered that she didn't know the stranger's name, it must be him.

"Put them through."

"Miss Crawford, I'm sorry for the intrusion. We met earlier and you had told me to meet you tonight. My name is Don, Don Williamson. I am at the Chelsea & Westminster Hospital waiting to be discharged."

Karen recognised him straight away. His voice melted her now as it did earlier in the day, as it did earlier in her shower when she sucked their encounter into her fantasy.

"Oh my, what happened?" She asked, whilst subconsciously writing his name on the bedside complimentary note pad. She liked his name, she wondered if he was Donald or Donny. *And they called it puppy love* briefly played inside her head. She'd been to an Osmond's reunion show with her American friend, Angie, some years ago in Vegas.

"My own stupid fault. I stepped into a cycle lane and was hit by a bike. Turns out I've cracked a few ribs and have some bruising to my shin. Painful though. They are telling me that I have to wait to be discharged so I may be late. I'm sorry."

She wanted Don Williamson. She wanted to nurse him, to change his bandages, to attend to his cuts and bruises, to touch him, hold him, kiss him.

"Are you in A&E, Don?" Even saying his name sent ripples through her body.

*Puppy Love* returned.

"Yes, they told me to take some over the counter painkillers for the pain and just told me to rest my leg," he told her.

"Wait there, remain seated. I'm coming to get you."

Did she really just say 'I'm coming to get you'? She felt herself blushing.

Christ, she felt so alive with this man. She had only just learned his name and she wanted him inside her. She just loved his voice, it drew attention to his mouth; a mouth that her lips brushed past when she kissed his cheek earlier. She wanted his mouth on hers right now, she wanted their tongues to touch and she wanted to reach down and feel how he felt about her.

"You really don't need to, Miss Crawford. I…"

She interrupted him in mid-sentence.

"Yes, I do," she told him. "And please, it's Karen."

She hung up before he could answer and within seconds was dialling her chauffeur's mobile phone.

"Luigi, meet me at Claridge's ASAP," she told him.

His answer was the standard, "Yes, Miss Crawford."

Luigi worked a 10 hour shift, if he needed to work longer his clients would normally tell him. Clients as high profile as Karen Crawford didn't need to give him advance warning that his services were needed. His employer, Shepston Limo Inc., had an office in central London.

Only the best and vetted drivers were allowed to work for them. Their office was private, nobody could just walk in off the street and ask for a driver, it was all done by telephone or postal mail. Their clients were the rich and famous, even royalty.

Luigi reached for the remote and switched off the plasma screen. Shepston Limo Inc. looked after its drivers, each of them had their own private facilities. A room, a TV and a shower.

Karen was already playing out in her mind what she would do to Don Williamson the moment he sat next to her in the limousine. Her heart was racing and her imagination was running wild.

She rolled the other stocking on to her left leg then slipped into her white Gucci dress and matching Gucci shoes. She dabbed her neck with Holygrace and grabbed a full length coat before heading out of the suite door and to the elevator.

# Chapter Twenty

Don was discharged just before twenty past seven, 7.19 to be precise (*1919*). He remained seated and turned his head to the door. Was Karen Crawford really coming to 'get him'? His shin was throbbing like a bitch and the pain in his cracked ribs would intensify at a sneeze or cough.

He loved the way she sounded. She had retained her American accent, even though she had lived in England for a number of years. He didn't know how long.

Why was this famous woman interested in him? His confidence had been knocked when he and Katy had split. He'd gone through the phase of feeling unworthy, gone through the phase imagining a much better looking guy than he fucking his beloved Katy, and gone through the phase of hearing those voices inside his head telling him that he was unattractive.

*That's why she dumped you Don, she found somebody much better looking than you.* Those voices had been hard to deal with, they had kept him awake at night, had accompanied him whilst he was trying desperately hard to forget her by watching *The Simpsons* on TV. Even the story lines in *The Simpsons* related to her, or he made them relate.

The voices had even started chanting to him at points of the evening, telling him, *We're not going away, we're not going away;* and *Kill yourself, kill yourself, kill yourself.* He was thankful that those voices had only lasted for the first few days after she told him.

He continued watching the entrance. A variety of drunken accidents staggered through the door at steady intervals. A man holding what was once a white handkerchief to his mouth (it was now red); the teenage girl in the pink mini skirt with vomit down her blouse and blood and scratches on her legs. The homeless man, clutching a can of *Special Brew*, singing *I can't help falling in love with you,* in his best Elvis impersonation.

He was actually quite good and charming, until security ushered him out of the door to an array of profanities. The homeless man raised laughs when he turned and said, "Elvis has now left the building." Even the two burly security guards laughed.

A teenage boy with a face full of acne was eating chips out of fish and chip paper. Security didn't allow him in at first, not until he'd discarded the food he was holding. Reluctantly, the youngster threw his vinegar smelling wrapper into the bin outside the entrance. Chips fell to the floor and a couple of pigeons and one single crow pounced upon them.

Don briefly thought about the crow that had followed him that day at the cemetery. As quick as the memory came, it faded. He continued looking and listening. He listened to the raucous behaviour of Mr Handerkerchief's friends who had accompanied him to A&E.

"Don't worry blood, we'll get the cunt, innit, he's fucking dead blood, innit."
And, "I'll stab him in the face blood, I'll mess him up, innit."

He listened to Miss mini skirt talking on her phone. "I tell ya, the fucking slut bitch is gonna get it; nobody messes wiv me, especially a fucking tramp like her."

Others walked through the door, those that seemed more worthy of using the British National Health services. A woman who looked to be in her 90's was wheeled in by a medic, her face partially disguised by an oxygen mask. She was in pain, and sadly, looked quite pathetic. She could be somebody's mom, somebody's Nan, Don thought.

A rather stout looking figure hobbled in. He was grimacing each time he placed his right foot on the floor. It's either a sprain, a break or gout, thought Don. Gout was a bastard; Don had it shortly after his wife left him. Drinking large amounts of vodka and eating junk food hadn't been a good idea.

The uric acid crystals grew on his over indulgence; excruciating pain being the result and the reason why he limped for the best part of a week until his doctor had prescribed him Colchicine.

An olive skinned man dressed in uniform, complete with hat was next to walk through the doors. There didn't seem to be anything wrong with him, maybe he was just visiting? Don watched Mr Olive approach the front desk. He couldn't hear what he was saying but he met his eyes when he turned his face to where Don was sitting.

The woman behind the desk, trying to look all official, was also looking at Don, she then pointed at him and Mr Olive walked towards where he was sitting.

He took off his hat and held it to his side.

"Mr Williamson?" Mr Olive inquired.

"Yes."

"Mr Don Williamson?" Mr Olive emphasised. Once again, Don replied in the positive, "Yes."

"I'm Miss Crawford's driver, Luigi."

Don's heart thumped and, for a brief couple of seconds at least, his pain lifted. His chariot awaited.

Karen Crawford had, indeed, come to 'get him'.

\*\*\*

She had looked in the mirror and decided on the black wig earlier that evening.

Tonight, she had gone for that Gothic look. It always made her look and feel younger.

She was cold. Standing three blocks from the street where she lived meant she couldn't be traced.

A taxi pulled up.

"De Kraken, snälla, förare," Katy instructed the taxi driver.

# Chapter Twenty-One

Don walked slowly to the black limo. His shin was on fire and with each (small) step he took his ribs ached. The back door was already open and Luigi had already climbed behind the steering wheel. Karen had told Luigi earlier to raise the tinted partition. She saw Don struggling and swung her legs out to the pavement.

Don caught a glimpse of them; first time he'd ever saw Karen Crawford's legs without a staple running through them. She was wearing white stilettos and black stockings, he caught a quick glimpse of the hem. Most women would never have been able to carry it off, black stockings, white stilettos and a short white dress would have most fashion experts shaking their heads in disapproval, but this was Karen Crawford.

She could wear a black bin-liner and get away with it. She stood and he saw the white dress clinging to her perfectly formed body. The cold December air brushing her nipples and making them visible to Don through her slinky body hugging dress. Her hair, unlike earlier, was in precision with her face. Those famous curls hung loose and went way beyond her shoulders. She, he thought, looked fucking stunning.

"Oh, Mr Williamson, you poor thing," she said, taking his arm and allowing him to lean on her.

He took a whiff of her perfume and said, "Holygrace, and please, it's Don."

"Well Don," she emphasised the word Don. "It looks like you need some pampering, and yes, you know your perfumes well; it is indeed Holygrace."

Don wanted to tell her how he knew but he didn't. The memory of Katy was fading fast again.

He watched her as she bent her head as she stepped into the back of the limousine, her short white dress stretching and amplifying her curves as she climbed in and slid along the seat whilst holding out her hand for Don to take as he climbed in alongside her. It was a painful manoeuvre for Don. She held his hand tight and saw him grimace before he managed to slide alongside her.

She leaned across him to reach for the door, her hair brushed against his face and, in front of him, he witnessed Karen Crawford's half naked back. His eyes averted to his right and he saw the white dress ride up the back of her thighs, she looked and smelled divine. She pulled the door shut, the motion of it all bumping the side of her rib cage into Don's stomach. He never grimaced.

She moved her body slowly back across Don, she knew exactly what she was doing, more importantly, she knew exactly what she was doing to him.

"Back to Claridge's please, Luigi," she ordered before switching the intercom off.

Luigi pulled away from the pavement to make the twenty minute trip.

"Claridge's huh, you do know that's pretty posh for average guys like me?" Don said.

"Is that a rhetorical question, Mr Williamson, or are you just fishing for a compliment?" She said this seductively before adding, "If you were average, Mr Williamson, you wouldn't be sitting in my car with me now." She inched closer to him. "You wouldn't be allowed within 10 feet of me as I normally have security with me when I go out in public at night."

She reached for the collar on his shirt and pulled him towards her. "If, Mr Williamson, you were average, do you really think I would want you in my bed?"

Don felt himself losing control.

She leaned in towards him, her lips meeting his, their tongues intertwining.

They were, once again, lost in the moment except this time it was physical. She sucked on his neck and moved her hand to his crotch. He was hard. He was breathing faster. He was powerless.

"Is that for me?" She asked, already knowing the answer.

"No, Miss Crawford, it's for Luigi," he told her, whilst giving her a wink of the eye.

His phone vibrated in his back pocket. He ignored it.

# Chapter Twenty-Two

Katy needed to hear his voice, hence the text message she had just sent him.

*Don, it's been a while. I miss you; can we talk?*

She waited then waited. No reply.

She wondered what he was up to right now.

She was back at The Kraken. It was early for her, normally she'd hit the bars around 9 pm when things were getting into full swing. Tonight was different; she felt compelled to hit the dance floor early. She had jet-black hair tonight, a wig that she had ordered online. She'd applied an ethereal, paleish foundation skin tone, her eye shadow was black, the same as her lips.

Black mascara was also a must for that Gothic look. She had exfoliated and moisturised before applying the make-up, it always looked better on smooth and clean skin. Her clothing was a plenitude of black velvets, lace, fishnets tinged with purple leather. All of her attire accessorised with a tightly laced corset, gloves, precarious stilettos and silver jewellery.

She looked the part, more importantly, nobody would recognise her if they saw her. She wanted it that way. For the next 4 or 5 hours, she was Lucy Ahlström.

Lance Foggarty, a 37-year-old suitcase salesman from Scotland, was handing over money to the buxom barmaid for the fifth and final time that night. 290 krona for a Tom Collins cocktail for him and a Negroni cocktail for the Gothic looking girl who had struck a conversation up with him whilst she was waiting to be served at the bar.

The Gothic girl was touching his hand as she spoke, she was also licking her lips and touching her jet black hair, brushing it occasionally to the side with her hand that had black nail extensions on each of her fingers protruding through her black lace gloves. She was straight and to the point. She, Lance felt, wanted fast sex with no strings attached. When she spoke next, this was confirmed.

"I have a car outside", she told him before adding, "It's a black Audi with a personalised number plate parked next to the food truck, meet me there in 5 minutes." With that, she took a sip of her Negroni and left the trademark lipstick mark around the rim of the glass before heading towards the exit door, the only door in The Kraken that had a blind-spot to the CCTV surveillance cameras inside and outside the bar.

She'd used it on a number of occasions.

Lance Foggarty left it a minute before following her footsteps. He'd never return to The Kraken again.

He'd never return to Sweden again.

# Chapter Twenty-Three

The passion had moved from the limo to the suite at Claridge's. The elevator ride up to the penthouse suite had saw Karen fall to her knees to take Don in her mouth, just briefly, just to lubricate him more than he already was.

She wanted him.

She had waited for him.

She wanted Don Williamson.

The elevator was nearing the rented penthouse suite, a special key card had meant it would travel straight up with no stops.

Karen removed Don from her mouth just as the doors opened, then rising from her knees, she gripped her hand around his firmness and offered him her mouth. Don accepted the offer and their open mouths met. The taste of salt as Don's tongue circled Karen's making him harder. As he grew, so did her grip on him.

Grabbing her hand, Don led her inside the suite. She wanted him to remain fully clothed. The prospect of undressing him made her wet again, made her tingle like she had never tingled before. They continued kissing, exchanging saliva and breath. His hands were on her back, moving slowly down to her rear. She was secretly begging to feel his soft touch on her buttocks and between her legs.

She began at the top of his shirt; one button, kissing his neck, the second, kissing his chest, the rest of the buttons flew across the floor as she pulled apart his shirt to reveal the whole of his upper body. She eyed the bruising to his ribs then kissed and licked the area gently.

Don then unbuttoned the buttons of her body-hugging dress, all the time kissing her neck and occasionally nibbling her ear. He felt the dress slip down her body then moved his hands to unfasten the clip on her bra. It was unfastened with no fuss and, just like her dress, it slipped down her body to the floor. Karen surveyed his face as her breasts came into view, his eyes now wide and showing intoxication whilst taking in every inch of her.

"Keep on the nylons," he told her, with a slight tremble in his voice.

"Oh, I intend to," she told him as she unbuttoned his jeans and slid them down his legs. He stepped out of them once they landed on the floor.

She next slid her hands over his shorts and, just like his jeans, slid them down to his feet where, once again, he obliged by stepping out of them.

It was her turn to grab his hand and lead him towards her bed. Once there, she gently pushed him onto the mattress before bestriding her knees either side of him. She leaned in and they kissed. Her limbs grew weak, her mind started to spiral uncontrolably as their tongues met once again.

He grabbed her upper arms and gently rolled her off him so she was flat on her back.

Karen's heart was racing in expectation as he started kissing and licking her neck, slowly moving down to her collar-bone before stopping at her breasts. Her nipples were raised and inviting for Don. He felt her quiver beneath him as his mouth encircled her right nipple whilst his hand caressed her left breast. Both mouth and hand brought the same degree of excitement for Karen.

Soon he was licking the underside of both breasts then moving slowly down her rib-cage, all the time licking and kissing as he went. He arrived at her hip bone with his mouth which was soon joined by his hand. She spread open her legs slowly waiting for the impending rush of joy.

He could feel her heart racing and her elevated breathing as he placed his head sideways on her midriff and moved his fingers towards her wetness. The anticipation was killing her, a result of which innately forced her to raise her hips towards his probing fingers. She placed both hands on the back of his head and gently guided him down where he almost immediately started licking, circling, and sucking.

"Oh God," she gasped.

His tongue was joined now by his fingers and opening her wide, he pushed his tongue deep inside, all the time sucking her , savouring her as she pushed herself hard down on him. She ran her fingers through his hair as he indulged in her. Electrical impulses ran through her body and her legs stiffened as she came hard on his tongue. She reached for the pillows and cushions behind her and gripped them hard as her orgasm inwardly reverberated.

Don came up and purposely rubbed his goatee beard against her opening. He cupped her face in his hands and once again they kissed and shared the most intimate of liquid nectar.

He then positioned himself on top of her, his hardness rubbing against her opening. She reached down and cupped his balls as he inched inside her.

"Fuck me, baby," she said as she looked deep into his intoxicated eyes.

That was enough for Don, he could not hold back any longer. He held on to her shoulders and was soon penetrating himself deep inside of her; both of them knew they were close.

"Oh, baby, look into my eyes," Don urgently gasped.

She complied and teasingly squinted them before opening them wide as she came again at the point of Don exploding deep inside of her.

# Chapter Twenty-Four

The angels were rejoicing. It was a celebration. As always, they had left the room while the chosen ones had copulated, that was their business. The angels just arranged it all. Sebastian and Anthony were always by Karen's side whilst Teresa and Sara guided Don.

All four had worked together to bring about the healing that both human spirits deserved. Don's circumstances were evident to anyone who knew him whilst Karen chose to keep her hurt close to her chest. Nobody but she, her mother and father, and the four angels ever knew of her pain.

Sebastian, Anthony, Teresa and Sara were angels of love. It was their first time working together, it was their first time they had joined love. The process was so difficult, they could only guide, they could never convince.

Teresa and Sara had been with Don from his birth, they already knew his journey, and they already knew that he was on a road to self-destruction. That's when Archangel Gabriel intervened; that's when Teresa and Sara were told of the *plan*.

Archangel Gabriel had showed them both Don's journal. It showed how Don would go through a series of relationships and face heartache. Archangel Gabriel told both Teresa and Sara that Don needed to experience the heartache and that they could not do anything about it. Don's journal had his whole life mapped out.

Everything had been planned, everything except the poem. That was down to Don and Don alone. It came from his heart.

Sebastian and Anthony had been with Karen since her birth too, once again they had been told of her future journey, and once again they had been given the duty of being Karen's Guardian angels by Archangel Gabriel. Karen had lost a child. She was just 13 when she gave birth. Lex Brampton was 16 and he had forced himself upon her in the barn at her parent's farm in Idaho.

Nine months later, she gave birth to a little girl and called her Odelia. It was agreed that she keep Odelia a secret. Her parents were strict Catholics and totally against the idea of abortion.

Adoption had been suggested but Karen told her parents that she would cycle around the length and breadth of the state distributing leaflets telling of her promiscuity if Odelia were ever taken from her.

Odelia was taken from her at the age of 4 months. Her blue lifeless body lay motionless in her crib as Karen went to check on her. Odelia was due a feed and Karen just wanted to see if she was awake; Odelia was sleeping, it was a permanent sleep. The cause of death was determined by the local coroner, Odelia died from Tay-Sachs disease, a genetic and degenerative condition that is always fatal.

Odelia lacked an enzyme responsible for breaking down specific chemicals in the nerve cells of her brain. Because these chemicals weren't removed, they built up, and Odelia lost her ability to function. The coroner told Karen and her parents that it was unusual to lose an infant of just 4 months to Tay-Sachs disease but he estimated that she wouldn't have lived beyond the age of 3.

He also warned Karen of future pregnancies. She remembered the conversation well, He told her,

*The chance of passing on a genetic condition applies equally to each pregnancy. Having one child with a disorder does not protect future children from inheriting the condition. Equally, having a child without the condition does not denote that future children will definitely be affected.* It was all so very vague, particularly for Karen, who, back then, was just a 13 year-old child.

Karen turned her back on the Holy Trinity after losing Odelia. She could just not understand how a loving God could be so cruel. In her final prayer to God, she held back tears and said, *"How dare you take my child from me, how dare you be the judge of who lives and dies, how dare you."*

Arrangements were made for a private funeral and Karen was given time off school to attend, to say goodbye to her little bundle of love. The school were told that Karen's aunt had passed away; they never knew of Karen's heartache.

When the human spirit cries, the angels cry with them; they join in their grief and they feel every ounce of their pain. Anthony and Sebastian had guided Karen through the trauma, sent her messages and signs and showered her with love. They'd even spoken with Odelia when she finally reached the other side. They had told

Odelia that they were going to protect her mother, going to bring her to a level of consciousness so she could, through all the darkness, realise that she was the light.

There were no ages on the other side. Time is irrelevant, and it's not measured. There was no sex on the other side either. All forms were just one, being both male and female.

Odelia was allowed to visit Karen in her dreams. The male figure that Karen had dreamed of, and still continued to dream of, was her daughter. Karen had often felt love upon waking, she didn't know that it was Odelia who was projecting that love.

Odelia Crawford left the earth 27 years ago. It was for the greater good.

Lex Brampton, Odelia's biological father and Karen's rapist, was found guilty by jury. Karen, because she was a minor, was known only as Jane Doe throughout the 4-day trial.

Unknown to the media and her millions of fans, Karen Crawford donated 30% of her annual earnings to various charities, all of which had one thing in common. Children.

She had, some years ago spoken with her agent, a catholic woman called Melissa. She had asked Melissa to arrange to have 30% of her earnings deducted.

Melissa had been wearing a striking pendant and Karen remarked on its beauty. "My mother left it me, it's St Osyth, an English saint."

Two days later, Karen bumped in to an old friend of hers, Dominic. He was a male model and had just got back from America where he had wed his long-time boyfriend, Nick. When deciding which three charities to donate to later that day, Karen thought it coincidental that the list she had been given by her researcher had The Church St Osyth's Children Foundation on there.

The timing of the death of Melissa's mother, the pendant being left in her will for Melissa, the offer of the job to Melissa from Karen's management—all part of the *plan*.

Karen put a tick next to three charities. She handed the list back to her researcher and told her to leave it with her secretary. Her chance meeting with Dominic, the mention of his marriage to his long-time boyfriend, Nick—all part of the *plan*.

Her donation was spread out equally between three charities. The Church of St Osyth's Children Foundation, St Dominic's Children's Hospital and the paediatric centre at St Nicholas Hospital. Each charity would help children in dire need. Each saint being symbolic to Karen's future.

St Dominic.

St Osyth

St Nicholas.

Karen chose her saints wisely. Sebastian and Anthony had guided her.

# Chapter Twenty-Five

*Sebastian Chantel Born 3 October 1955*
*Gers, Midi-Pyrénées region, southwest of France*
*Died 19 March 1969*
*Anthony Chantel Born 3 August 1954*
*Gers, Midi-Pyrénées region, southwest of France*
*Died 19 March 1969*

Anthony and Sebastian Chantel were brothers. They lived on a farm in the Midi-Pyrénées region, southwest of France. They were killed by the hands of Clément Dubois, a 45 year-old army veteran. Dubois was arrested and charged with kidnapping, rape and the murder of the Chantel boys. He committed suicide in a Toulouse prison in 1970 while on trial.

Anthony and Sebastian's father, Claude, and mother, Simone, buried them both on the 27 March 1969.

Anthony and Sebastian, just like Teresa and Sara, had witnessed their own burials, they were comforted that day by both Sara and Teresa. They were, as Sara had put it, the penultimate piece of the jigsaw.

Everything was now in place.

Sara and Teresa took Sebastian and Anthony across to the other side and left them with Archangel Gabriel. Over the next 5 years or so, they would be prepared and instructed by Archangel Gabriel and when the time was ready would become the guardian angels to a baby girl, born in Idaho. Karen Crawford.

Sara and Teresa had headed back to the side of the then 4 year-old Don Williamson.

# Chapter Twenty-Six

Karen was allowed the luxury of smoking in her suite at Claridge's. At just over £4,500 a night, she could have broken every rule in the book if she wanted to. The staff were always briefed before her arrival. *Give her what she wants, let her do whatever she wants, and always be polite and courteous.*

They were lying side by side, both exhausted from their love making. Three times, a record for Karen. Previous lovers had rolled over and fallen to sleep. Don was different. He held her after he came the first time. He spoke with her, kissed her, and snuggled up close to her.

He made her laugh with his jokes, moreover he made her laugh when he laughed, it was infectious, it was fun, and it was companionship. In between they had ordered room service, bacon, eggs, toast and champagne. Karen was really falling for this guy, Don was falling for her too.

One minute, he could be so serious, the next he could be funny, followed by a deviant side to him that she just loved. They talked into the small hours, classical music played from the radio channel via the TV.

He was melting her. He was making her feel human, more importantly he was seeing beyond her beauty and reaching in to her heart. She reached across him for a cigarette on her bedside cabinet, her breasts gently gliding over his hairy chest. Duty free American Spirit's that Don had never seen or indeed smoked before. "Can you pass me the matches please lover?" She asked.

He reached for the complimentary book of matches that were on her bedside cabinet. It was a game. She wanted to feel him brush against her body as he leaned across her just as much as she wanted to tease him by leaning across him.

Don tore a match from the book and struck the red phosphorus against brown strip on the bottom of the open book, the flame was instant and Karen leaned in to it to light the cigarette between her lips.

"Do you believe in karma, Don?" She asked as she exhaled smoke.

"I'm not really sure, I've never really thought about it," he answered.

She handed him her lit cigarette. "Are you familiar with the law of connection?" She asked.

He inhaled on her cigarette then handed it back to her, answering, "No, I don't think I've heard of that before. Law of attraction, yes, but not law of connection. Tell me more."

"I have a close friend from back home, she's a very famous psychic medium. She told me that we would meet; she never told me your name or anything like that but she did say that I would know. When I saw you today by the traffic lights and we both looked at each other, I knew you were the one Angie, my friend, was talking about. We connected right there, right in that moment. I know you felt it too, Don."

He was going to interrupt but he allowed her to continue.

"The law of connection is fundamentally a law that tells us that each step we take leads us to the next one. If something we do seems insignificant, it is very important that it gets done as everything in the universe is connected. Past, present and future, they are all connected."

"Are you saying that it's down to the universe that we met today, Karen?"

"I believe that us finding one another was no coincidence, Don. I believe that someone or something has been working behind the scenes to bring us together. Tell me, why did you turn today at the traffic lights, what made you turn, Don?"

"Your perfume, Karen, I recognised it immediately. My last girlfriend used to wear it; it was her favourite."

"Did you turn because you thought it might be her?"

He felt uncomfortable with her line of questioning. He'd been around the block a few times to know how jealousy could creep into relationships, even at this early stage, when ex-girlfriends or boyfriends were brought up in conversations.

"Good question, I don't actually know why I turned. I think it was because I really like the scent and I'd only initially got a small whiff of it."

"I saw heartache in your eyes, Don. Have you recently split with your girlfriend?"

"As a matter of fact, yes, she ended things with me fairly recently," he told her. He went on to tell her how he had struggled to cope with the sudden loss of Katy in his life; how he had gone through the phases of shock, anger, depression, suspicion and finally acceptance.

Karen listened intensively.

"Poor baby, I'm sorry your heart was broken. It's not nice is it, not nice at all?"

"No, to be honest I can't think of anything worse than losing the one you love."

"Are you still in love with her, Don?"

"I thought I was, Karen, but after today I know that I can't be."

"Why's that?"

"Well, call me old fashioned but I believe that any man, or woman for that matter, that profess to love a person and then have sex with another person are pretty pathetic human beings; spiritless, heartless, cold, you know what I mean? If I truly loved her then I wouldn't be in your bed right now."

She loved his answer, it showed he had a heart full of love, full of pureness, full of compassion and morals. He was a keeper for sure. Of course, he could have just been saying what he thought she wanted to hear but Karen felt his truth just as much as she felt the love pouring through him. She could feel her own love rippling through her own body.

Don Williamson was the one. He was the connection, he was everything those glossy magazine agony columns told teenage girls.

Karen leaned in towards him. "Give me your mouth," she said. They kissed and she grabbed his top lip with her teeth. She giggled.

Her cigarette had burned out so she leaned across Don and stubbed it on the empty plate.

She positioned herself in front of him again and ran her fingers gently over his hairy chest whilst looping her leg over his pelvis.

"What's your birth sign, Don?"

"Leo," he told her, before adding, "31 of July."

She smiled and thought how her friend Angie had never once made a prediction that never came true. *I also know for certainty that he will be a Leo, born towards the end of July.* Angie had told her some 3 years ago.

Don's arm was underneath her, his hand rubbing her shoulder, rubbing over the tattoo.

"What's with the tattoo? What does '1111' signify?"

She smiled again; she was happy he had asked her and equally happy to offer him an answer.

She answered his question with a question first.

"Do you believe in guardian angels, Don?"

97

"I've never really felt that I have anyone guarding me but my dad once told me a story about when he believed he once heard angels singing to him."

"Really?"

"Yes, really."

"Tell me more," Karen asked.

"Your turn first, the tattoo, what does it mean?"

"Well," she said. "I'm a firm believer in angels and also believe they show us signs to warn or guide us. About 3 years ago, I kept seeing the number eleven appear. On clocks, watches, flight numbers, even when I looked at my microwave back home, I'd always manage to catch the countdown timer at 11.11 or just 11.

"Walking through London I'd overhear conversations, people talking into their phones mainly, people setting up meetings at eleven or meeting outside a tube station at eleven. It was more than just a coincidence."

Don raised an eyebrow and asked, "Do you think so?"

She snuggled up close to him, her hand reaching to the back of his head where she started gently rubbing him.

"There are no such things as coincidences, Don. I got in touch with Angie and she told me about the number eleven and the significance of it. In a nutshell, it's a sign of awareness, one that we should pay heed to. It means the angels are reaching out, yelling at us to pay attention to what is going on around us. When you saw me earlier today, Don, did you notice anything strange?"

"Well, it was a feeling that I've never experienced before, that's for sure," he told her.

"Do you remember seeing me do something when I broke my gaze with you?"

"Yes, you looked at your watch."

"And do you know what time I saw on my watch, Don?"

It was one of those moments when a reply wasn't needed; her previous information she had fed him about the number eleven and her belief that the number was a sign told him that it was 11.11.

"It wasn't?" He asked her, already knowing it was.

"You still believe in coincidences?"

"It's very strange, I'll give you that," he said.

"Kiss me, Don, and hold me, hold on to me all night. Tell me the story of your dad tomorrow. Let's drift, babe, let's drift together."

They kissed passionately, neither became sexually aroused. Neither bit the lips of the other.

"You're for keep," she told him as she drifted.

The bedside clock showed Don that it was 5.55 in the morning. He offered himself a wry smile. Karen had already started drifting as Don held on to her tight.

# Chapter Twenty-Seven

Katy woke around 9 am that morning and did two things. First, she reached across her bed to feel Don. He wasn't there, and her heart sank as reality set in. Next, she reached for her phone to see if he had left a message. For the second time that morning her heart sank.

She pulled out her journal from her bedside drawer, she wrote:

*I don't know why I am feeling like this. I feel empty and my heart aches for Don. I wanted him out of my life and now I want him in it. The despair I feel is eating me away. Should I try to contact him again today or should I just leave it be? I love him and need him in my life.*

*My heart aches without him and I feel bad for cheating on him. I want to make it up to him. I just want to be next to him again, I miss him so much.*

*Possible options:*

*\*\*Email Don and tell him how much you miss him. Tell him you were stupid for letting him go and you need him in your life. Don't mention Hjalmar or you will ruin your chances of getting back with Don.*

*\*\*Send him another text message—don't be pushy, just ask him how he's doing these days.*

*\*\*Fly to England.*

She made no entry regarding last night's events. They were locked away, at least until the next episode.

She closed her journal and tossed it to the floor, it landed next to the black wig she had worn last night. The steady rhythmic sound of a drying tumbler could be heard in the background. Katy's small apartment had no respite from sound that came from within.

She knew that she'd been sleeping for less than an hour, the washer/dryer cycle was 60 minutes. She had thrown her clothes in the machine, as she always did when returning from her night's out. She'd throw the wig out later or maybe burn it because evidence of the suitcase salesman was now on it.

Blood splatters and probably saliva droplets as Katy's alter-ego briefly invaded her mind and recalled he had coughed hard before taking his last breath last night.

Katy went back to sleep. She smiled as she dreamed.

# Chapter Twenty-Eight

The four angels had returned to the suite. They had heard the conversation about the law of connection between Karen and Don. They had smiled and rejoiced at Karen's spiritual awakening and of her relaying the story to Don about the significance of the number eleven.

Don, it seemed, had a lot to learn. That's why they sent him a sign just before he held on to Karen, just before they both drifted off to sleep. They were pleased he smiled at their sign.

Archangel Gabriel had summoned them. They left Karen and Don as they slept and returned to the *other side.*

"We need to talk," he told them.

"We need to send Odelia back."

Odelia had been back many times to earth. She had been looking after Lex Brampton. She forgave him and tried surrounding him with love. Her natural father was just 16 when she was conceived. He had been abused by his father on countless occasions. His father, Bill, was an alcoholic, who had also been abused as a child by his grandfather. It was a bloodline of sexual abuse.

At 16, Lex was serving time for the rape of Odelia's mother. He did 2 years in a young offenders institute then was sent to an adult prison. Just his luck (*no such thing as luck*) that he shared a cell with a paedophile. Lex had two guardian angels, they could not stop the rapes or the abuse from the landing paedophile, it was penance handed down by a higher authority.

They (*Carmel and Richard*) were told to pull back when the rape and beatings started. If Lex called upon help from spirit, then they could return but they could never intervene.

Lex never called upon help from spirit.

Upon his release, Odelia was summoned by Archangel Gabriel. She had a task that she needed to perform and it would take many years of planning. She would meet her father again in 2015. Their meeting would be brief; they would pass like two ships in the night.

# Chapter Twenty-Nine

*A tranquil heart gives life to the flesh, but envy makes the bones rot.*
Proverbs 14:30

Katy booked her flight to England. It was more expensive than usual; this time of the year it normally was but she didn't care, she needed to see Don again and was sure that a surprise visit would be just what he wanted.

Stockholm to Frankfurt with Lufthansa would take just over 2 hours. A wait of just 50 minutes for her connecting flight to Birmingham, which would take another 2 hours, then she could jump in a cab from Birmingham Airport. She'd be in Don's arms once again, feel his lips on hers, and feel him deep inside her within minutes of him answering his front door.

She ran a bath and added a handful of Epsom salts. She'd read that adding the salt helps you look better, feel better and gain more energy. She'd had a long, hard day at work, a job that was fulfilling. Katy was a paediatric nurse who worked as a locum at paediatric hospitals across Stockholm.

Today, she had been at *Södersjukhuset* (Stockholm South General Hospital) and the *Valkyries University Hospital* training staff members. Katy had been a paediatric nurse for the past 10 years. Her experience and dedication was noted by senior staff and they offered her the job of training students. She enjoyed it immensely, particularly when the male students gave her the attention she craved.

Katy immersed herself in the water and pictured Don answering his front door. His look of complete shock and excitement upon seeing her would be enough to rekindle what they had. Katy was sure of it.

Her flight was booked for tomorrow, 28 December.

Her hot bath was invigorating and gave her a dry mouth. She changed into her pyjamas then poured herself a cold glass of *Linoti Pinot Grigio*. She headed to the couch in her living room then turned on the TV to occupy her mind. *SVT News* was covering the story of the grisly murder that had made headlines.

An unknown male, believed to be an English tourist, was found in dense forest, not too far from where Katy lived. He had been battered to death and had died, according to the coroner report, from blunt force trauma. Swedish police were appealing to the public to come forward with information. Detective Johan Hedman was asked by the news anchor if he thought the latest murder was related to the other three murders in the same area.

Two males and one female—two had died from blunt force trauma, both were tourists; the other victim had been stabbed multiple times, his testicles had also been dissected and stuffed in his mouth, although this wasn't publicly known. Hedman told the anchor that, "It can't be ruled out at this stage."

Hedman was holding something back, thought Katy. Detectives making appeals usually knew more than they let on. Four bodies found, others were yet to be discovered, and not one single lead for Hedman and his investigative team.

Katy noted that Hedman looked tired. "Useless prick," she said before reaching for the remote to change channels. She flicked on MTV, drum and bass, her favourite type of music. She stood from the couch after turning the volume up on the remote and started dancing around the room to Sebastian Ahrenberg, better known as Seba.

She'd actually saw Ahrenberg perform some years previous at the nightclub he owned called *Secret Operations* in the basement club Tuben in central Stockholm.

She danced for the next hour then, as midnight approached, she turned off the TV and went to bed.

The voice came to her in her dreams.

It told her a new kill was on the horizon.

# Chapter Thirty

*O, Star of wonder, star of night Star of royal beauty bright Westward leading, still proceeding, Guide us to thy perfect light.*
John Henry Hopkins, Jr—1857

Angie woke from her sleep. Archangel Gabriel had come to her again, in her dreams. He was relaying a message to her and it was one of surprise. Karen needed to come home, home to Idaho, and she needed to bring him with her. The message was garbled but Angie deciphered it with her gut instinct. She knew all about numbers and crucifixes appearing in dreams.

The symbol of the crucifix followed by a number meant something relating to the Bible. She had seen 120, a crucifix and the word 'Reveal'. She also saw an airport, one she had frequented many times, it was her hometown airport, Idaho. The vision she saw was the arrivals section of the airport.

In her vision, she was there, standing and waiting for something. In her vision she saw a full length advertisement, on it a photo of Karen Crawford, underneath were the words, *All Envy Us.* Angie knew the meaning of this. She and Karen had had t-shirts printed with the slogan on.

They had each worn them some weeks ago when they had spent a week together in Turin, New York. People had asked what the slogan meant but neither Karen or Angie had told them. It was just a bit of fun and it bonded their friendship even though they lived miles away from one another.

The whole dream had a soundtrack, an old hymn. She couldn't get it out of her head upon waking and she had no idea what part it played in the vision Archangel Gabriel was trying to make her understand.

*'We plough the fields, and scatter'* was playing like a stuck record but she had no idea what it meant.

She reached for her Bible, she knew which scripture she had to read, *he* had told her.

## Revelation 1:20

*The hidden meaning of the seven stars that you saw in my right hand and the seven gold lamp stands is this: The seven stars are the messengers of the seven churches, and the seven lamp stands are the seven churches.*

Angie didn't quite understand what *his* message was but she knew it was important. She knew what she had to read, she just didn't quite understand what it all meant. She reached down by the side of her bed and raised her laptop, bringing it to her lap she Googled *seven stars,* and this is what she saw.

*The constellation of Ursa Major lies far away from the plane of the Milky Way, and so these seven bright stars stand out noticeably against the somewhat faint stars that edge them. Their distinguishing pattern is therefore, especially easy to pinpoint. The stars of the Plough belong to the northern sky, and rotate around the Northern Celestial Pole.*

Angie opened her email and hit the compose button. She started to type Karen's email address into the contact tab. Typing the letter K was enough. The rest was auto filled.

*Karen, we need to talk urgently. Please call me at your earliest convenience. It's important.*

She hit send.

# Chapter Thirty-One
# (13 years ago)

Don was shattered by his wife's infidelity. He never saw it coming.

Hindsight is a powerful tool and he was running through the events that led up to her telling him that she had been having an affair. Dressing differently, wearing perfume to work, in a bakery for fucksake! The abrupt disinterest in sex, working longer hours, how she had become defensive, how she had changed her Nokia 3210 phone setting to vibrate instead of the ring tone and how he had caught her secretly reading text messages while they were together, watching a movie, on their couch.

He never asked her whose text she was reading but she smiled whilst reading it. It was all textbook stuff, the classic cheater and classic duped husband. Pick up any magazine and all of the above point to someone who cheats, Don was too trusting.

He should have read the *signs* more clearly.

The pain of her infidelity took months of endurance to wade through. He knew who the other guy was, he'd gone to his *My Space* page. The day his wife of 6 years told him that she had been seeing someone else was the same day, 7 January, that Dan Pallatt had uploaded a photo of himself holding a self-made love heart, underneath it he had wrote, *The beginning!* Pallatt had often taken pictures of himself and uploaded them to his page.

He was vain, Don thought. He came to the conclusion that Dan Pallatt selfie's were akin to a tampon string. Always a cunt at the other end. She was welcome to him and he her. The irony of it all was that Pallatt had used a tagline on his profile, *No more Mr Nice Guy*.

Don had asked her about Dan Pallatt before, she said she didn't really know him that well as he worked in a different part of the bakery. "He's a friend of a friend of a friend, that's why he is on my list of friends on My Space," she told him. That was over a year ago and Don wondered just how long they had been seeing each other behind his back.

It ate at him like a cancer, more because he had been duped. The deceit hurt as did the thoughts of her thinking about Dan while he had made love to her, which was a rare event in the lead-up to the split.

Researching Pallatt gave Don some comfort. He learned that he was an active member in no less than five online dating agencies, two of which where he had profiles stating his interest in women between the ages of 18 and 25. *Active and Awesome singles* (aka AAS), *Match Making, Birmingham Singles* (30s and over), *Up for Anything* (UFA) and *Thrillseekers* (18 to 25).

Pallatt's profile on the latter had suggested that he was 24. Don's wife, Trudy, was, at the time of her infidelity, 38. Pallatt was 40.

Upon learning of Dan Pallatt's internet activities Don shrugged his shoulders. He did not gloat, did not gain any satisfaction. He knew that he could never trust his wife again and needed to draw a line under the whole experience. He never made any effort to tell his wife, she'd have to find out forherself.

He avoided contact with most of his friends and revisited his childhood, a time where he was an avid writer of poetry and budding astronomy enthusiast.

He took an interest in the night sky again, searching for answers, searching for reasons why, that's when he felt compelled to write the poem.

After seeing that Don had penned the words, Archangel Gabriel pulled back.

He was safe in the knowledge that Don, at some point, would make the psychic connection between what he had just wrote and an event that would happen some years later, around the stroke of midnight, as 2015 said goodbye to 2014.

Don was proud of the poem. It was straight from the heart. It was reaching out to a God that he did not believe in but was asking, just in case one did exist. He was unsure where the lines had come from, certainly not his head, he thought. It has to be my heart, no way I could write something like this, he said to himself as he read the poem over and over.

He showed it to friends over the years, even learned it off-by-heart in the small hope of impressing people.

There wasn't one person who understood two particular lines of his poem. He'd asked many and when they couldn't answer him he told them to read it again then look up at the night sky.

Nobody ever did, well, nobody ever came back to him with the answer. Archangel Gabriel knew though.

Those two lines would play a major role in Don's life. They'd play a major part in Karen Crawford's life too. Two lines that predicted an event, two lines that would indicate the beginning of something that all four guardian angels and Archangel Gabriel had known about for many years.

Those two lines were the hidden code that The Vatican were trying to get their hands on.

# Chapter Thirty-Two
# 28 December 2014 Cobham,
# Surrey – The Crawford Residence

Karen had read the email from Angie and had immediately phoned her.

Angie woke from her sleep and told Karen of the dreams, of Archangel Gabriel and the message he had given her.

She needed to head home to Idaho, Angie had told her, and she needed to do it today. Two tickets, one each for both her and Don.

"You remember what 'all envy us' means?" Angie asked her.

"Yes, of course," Karen replied.

"Well, I saw it in my dream last night, that's how I know you have to come back to Sun Valley."

Karen never questioned Angie's reasoning. Karen trusted her friend and her psychic abilities.

She told Karen about the biblical message and how she couldn't decipher what it meant. She read Karen the passage to see if she could throw any light on it. She couldn't. She then asked Karen if she could throw any light on the hymn that she had heard. Again, Karen drew a blank.

"I'll text the scripture to you, Karen." Angie told her, adding, "Keep reading it and let me know if it makes any sense to you."

Don was downstairs; she'd insisted that he return to Cobham with her. How could he refuse? This was a world that he had only ever dreamed about; a world of the rich and famous, a reversal on the Cinderella tale where he was the girl in rags and Karen was the prince.

He was flicking through the TV channels when she came down the stairs, she had showered and changed again. They had both shared a shower together earlier that morning at Claridge's. She had, once again, brought him to climax, as he had her.

"How are you up for a trip to America, Don?"

The question came left of centre.

"Um, when?"

"Tonight," she told him, studying his face for his reaction.

He started to tell her how he couldn't afford it but she interrupted him.

"Look, Don, here's what you have to understand. I'm rich, filthy rich, wealthy beyond my wildest dreams. If you and I are going to be together, you need to come to terms with this. In my world, there are no bread winners, Don. I have more than enough at my disposal to accommodate us.

"It's great to have the security of money, Don, but I want more than money to make me feel happy. I want you so please don't have any hang-ups about who should be paying for what. I want my world to be your world, Don; it will take some getting used to but I will help you with that. I come from a very modest background.

"A small town that others refer to as butt-fuck Idaho, it's in the middle of nowhere, Don, yet it's quite beautiful and serene. I want you to witness it with me. I want us to see in the New Year together and I can't think of a place where I would rather be or of a man I would rather be with than you. The woman behind the kitchen sink while the man goes out to earn is old fashioned, Don."

"I'm an old fashioned type of guy," he told her.

"I know you are, Don, and fuck do I love you for it."

She mentioned the 'L' word and it threw them both off kilter, even though they both felt it in their hearts.

She interrupted the silence.

"Do you have an up-to-date passport?"

Don's passport was renewed only 2 years ago, he liked to travel.

"Yes, I do but…"

"Right, that's it then. We will head back to where you live, grab your passport and fly from Birmingham. No need to pack, we can travel light and go shopping when we land."

The world he was in right now was moving at a fast pace. Is this how the rich and famous lived their lives, at the drop of a hat jetting off overseas? He was excited at the prospect of flying, of flying with the world famous Karen Crawford. In all his years of travel, he had never once flown with a woman.

"Okay," he said, adding, "When?"

"I will call my agent and tell her about the timescale of getting to Birmingham and then flying from there to Idaho, she'll arrange it all while we are heading to your place. Let's get ready."

"You mean right now?"

"Yes, Don, no time like the present," she told him.

Sebastian, Anthony, Teresa and Sara smiled in unison.

# Chapter Thirty-Three

The penny dropped for Angie when she saw the obvious signs that day.

Sign #1—A phone call from an old friend of hers from Minnesota. Gabrielle Barker-King had not been in touch for at least 7 years. She fell off the scene when she had married a property developer. They had moved to Wisconsin but her husband had a string of affairs which, in turn, led Gabrielle back to Minnesota.

She was in the process of filing for divorce and needed guidance or, more importantly, needed Angie to tell her if she was doing the right thing. She came from a large family of four brothers and seven sisters.

Sign #2—It was all over the news. A huge traffic accident that had killed seven kids on a school bus. Apparently, a FedEx tractor-trailer had crossed a grassy freeway median and slammed into the bus. The accident happened in the San Gabriel Valley region of southern California.

Sign #3—Angie was driving through Meridian in Idaho. She was mulling over her dreams when a boy ran in front of her car. She braked hard and, luckily, the boy was unharmed. The boy, who was probably no older than 10, picked up his yellow ball and headed east into North Bright Angel Avenue.

He was wearing a red English football jersey, the number 7 was on the back. By the law of averages, she should have hit him, instead it was the little boy's actions that hit Angie.

Angie slapped the butt of her hand on her forehead when the penny dropped and said aloud, "Of course!" She then remembered that Gabriel, as the archangel of communication, frequently announces what's on the horizon, and acts like a manager or go-between in synchronising new projects related to one's soul purpose. Angie cussed herself for not making the connection earlier.

The message was crystal clear. Gabriel had given her valuable guidance for the future, for Karen and Don's future.

Archangel Gabriel, after seeing that the little boy was okay, left Angie's side.

Angie pulled over and opened her glove compartment. She pulled out a pocket guide to astronomy, a gift given to her by one of the clients she had done a reading for a week or so ago.

She looked in its index and found the two words she was looking for, *Seven sisters.* She then read how the 'saucepan' was more commonly known as the seven sisters, in the UK astronomers had given it the term, 'the Plough'.

*We Plough the fields and scatter.*

She put the pocket book back in the glove compartment then, after phoning him, headed to Richard Butler's place. He was the client who had gave her the pocket book, he was also a keen astronomer.

# Chapter Thirty-Four

"And so it is," he told the four.

"Odelia will return as the event, she will become not one but all seven. She will tilt its axis so they know, so he knows. The sign will trigger the past and that will trigger the now. He will recognise it immediately for he is already connected to it; it will be the definitive moment.

"Odelia will be all of the sisters and she will shine down upon them the message of love; she will, in that instant, unlock the answers. Odelia will then return to humanity, back to the womb of her mother."

All four applauded.

Gabriel hushed them by raising a single hand.

"It won't be plain sailing, from this point on we all have to be ready to tackle the opposition. Our subjects are vulnerable and we must never forget this. We must watch them carefully and surround them with our wisdom and protection. The evil one is lurking and, as you all know, he will work through others to stop the wheels that are already in motion.

"I know who he will work through. There are two of them, one female and one male. I will give you more information as the time nears."

# Chapter Thirty-Five

It took Luigi just over 2 hours to make the journey from Cobham to Birmingham, he waited outside while Don and Karen went inside.

Don's place was small. A two bedroom affair with the minimum of wall paintings and photographs. His kitchen was your typical single guy type of unit, compact, dishes and plates left to drain and a hob surface that looked like it hadn't been cleaned in years. There was a washing machine, Karen could see that it still had clothes in.

It never bothered her. Don would never be coming back here anyhow. She knew that much.

"I've found it," he said, waving his passport at her. She noticed that he'd changed into jeans and a white tee-shirt, finished off nicely, she thought, with a soft beige leather jacket. Fuck, he looked good, she thought.

"Good, then let's head to the hotel," she told him.

Karen's agent, Melissa, had booked the flight earlier. She'd even reminded Karen that Don, as a non US citizen, needed an ESTA, a visa to travel to the US under the Visa Waiver Program, she'd book it via the ESTA website as soon as she had Don's passport number. Melissa booked the shortest possible flight time that was available, a journey just under 22 hours, actual air time was just over 14 hours.

"One small problem," she had told Karen over the phone. "It doesn't leave until the 29."

Karen told her two words, "Book it."

They'd land in Boise just before 9 pm. Because of the time differences, it meant that they would not lose anytime, in fact they'd gain.

Once again Karen had left the hotel arrangements to Melissa. Tonight, they would stop as close to the airport as possible, their flight left at 6 am in the morning. She booked them a Queen Executive room at the Hilton. Luigi had already been informed of this and had programmed his *TomTom* navigation system accordingly.

Don locked up, he didn't know whether or not he would be returning, his head was in a spin as everything had happened so quickly. One minute he's on a train to London going to see a concert, the next he's in the arms of the hottest woman on the planet, in between all of that he'd cracked two ribs and severely bruised his shin.

Thinking about the pain brought it to the surface but he hadn't taken any pain killers since he first set foot inside the limo. Karen Crawford and his adrenaline had kept the pain at bay.

Inside his apartment, buried in the back pocket of his trousers, was his phone, on it two text messages from Katy. The last one read, *Don, I've just landed at Birmingham Airport, I'm heading over to your place as I type this.* Don's battery had died last night when his tongue was deep inside Karen Crawford.

Luigi was holding the door. Karen stepped in first then Don climbed in beside her. She reached towards the cabinet, as Luigi pulled out to head down Fentham Gardens to make his U-turn, and pulled out a bottle of Jameson's Whiskey, her favourite tipple. "Fancy a stiff one?" She said, winking. Don loved her humour.

"Yes," he said, before adding. "Make mine a large one."

They both giggled like they were teenagers again as Karen poured the neat Jameson's into two glasses. She handed Don his and gave him a wink; he loved her wink. "Down the hatch," she said. They both knocked back the whiskey. They both pulled faces as the whiskey hit the back of their throats. They both had another.

"Come here and kiss me, you sexy fuck," Don ordered.

That's when *she* saw them.

# Chapter Thirty-Six
# Katy Takes a Taxi

"Fentham Gardens, Olton, please," Katy told the taxi driver outside Birmingham Airport.

The last time she had caught a taxi to Don's place, he had been with her. They had kissed passionately and fondled one another, completely oblivious to the driver who was looking in his rear view mirror at them.

She'd travelled light, she only wanted to see Don and maybe spend a couple of nights with him. She hoped he'd see how broken-hearted she was. She hoped that he would forgive her for ending their relationship. She couldn't get him out of her mind and she wanted him again—her man, her baby.

She'd made alternative arrangements just in case Don wasn't at home, a bed and breakfast close to where he lived, the pub. They had knocked back shots there one night and the staff seemed friendly.

She had booked the room via email. Worst case scenario, Don wouldn't be at home and she could have a few drinks then just walk to her room from the bar. She had texted him while she was waiting to have her passport details checked, no reply. She tried calling him when she walked out of the arrivals section at the airport, she got the message, *The mobile phone you are trying to reach may be switched off, please try again later.*

She was shaking as the taxi driver turned on to Barn Lane, it all came back to her—the romantic walks they had taken, the meal at the Indian restaurant they had eaten, even the shop, 'Grundy's Newsagents', where they had bought cigarettes together. She'd only spent a week in Olton but she remembered every detail about it.

Her heart was racing as she neared Don's apartment. Would he be at home? What would his reaction be? Would he still want her? She reassured herself, 'Of course he would still want me. The emails he had bombarded her with after he had returned home showed her that he was hurting, showed her that she was in complete control of the situation'.

Her mind drifted and she wondered what he would be wearing when he answered the door, if indeed he was at home. Maybe he'd be at his local and she could walk in there and surprise him. She hoped that he'd be alone and not with his friend Jake. There was something about Jake that Katy didn't like, and that cunt of a whore wife of his, Jade.

"Turn right just after the pub," Katy told the driver.

The taxi turned right into Fentham Gardens, Don's road. Katy remembered it well. She even remembered the white van opposite Don's place, it was owned by a builder as was evidenced by the lettering on the side of the van, 'Brackley's Construction—No Job Considered Too Small.'

As the taxi neared Don's driveway, Katy saw a big black car parked outside on the curb; it was a limo and was indicating to pull out. The taxi driver pulled up behind the limo. Seconds later, the limo pulled out and drove to the bottom of Fentham Gardens.

"£15 please." the taxi driver said.

"No, wait, I may want to go somewhere else first," Katy told him.

Katy watched the black limo head towards the bottom of Fentham Gardens.

Once at the bottom, she watched the driver manoeuvre a perfect U-turn then head back towards where Katy was sitting in the private hire taxi. Don's road was maybe 50 yards in length, a cul-de-sac. She looked out of the back passenger window as the limo drove past. It slowed as it approached the junction and Katy had a great view of the olive skinned driver and the two passengers in the back.

That's when she saw them.

Fucking kissing.

And that's when Katy said, "Follow that black limousine please."

# Chapter Thirty-Seven

Archangel Gabriel had summoned them again. They had been in the limousine when they were pulled back. They had felt the impending danger together, they knew upon feeling it that Gabriel would pull them back, it often happened like that.

"And so it is."

"There has to be a sacrifice so we can move forward with the plan. Nothing can get in its way. You all felt the impending danger but do you know where it came from?"

The four shook their heads from side to side.

"She is hurting and she carries blackness in her heart. She is full of rage and jealousy and wants avengement. She is already planning retributive punishment and is being pushed forward by the evil one. We cannot allow this to happen.

"She will stop at nothing because the evil one is working through her; he is giving her great strength and clouding her judgment. She plans to kill them both."

"What can we do?" Sebastian asked.

"We need to pray; we need to join forces so that we can protect them. We need to make a human sacrifice of her. We must all pray to the Lord and ask for forgiveness at what we are about to do. We must ask him to grant her with grace, faith, love and power of God, and we must pray to the Lord so that she can be uplifted to greater heights."

Teresa asked Gabriel, "Is she the female that the evil one is working through?"

"She is," Gabriel replied then added, "The evil one has entered her heart before, and this is not the first time. He knows that she has great strength and he also knows that she has great weaknesses too. He will be working on those weaknesses to get her to do his work. I can feel what he is doing. She can hear him but she does not know his pure evil as we all do.

"This is not her fault; he has her in his grip and is playing on her insecurities and jealousies. This is making her strong, this is giving her no fear. She has tunnel vision and is not thinking straight. He is not allowing her to."

Gabriel and the four bowed their heads and one by one the four angels left Gabriel's side and re-joined Karen and Don.

And so it came to pass.

All four returned to the back seat of the limo. Just in time to follow Karen and Don into the lobby ofthe Hilton Hotel.

# Chapter Thirty-Eight

She saw them get out of the limo, they were laughing and she had linked arms with her man.

She would pay dearly, as would he.

She paid the taxi fare and walked through the lobby of the Hilton. They were still linking arms, still laughing. She knew the woman, it was that cunt whore who sold her soul and body to men, making them weak, those pathetic fucking men who would purchase magazines and think about nothing but her.

Those fucking perverted creatures who couldn't wait to find time so they could open the centre pages to look at the cunt whore and then carry out self-gratification whilst thinking about her. She needs to repent for her sins; she needs to beg for mercy.

The fucking cunt whore was even in a magazine she had read whilst she was flying across to Birmingham. The in-flight magazine had showed Karen Crawford's famous curves and long curly hair in an attempt to get passengers to buy duty free chocolate. Katy hated the whole marketing business, she knew how fake it was.

As if someone would have a figure like the Crawford cunt if they gorged on fucking chocolate, she had thought when skimming through the pages just hours ago. Rage was building inside Katy.

*She needs to beg you, Katy.*

The evil one had control of Katy, he had her in his grip.

*Look at them, look at them, so fucking happy, so in love. She stole your man, Katy. She has been fucking him senseless and he has enjoyed every minute of it. He was fucking her when you sent him your first message. He laughed and showed her how fucking pathetic you was.*

*You know what she said when she read your message to him, Katy? She said that you were obviously not ready for him like a real woman was, like she was. Kill the cunt whore, Katy.*

Katy was trapped in *his* lair. He increased the flow of hatred into her heart.

*She asked him about you, Katy. She asked how good you was in bed. He told her you were frigid. She was stroking his chest lovingly while he was belittling you. Does that make you mad, Katy? Do you want to get even, do you want retribution? Watch the elevator, Katy. Watch what floor they get out of.*

*He'll be kissing her on the way up, she'll be putting her hands down his jeans, just like the way you used to do. They both need to pay, Katy. Kill them. Kill them both. Use the rage within you. You did it before, Katy, you did it to that tall man, remember the one who was pestering you, the tall one with the bulbous eyes? How did it feel to kill him?*

*Thud, thud, Katy, the sound of metal meeting flesh. Good girl, Katy. How will it feel to kill Don and his gorgeous looking cunt whore? He will be fucking her tonight, again and again, each time telling her how special she is and how he has never loved anyone like he has loved her.*

*And what about Hjalmar, Katy, you remember him don't you? You dumped him and then learned that, on the very same night he ate with you, that he fucked Viktoria. You did a great job on him. Cutting off his testicles and stuffing them in his mouth was a stroke of genius. Katy, I'm so proud of you. Do the same to Don and the cunt whore. Remember me, Katy?*

*Remember me coming to you 4 years ago? You told Don that Rikard had left you, didn't you? You hide your lies well; I'm proud of you, Katy. Even when they lowered Rikard's body into the ground, you played the grieving lover so well, but we both know the truth. We both know he was your first and we both know how you did it.*

*The authorities are still looking for the man you described as Rikard's attacker. They had never seen anything like it, a frenzied stabbing they had called it, 62 stab wounds. I'm proud of you, my sweet, sweet Katy.*

Katy watched the elevator, it stopped on floor 46.

*Now follow them, Katy. Nobody has seen you, just as nobody saw you those times when you walked through the exit door to entrap your prey back at the bar, right, Katy. Follow them up to the 46th floor and put an end to your misery, Katy. Put an end to the sorrow you are feeling. The cunt whore is causing that sorrow so start with her first.*

*Feel my strength, Katy, feel my strength today as you did when you stabbed Rikard or when you strangled Hjalmar or even when you used the wrench on that English pig who reminded you of Don. They all reminded you of Don didn't they, Katy? Kill her first, Katy, then kill Don."*

Katy pressed the down button and within seconds the doors to the right of the elevator, ridden by Don and Karen, opened.

*That's my girl, Katy, now press 46 and seek them out.*

Katy followed *his* instructions and pressed the button marked 46.

*That's my girl, Katy.* He told her once more, then added, *There will be empty wine bottles outside a room on the lobby, take one and smash it, Katy, then use it. Stick it in the cunt whore's neck.*

The elevator doors closed and she ascended.

# Chapter Thirty-Nine

The elevator stopped on floor 46, the doors opened and Katy walked into the corridor. A scent of Holygrace lingered next to the three elevators. She had used Holygrace for Don, she used different perfumes for different men.

She had panties in her drawer back home, each pair individually scented, each one given a name, a male name. Rikard's were red, the colour of blood; that's how she last remembered him. He had wanted to end things with her so she killed him, stabbing him multiple times with a carving knife from his kitchen. She had entered his apartment with her own keys; Rikard had agreed that she have a spare set.

He was surprised to see her, but more surprised to see what she was wearing. She had loved the look of surprise on his face. The Swedish authorities were right, it was a frenzied attack, but he deserved it. She had remembered the useless prick, Hedman, and his appeal on TV.

"We are looking for a white male, blue eyes and about six foot tall. He was wearing a t-shirt with a clock face logo. He has shoulder length hair and a poor skin complexion. Please, if you see this man do not approach him."

Throughout Hedman's appeal, an incident number was scrolled from left to right across the bottom of the screen. Katy had smiled when she saw the ageing officer on TV describe the assailant. It was Katy who had gave him the description.

No man had the right to end relationships, no man. She played the victim so well, especially when Hedman had interviewed her back at her apartment wanting to know what she witnessed.

She told Hedman that they were attacked as they entered Rikard's apartment. The assailant, she told Hedman, had lunged at her with a knife, Rikard had jumped in front of her and the knife went through his chest. She managed to escape as Rikard put up a fight. She told Hedman that Rikard had held on to the assailant and had yelled, *Run Katy, run.* Hedman was taking notes and watching Katy's body language carefully.

"I ran as fast as I could home to my apartment and that's when I called the police and fainted."

She broke down crying then vomited. She'd chewed on some charcoal after leaving the back entrance of Rikard's apartment, she'd read that it induced vomit. That's when she headed for the overgrowth in his garden and removed the Keep Safe Disposable Coveralls she had worn over her clothes for the kill just under a half an hour ago. Everything she wore over her clothes that night had been stolen from the various hospitals she worked at.

Being a paediatric nurse allowed her access to such attire. She had, minutes before entering Rikard's apartment, placed a black bin bag in the overgrowth. Once home, she threw bin bag containing the blood stained coveralls onto the open fire; they burnt in seconds. Along with it went the evidence that the coverall had been taken from Valkyries *University Hospital.*

She then threw her blouse and jeans into the flames, the coveralls had done the job and protected her clothing but she knew how forensics could pick up on fragments. That's why she wore the jet black wig tonight, a wig that she also tossed into the fire.

She'd washed her hands then jogged vigorously on the spot for one minute before calling the police. Out of breath and turning on the water works she told them that her boyfriend had just been stabbed in his apartment. She was hysterical. She threw a chair on the floor and left the phone receiver next to it. Katy was a seasoned pro.

The police operator at the other end of the line had presumed Katy had fainted. She jumped in the shower, and scrubbed her nails. She'd worn extra strength surgical gloves but just wanted to make sure. The gloves were in the pocket of the coveralls that she had thrown onto the open fire as were the medical shoe covers. She tossed her trainers in there too.

She spent just 3 minutes in the shower then quickly dried herself and changed into jeans and a pink blouse, they had been placed on top of the wicker linen basket earlier in the day. Once dried and changed she positioned herself onto the floor, next to the overturned chair. That's how they found her when they broke into her apartment. That's what Officer's Andersson and Lowenberg wrote when they filed their reports later that night.

The forensics team, two days after the killing, had even searched her apartment. They told her it was just routine, but she had already burned the evidence—the clothes, coveralls, gloves and medical shoe covers she had worn over her Nike trainers. They found nothing.

Hjalmar's were yellow. Piece of fucking chicken shit he was. No morals, a pathetic weasel who thought he could just jump from bed to bed. She'd pissed her panties when he took his last breath. She saw him coming out of Viktoria's apartment at 5 am that morning. She saw them kiss on her doorstep. She followed him home in her car.

She watched him enter his apartment and waited 5 minutes before she knocked on his door. The idiot let her in after she had told him that she was sorry. It was easy. She tied his wrists and told him that she wanted her wicked way with him. He couldn't fight back with his hands behind his back, tightly bound.

She even got him to turn around and close his eyes. That's when she removed the second piece of rope she had brought into his apartment that morning. That's when she strangled him to death. That's when she pissed her panties. She wasn't finished with him. *Men like that deserve to have their balls cut off.*

She went to the kitchen drawer and pulled out a bread knife, its serrated edges perfect for splitting the skin on Hjalmar's ball sac when, once split, would allow her to reach in and pull his testicles out. She placed them in Hjalmar's mouth. Once again she had worn the same attire as she did when she killed Rikard. She wiped the bread knife on the kitchen towel, folded it four times before putting it in her pocket and leaving through the back door.

The police were called to Hjalmar's when Viktoria had phoned them after she discovered his body the next day. She had gone over to his place at 5 pm, just like he had told her to when he left her place that fateful morning. He'd told her about Katy, although he only knew her as Isabelle, because that's the name Katy had given him when they exchanged phone numbers. He'd remarked that she had changed her hair on their second date. It was, in actual fact another of her wigs.

The forensics team, two days after the killing, had even searched her apartment, they told her it was just routine, but she had already burned the evidence—the clothes, coveralls, gloves and medical shoe covers she had worn over her Nike trainers. They found nothing.

On interviewing Viktoria, the police had learned that Hjalmar had a previous girlfriend with red hair. She was called Isabelle. Katy had, after strangling Hjalmar and returning home, tossed the pay as you go Blackberry into the open fire along with the rest of the murderous attire. No blood but better to be safe than sorry, she thought.

Her blue panties were called 'English', the guy Luke, from the stag party, the English pig. He was easy too. She'd purposely left her fake calling card under his glass. She watched him lift the glass, her lipstick grabbed his attention first then the card she had left underneath the glass. The calling card had a photo of her with a jet black wig.

'CALL SUZY SUXX FOR THAT SPECIAL MASSAGE' was written across the top of the card. He didn't need to call her, his eyes followed her to the door and when she turned to offer a gaze he practically ran over to her. She and the English man left via the exit door where she unlocked her Audi and invited him inside.

She'd made out that her husband was at home so they couldn't head back to her place. Instead she drove him to a quiet spot near dense forest.

She pulled down the front seats and laid him down. Unbuckling him before sitting on his erection. He didn't know about the wrench behind his head, wrapped in a stained kitchen towel. In the throes of passion, she had leaned forward for him to suck on her nipples. That's when she grabbed the wrench and hit him hard across the crown of his head.

It was perfect. One swoop and he was unconscious. She finished him off by dragging him out of her car. He'd stirred so she hit him with the wrench again, then again, and then again.

She dragged his lifeless body into the thick dense forest. He was found the next day by a woman walking her dog.

Luke Cooper was a random kill for Katy. She had not prepared well. His blood was on her clothes. His blood was on her hands. And, more importantly for Detective Johan Hedman, fibres were found on the body.

She would, when she returned home from the UK, pick out a colour for Don but first she had to find him and the cunt whore. She also had to find different colours for her most recent kills, but they could wait.

*Smell it, Katy, smell the perfume, it's the same scent that you wore for him. She wears it for him now. He loves the smell of her, Katy, and has completely forgot about you. Seek them Katy. Seek.*

*His* voice disappeared. It was just Katy, just her and a cacophony of the multiple voices from the personalities that followed her around. She was in the midst of yet another psychotic episode.

128

She started to walk down the corridor, trying to follow the scent of the cunt whore's Holygrace but it had faded and was gradually replaced by a smoky aroma.

The fire alarm sounded.

# Chapter Forty

Colin Turner's flight had been put back 24 hours. Virgin Atlantic had, as a way of compensation, offered him a room at the Hilton and a £50 voucher to spend. Colin Turner was a reformed alcoholic. He was, as he had told his sponsor back in Missouri, still an alcoholic; most 'reformed' alcoholics still are.

Colin had stacked up a serious amount of air miles over the years. He was a statistician and his expertise was often called upon in complex tax evasion court cases. He could speak many languages and this, combined with the art of crunching numbers, meant he was in high demand as an expert. His credentials had never been called into question. He guarded his alcoholism well, as most alcoholics did.

Colin had always phoned ahead to inform hotel management that he wanted his mini bar to be 'dry', the temptation was just too hard to fight. Tonight, however, was different, he had no control over the booking. He could not resist temptation. If it's meant to happen, then it's meant to happen, he told himself.

The miniature Smirnoff vodka was first, just one wouldn't hurt, but hurt it did. One small drink led to another, each time Colin's warped inner voice telling him that one more wouldn't make any difference. *You've had one already so another wouldn't really make much difference, go on just drink it.*

It was a vicious cycle, one drink would cancel out the guilt of having the previous drink, then a third would cancel the guilt of having the second, and so it went.

Within the space of 2 hours, Colin had gulped three miniatures of Smirnoff Vodka, three miniatures of Bells Whiskey, three miniatures of Gordon's Gin, three miniatures of Bacardi and two miniatures of Baileys Irish Cream. He was drunk, beyond drunk in fact. But he felt so good.

He lit a cigarette inside his non-smoking room on the 45th floor. The smoke alarm detected it first then, as he fell into a deep sleep, the cigarette dropped from his fingers. It landed to the left of his bed, on top of the loosely crumpled complimentary newspaper, which was on top of the plastic miniature bottles that his guilt had tried to conceal.

Heat turned to flame and in an instant the hotel fire alarm sounded. The sprinkler system, that had been designed to switch itself on, failed.

Archangel Gabriel and Colin Turner's guardians pulled back. They took Colin Turner's soul with them. Pathios also returned.

# Chapter Forty-One

There were three elevators in the Hilton hotel lobby. Katy had used the one on the right, the same one as Karen and Don. If she would have waited, she would have seen that the middle elevator had been called to the 46th floor. If she would waited she would have seen Don and Karen return to the lobby.

She could have watched them again as they left the front door. She could have watched them climb into a taxi. If she felt the need, she could have followed them to the Tai Po Chinese restaurant. Instead, she was stuck on the 46th floor where smoke was rising through the elevator shafts.

Being the coward that he is, the evil one left Katy's side. He was needed elsewhere. He pulled back then found himself in Idaho, back with Lex Brampton.

And so it was.

# Chapter Forty-Two

In all there were 17 angels present that night. They had each brought with them love and peace. They were the angels of termination, those that are given instructions in advance of the impending death of those they guard. Those instructions were laid out to them by the Archangel Gabriel.

"Comfort them and offer them the grace of God," he had told them. Katy's angels, Daniel and Hannah, were with her when she crossed over. She was now at peace and awaiting her judgment.

An investigation into the fire at some point in the future would show that The Hilton was evacuated efficiently but sadly eight perished. There were just five rooms booked on the upper 45th and 46th floors that evening.

Rachel and Sandra Beattie were sisters. They had saved long and hard for their trip to Australia, a one month holiday visiting their parents who had immigrated to Melbourne some 2 years ago. They were asleep in room 4506.

Next to them, in room 4508, was single occupant and *former* reformed alcoholic, Colin Turner. This is where the fire started, it was a cigarette.

On the 46th floor, Peter and Janet Rathbone were situated directly above room 4508. They were celebrating their 25th wedding anniversary. Janet had multiple sclerosis and Peter, it appeared, could not get her out of bed and into her wheelchair before the flames hit them.

In room 4606 was journalist, Simon Hopkins. He was married with three children but was sharing his bed that night with fellow journalist, Ruth Delaney. They died from smoke inhalation. The fire alarm, it seemed, had not roused them in time.

The sprinklers on the 45th and 46th floors had malfunctioned, a later investigation would not determine why they had failed. In truth, the investigators would never learn that the water had turned to ice, blocking any attempt for it to be sprinkled onto the flames. Once the flames subsided, the ice had returned to its liquid form again.

Pathios had made sure of it.

Room 4610, the only other room that was booked that night on the upper 45th and 46th floors, was also destroyed in the fire; its occupants, Karen Crawford and Don Williamson, were out at the time.

*And then there was one.*

Katy Johansson, a Swedish tourist. It was unknown why she was on the 46th floor.

They'd found her body in the corridor lobby. Smoke inhalation had caused her death.

They knew little about her but suspected she was an escort of some sort. Her calling cards and passport found in her handbag and jet black wig that had started to come away at the side revealing her natural blonde hair had made investigators assume this. She wasn't on the hotel reservation list but investigators found a return airline ticket to Stockholm among the contents of her handbag.

The 17th angel present that night was the incarnate water angel, Pathios. Her mission complete, she returned to the other side.

# Chapter Forty-Three

Karen Crawford's $6 million 1,000-acre ranch was easily accessible to the year-round resort amenities of Sun Valley. It was meticulously maintained, thought Don. There was a horse barn, hay and machinery storage, cattle handling facilities, and even a spring creek and several spring-fed lakes. It was, Karen told him, one of the few remaining large, intact ranch properties in the Sun Valley area.

Karen's nearest neighbour, and long-time friend, Angie Jakobs, lived just over 2 miles away. It was her haven and just one of the many properties she owned in both the UK and America. She now had a reason to be there. She now had a companion, a soulmate, and someone to share her life and love with.

Her $6 million home had never felt like home. Today, upon returning, it did. It felt sacred and Karen knew as she surveyed the thousand acres that it was going to be the place where she and Don would tie the knot, unite, tie the binds. She wouldn't invite all and sundry, just a few close friends.

Just as her home in Cobham, Surrey, there was no evidence of who she was or what she did for a living. Karen had built up her wealth over the years and had decided, at an early point in her career, that home was home and work was work the two should never cross over.

\*\*\*

Their flight from Birmingham was long but Karen had upgraded both herself and Don. The first class trip cost her over $13,000, her website had made her treble that as they flew across the Atlantic Ocean.

They were both thankful that they wasn't at the Hilton when it had caught fire that night.

"Talk about luck," Don had said during the flight.

"It's nothing to do with luck, baby," she had said, adding, "everything happens for a reason, it's beyond our control. Chance or luck does not exist, it's just an idea of the human mind. Everything is planned, Don. Everything. There is a reason you were insistent on taking me to that Chinese restaurant, it wasn't just about the hunger you felt in that moment.

"Our spirit guides can make us feel things, Don, particularly when they are trying to warn us. Have you ever walked into a place and felt fear, Don' have you ever felt a feeling that makes you feel as if you shouldn't be somewhere?"

Don had, in the past, been to places where he felt uncomfortable, so much so that he had left. He always felt he had an inner sense that could predict negative energy but he had always put this down to 'streets smarts'. Karen nodded in agreement when he explained this to her but added that to get out of danger quickly the spirit guides would often speed up the process by making a person have physical feelings rather than thoughts.

"You felt hungry, we could have had food sent up to our room but you were insistent on Chinese food, something the hotel didn't serve so we had to leave the building. Don, if we hadn't we would have been caught up in the fire."

Don didn't want to debate the who's and how's and Karen sensed this, so changed the subject and started to tell Don about Odelia. They were halfway over the Atlantic at this point. She told him how her life, however brief, was planned, once again emphasising 'everything for a reason'.

"Whatever happens in our lives shapes us, Don. We have to take the rough with the smooth." Don felt her pain, he wiped each tear drop with the tip of his thumb as she painstakingly recounted the events of 27 years ago. Through tears, Karen told him, "I will take you to her final resting place, lover."

He loved the term of endearment (*lover*) she used for him. He loved that she wanted him to be introduced to Odelia.

\*\*\*

Don had lit the open fire around 6 pm that night. They had eaten and drank wine then, after an hour or so, they had made love in front of the burning embers. She had run them both a bath, complete with Jacuzzi jets and big enough for a family of four.

They had brought the wine in with them and had each returned the favour of back rubs. They were both very much in the moment where nothing else mattered but contentment.

With marriage still firmly in her mind Karen, whilst receiving the shoulder rub from Heaven, asked Don about his friends and family back in England.

"I have very few close friends, babe. Jake, his wife, Jade, are like family to me. They've always been there to pick up the pieces when things have gone pear-shaped in my life. I have a brother, Danny, who lives in a suburb of Melbourne in Australia, a sleepy little town called Colac. We've not spoken for a number of years.

"My only sister died when I was just a kid. Kim, she was in a car accident with my mom, Maria. Dad died 4 years ago."

"Tell me more about your brother," Karen asked while moving behind Don to return the shoulder rub.

"Ah, he's one of a kind, babe. He's 2 years older than me and is the brains of the family. He studied hard and reaped the rewards at an early age. He was a veterinarian surgeon, owned a string of rescue centres in the UK before branching out. He moved to Sydney where he met Tayla, his current wife. They both moved to Colac after he extended his business to Melbourne.

"He ran into debt and when dad died, he really dug in his heels on the will. He hired a lawyer and contested much of what dad left behind. Dad had split everything down the middle for me and Dan; it wasn't a great deal but it could have been if Dan had agreed to hold on to the house dad had left us. The house market was on the rise again just before dad died.

"We were both given advice to hold on to the house and sell when the seller's market was at its peak. Dan, because of the debt he was facing, disagreed and it was sold for peanuts. Had he have held for a couple of years we would have sold it for an extra thirty thousand. Things between us became toxic.

"I couldn't get to grips with the fact that he just wanted to rid himself of any memories of dad. I was prepared to buy him out over a period of years but he just wanted the money right there and then. As I said, we haven't spoken in years."

Karen lathered her hands and pressed her thumbs into the knuckles of Don's spine. "Tell me about your dad, lover?" She asked.

"We had a pretty good relationship. He kinda raised both Dan and I single-handedly after mom and Kim died. He was a hard worker, often working double shifts to help put food on the table. He had a great sense of humour despite the tragedy. I miss hearing his laugh."

Karen sensed the croak in Don's voice. "And tell me about his experience with angels, you told me he heard them sing?"

"Yes, that's what he told us. He was a kid and was swimming on a beach somewhere in the south of England. A wave washed over him and took him under the water, he swallowed water and feared the worst. He told Dan, Kim and I that he didn't fight it; he felt calm, almost peaceful, that's when he said he heard the most beautiful choir of angelic voices.

"He said that he'd never heard anything quite so beautiful. Next thing he knew, he felt a pair of hands on him then he remembers coming around on the beach. A passer-by had seen him. Luckily, this guy was an off duty lifeguard. He pulled dad out of the water and gave him the kiss of life."

"Interesting," Karen said, then asked Don why he didn't believe in guardian angels.

"I've never really felt them around me. In any event, if such beings did exist why do they not intervene when kids are being abused, why do they not guard old people when they are attacked in the street?"

"That was something I struggled with too, Don," she told him. "Here's my take on it. It's a misconception that they guard us. They merely guide us, show us signs, you know, like the number eleven with me. The suffering you speak of is hard to explain but I believe it is for us as individuals to experience sorrow, loss, tears and anger because without them we cannot, as humans, grow.

"Think about it. You had your heart broken by Katy, you experienced heartache, loss and, no doubt shed tears too. Would you say that you have grown since your separation?"

"I guess so, yes but on a scale of one to ten, my loss was a one compared to that of you losing your daughter," he told her.

"Oh, I struggled when Odelia went, struggled really hard but, as I say, it's not down to our guardian angels to intervene. Mine have just guided me since her passing, that guidance has given me strength and, to an extent, hope. I've realised Odelia was meant to be born and she was meant to die, that whole experience was for me and me alone.

"Would I give up the fame and fortune so I could have her back? Absolutely. Would I sacrifice my own life so she could return and live her life? Of course I would but that wasn't the plan God had for her, for us. There is a reason God chose her, a reason God chose me and there is a reason why you and I met the way we did, Don."

Don wasn't convinced but didn't want to push it. Karen felt his scepticism so changed the subject.

"You told me you were married but divorced because of your wife's infidelity. Tell me about that," she asked.

"Yup, I was married for 6 years. Her name was Trudy. She was basically seeing someone else behind my back. Her close friends knew, many of whom egged her on, you know, told her that she was doing nothing wrong and that she should do what made her happy. It's funny, Karen, you really think you know someone inside out, then wham! they hit you for six.

"The shock was hard to deal with, you know, the disbelief and coldness of it all. Hardest, for me at least, was the aftermath. Her new lover had posted about her on his MySpace page. He didn't mention her by name but I knew. It was the day she told me all about him.

"She must have told me she wanted to end things then either phoned him or sent him a text message. She told me around 3 in the afternoon. Her new lover had posted a photo of a love heart and the words 'The Beginning' on his page at 4 that very same afternoon."

"I'm sorry, Don, I truly am. Nobody should have to go through such heartache and torment. When did all this happen?" Karen asked.

"Oh, it was a long time ago, Karen, 2001."

"And do you know, or even care, if they are still together?"

Don shook his head from side to side.

"Nup, she left him 6 months or so down the line. Turns out he was cheating on her with both his and her boss. I felt kind of guilty about it because I researched the guy after she left me. He was a player, had a number of profiles posted online. Was even active on them while he was with Trudy."

"Well, serves her right. What goes around comes around, Don."

"Oh, I know, Karen. At least I've always thought that people who do wrong will eventually have a wrong done to them. I wish her no harm though. As a matter of fact, I wished them both well, not to their faces as that would have been too difficult. I just looked up to the stars one night and sent my well-wishes out to the Universe."

Karen was falling more and more in love with Don. He was the one for her.

"That was a beautiful thing to do, Don. You have a terrific heart." She once again changed the subject.

"Would you want to build bridges between yourself and your brother, Don?"

"I've thought about it a lot, babe, you know, life's too short and all that," he told her.

"Life is too short, lover," Karen told him then added, "You know in your heart what needs to be done, sweetheart."

She felt Don's unease.

"Would you like to go and see him in Australia? You know, just me, you and our engagement rings." Fuck it, she thought, no harm in throwing the idea of marriage out there.

Don turned his head around to her. He had a radiant smile on his face.

"Why, Miss Crawford, is that a proposal?"

Karen moved her thumbs from the knuckles of his spine and reached around to his waist, slowly moving her right hand over his tummy then between his legs.

"One time offer, Mr Williamson, now say yes and give your girl what she wants."

"Oh, I will, babe, but you know so much about me. What about you. Tell me a little about your family."

Karen moved her hands up to his chest. "Fuck, I could give you a whole chapter on my past," she told him.

Don moved to Karen's side and laid his back against the tub. He placed his hands behind his head, looked at Karen and, with a smile, said, "So, read to me."

"Well, you probably know more about me than I do, that's one of the drawbacks of fame, your private life is just not private. You know pretty much what happened when I was 13, you know about the rape and Odelia but I guess there is more stuff. Nothing newsworthy though but there is stuff that many people, apart from Angie, don't know about my upbringing. Mom and dad were strict Catholics, you know, the type that went to church every Sunday and confession at least once a week.

"We survived from their hard work. Idaho is a potato state and we had a farm that I will take you too soon. We weren't rich by any means but we weren't poor either. I kinda blamed myself for going through with the birth of Odelia for a while. The shame I brought on mom and dad showed, it was almost as if they aged overnight.

"We still had a great bond but something was gone between us. I felt that I had let them down by not agreeing to the adoption idea. After Odelia died, things became a little strained. I dropped out of school and helped on the farm for a while but there was something inside me telling me that it wasn't where I was meant to be. The job offers came in and I pretty much saw them as my escape from the potato picking world that I had become so used to.

"Mom was able to hold her head high again at church when the first photos of me appeared around the town. I did some modelling for girl's dolls and clothes which resulted in huge cardboard displays of me around the main stores. My name was perfect for the dolls, the advertising departments loved it. Kitty dolls were new on the market and they, with the aid of an air-line and pump, crawled across the floor.

"My name basically gave them carte blanche to use plays on words. The Kitty Crawler endorsed by Karen Crawford' had a certain tonality to it. I got lots of attention and dad didn't like it. We'd argued one night and he let it out that I probably egged the Brampton boy on. He and mom didn't talk for a week after that."

"I'm sorry," Don said sympathetically.

"Don't be, lover. Had dad not have told me his true feelings then I probably would have continued being the girl on the farm from butt-fuck Idaho. His opinion of me made me get off my ass and pursue the modelling career. Some years went by, more cardboard cut-outs appeared around the stores and then I hit bigtime.

"The Cornflake ads took me to a new level. It was a job that paid well, enough for me to help buy the farm for mom and dad. Tragic thing is, my final payment bought the farm outright. Two weeks later, mom and dad were killed when the tractor they were on punctured a gas line that was above ground. You heard about that, right?"

Don shook his head and offered "Uh huh."

"It was a part of the farm that they had not previously used. Me paying the mortgage meant they could invest more time and their own money, they did so by cultivating some land that they'd previously used to store equipment. Mom had been riding with dad on the tractor when it went over an exposed valve of a natural gas pipeline. The steel pipe had been obscured by the overgrown brush.

"Apparently, the line was punctured and that allowed natural gas to escape and caused the explosion. By the time the first firefighters arrived on the scene, the fire had destroyed the tractor and had burned a 40-foot circle around it. Mom and dad were found lying on the ground near the tractor, but the firefighters could not reach them until the fire was contained almost an hour later. The coroner was called to the scene and pronounced mom and dad dead at around 4 pm that afternoon."

"Oh, baby, I am so sorry," Don said whilst turning his body towards her.

"Please, don't be. It could have been me, I guess. I'd often jump in that old tractor. It was the same coroner who came to the house when Odelia passed, he was a good friend of mom and dad and kinda took it upon himself to become my adopted dad, not in a parenting kinda way, I was too old for that by then. He just said that he would do his best to keep the media away. I'm surprised you haven't heard about the accident, Don?"

"Well, I'm a fan of yours, Karen, but I never really went too deep into your background," he answered.

Karen's mobile phone bleeped. It was a message from Angie.

# Chapter Forty-Four
# Kawarren, Australia
# New Year's Eve 2014

"You lucky, lucky bastard." Danny Williamson was laughing in disbelief at the TV screen.

Photos of his brother and Karen Crawford had hit the news media after it was leaked that they had booked a room together at the Hilton in Birmingham. As always, whenever Karen Crawford's name was mentioned, the news went global.

Danny and Tayla had moved away from Colac, but not too far. Their home was in a private, secluded pocket of Kawarren, just south of Colac. They even had a creek running through the 170 acres of land they owned.

"Tayla, come and look at this, darling."

Tayla, Danny's wife, had jet black shoulder-length hair. She had a golden suntan and large deep blue eyes and a cute curved nose and small mouth outlined by puffy lips that she often accentuated with glossy pink lipstick. Tonight, she was wearing no make-up.

"What is it, Dan?" She asked as she entered the room cradling a coffee mug between her hands.

Dan hit the volume on the remote and put his finger to his lips, gesticulating to Tayla that something important was being said. She turned towards the screen.

*Don Williamson, a 50 year-old paralegal from Birmingham, is thought to be the new man in Karen Crawford's life. Crawford, who earlier this year told Time magazine that she would consider having a relationship outside of the celebrity circles, is thought to be besotted with the Birmingham man. BBC correspondent Philippa McAndrews speaks here with Hilton staff members.*

Both Dan and Tayla watched with open mouths.

*Thanks, Brian, I'm here with Lucy Sullivan, a receptionist at the Hilton.*

Philippa McAndrews then introduced Lucy to the cameras. *"So, Lucy, you saw both Don Williamson and Karen Crawford together, I believe it was you that checked them in. Can you tell us a little bit more about that? How did they look together, were they happy? Do you think they looked like they were in love?"*

Lucy looked in to the camera. *"Well, I knew that Miss Crawford was staying overnight as we had been told by senior staff that she was coming. Her room was booked earlier that day and when she and Mr Williamson arrived I was on duty. They were laughing and holding hands, they seemed to be having a good time and seemed to be very much in love."*

"Bwahahahahaha," Danny let out an uncontrollable laugh. This was followed by, "Go on, my son."

It was Tayla' turn to gesticulate silence by looking at him with her finger to her lips.

*Another source tells us that they avoided the fire as they had left the hotel shortly after checking in. Karen Crawford's agency have refused to make any official comment but it is believed that she, along with Don Williamson, flew to America a few days ago. Back to you in the studio, Brian.*

"Lucky bastard," Danny said again.

"She looked better 10 years ago," Tayla remarked before heading back to the kitchen for more coffee.

# Chapter Forty-Five

It was 11.23 pm in Idaho (2323). They were just over half an hour away from 2015. More importantly, to Karen and Don at least, they were minutes away from sending an email to the editor of *The Washington Post*. Karen knew him personally, she also knew not to use the standard email address advertised on *The Washington* Post website. She had his private email address. The email was short and sweet.

*From: Karen <karencrawfordodelia@crawfordodelia.com>*
*To: Richard G*
*Subject: Announcement*
*Date: Wed, 31 December 2014 23:31:17*

*Dear Richard,*

*I always told you that you would be the first to know. I stick to my word. I am engaged to be married. Check the BBC website for his name.*

*Will call you tomorrow and give you the exclusive. Your end of the bargain still remains!*

*Karen.*

A text message had been sent to Karen's phone from Angie while she was telling Don about the death of her parents. She had read it aloud to Don in the Jacuzzi. *The cat is out of the bag; check the BBC website.* They both looked at the news, they read the quotes from the hotel staff, they even read Don's background—a paralegal working for a Swedish law firm, previously married, no children.

Even a quote from his old neighbour, Bridgette Gillespie. *I knew Don for years. He's a very sweet, genuine guy and I wish him all the best for the future. He thoroughly deserves love in his life.* The BBC had even tracked down where he lived.

"Williamson lived in Fentham Gardens in a small two bedroomed flat. He was partial to a drink at his local pub, the Lyndon Poacher, and his preferred choice of drink was whiskey and coke."

Smiling, she continued to read aloud to Don.

"Neighbour, Jimmy Ryan, who has his own building business, said of Williamson, 'He keeps himself to himself, works from home and has the occasional pint down the local. He's an affable guy so good luck to him'."

There was even a photo of Jimmy Ryan standing next to his white van; 'Brackley's Construction' had been airbrushed away.

"Oh my God!" Karen said, before adding, "They've even quoted Bella."

She read the following to Don.

"Bella Thornton, a long-time friend of Crawford told reporters, 'Karen will have gone into hiding as she knows about the media interest that her relationship will create'. Thornton added that there were far more interesting events happening around the world than a relationship between two people. 'My apartment was burgled but that didn't make the news, you guys should be chasing the culprit who stole my belongings'."

Karen couldn't stop laughing when she saw the photo of Bella. She was wearing the tightest t-shirt ever, emblazoned across her breasts was the word 'JUGS'.

"Ah, that's my Bella, never one to miss a photo opportunity."

Still giggling, Karen turned to Don. She held his hand and simply said, "Welcome to my world, lover."

Karen took control of the situation. She knew there would be a media frenzy and she knew that the digging wouldn't stop. She told Don that she would make an announcement in the press that would hopefully keep off the hounds from snooping too much into Don's private life. The editor at the *Washington Post* had promised a $50,000 donation to a charity of Karen's choice should she ever give him an exclusive into her private life.

Don was given the pleasure of clicking the 'send' tab on the email she had just composed.

"Let's put some champagne in the ice bucket and take it out to the patio, lover. Let's see in this wonderful new year together." She handed Don a blanket. "We can share it, you can wrap us both in it and I'll unwrap you later," she told him, whilst offering a wink.

"Here, take this," she said handing him a hip flask. "It's whiskey, we can do some shots when 2015 arrives."

Don put the hip flask in his inside coat pocket before taking Karen's hand and leading her to the patio doors.

# Chapter Forty-Six

*He* came to him in his dreams at first. He was 15 at the time and had, just like Don and Karen, been chosen. Unlike Don and Karen, he had been chosen by the evil one, the same evil one who had blighted the life of Katy Johansson. His mission was simple. He had to destroy the womb of Karen Crawford. He'd tried but failed 28 years ago.

*He* was back with him again. The disaster with Katy meant *he* needed another tool to work through. Lex Brampton would be that tool.

Lex Brampton was just 16 when he raped Karen Crawford. He'd been sent to a juvenile detention centre in Fort Worth, Texas for his crime. Once he reached the age of 18, he was transferred to a state prison in Lubbock. Whilst there, Brampton fell afoul of inmates and prison guards.

He experienced what 13 year-old Karen Crawford experienced. He was sexually abused, forced to swallow the semen of men three times his age and buggered with fists, penises and any phallic object that could be found. His soul was eaten away on a daily basis and, particularly, after his claims of sexual assault were investigated and dismissed by the Office of Inspector General.

He'd walked into the Lubbock correctional facility in 1988. His 2 year stint at the juvenile detention centre in Fort Worth had gave him a certain cockiness. His first night on landing 5 saw that cockiness ripped out of him as his cell mate, Luiz Gonzales, beat and raped him. He was easy meat and Gonzales became his pimp.

Half an ounce of tobacco and the young buck would swallow. Items stolen from the prison kitchen equated to a spit roast between any two prisoners who could manage to get their hands on tins of pineapple, bags of sugar or anything that pleasured the sweet tooth of Gonzales.

When Gonzales was released, Brampton breathed a sigh of relief, he spent just one night alone in his cell. In the morning, he woke to Warden Estevez who was standing over him, trousers and pants down by his ankles waiting to be sucked by the landing 5 bitch. *You are going to swallow my load and you are going to do it without making a single sound, you hear me, boy?*

Brampton had become accustomed to the salty tasting semen. It had become a blessing to swallow rather than have his teeth and ribs broken.

His father never came to visit him. In fact, during his time spent at the Lubbock correctional facility ,he received just one letter from his drunken father. It did lift his spirits though. Revenge tasted oh so sweet.

The rapes and beatings continued. His only saving grace being that none of his sexual predators carried any sexually transmitted diseases. He was the bitch of landing 5 for the duration of his detention and was released on the 3 of October 1997.

On his release, Brampton returned home to Idaho. He'd read about how Karen Crawford had turned her life around. How she had become rich overnight and how she was the face of 'Crackle Corn'.

For the next 17 years or so, Brampton kept an unhealthy interest in Karen Crawford. His current apartment, a rented studio in Pocatello, was decorated in posters of her. The cheaply plastered walls in his studio apartment adorned in magazine pages and posters. He even had a signed one sent to him, although he had used a PO Box for that delivery.

Her DVD's, all pirated, lay strewn across his breakfast table where he spent many days and nights masturbating. He'd had her, he thought, he'd fucked her when nobody even knew who she was. He will have her again too. He knew he would. The voice had told him in his dreams.

*Fuck her good this time, Lex. Fuck her and damage the inside of her cunt; she deserves it. It was she who put you through that hell in prison; each of those thrusts you felt was down to her. It's payback, Lex, bide your time. She is coming home soon and I will give you the strength to find her, to fuck her, to destroy any chance she has of giving life again.*

Lex Brampton had also read the news that day. It had been suggested that Karen Crawford had returned to the United States and he knew exactly where she would be if the media had suggested correctly. That fucking big place of hers up in Sun Valley, where all those rich cunts lived.

He'd been up to her place a number of times since his release from prison. She was never at home. Her home, he had read, was now in England.

He left his apartment on the morning of 31 December. It would take him around 3 hours to drive the 170 miles to Sun Valley. Karen Crawford was the only woman he had ever been with, even though she was just 13 at the time. He would have her again tonight, at least they couldn't throw a 'sex with a minor' charge at him.

In any event, nobody would know. She wouldn't be able to squeal to mommy and daddy this time. She wouldn't be able to squeal to anyone for that matter.

*Kill the fucking cunt, he* told him.

# Chapter Forty-Seven

It was a clear night and the sky was illuminated with the moon and stars. They were sharing the sheepskin blanket and sitting on the swinging bench on the patio.

"Champagne and stars, just perfect," Karen remarked.

"I'm a big fan of the stars, especially the ones called Karen," Don quipped.

Karen fired back with, "Well, you're the one being discussed in the British press, you big star." They both laughed. Karen, because she knew that laughter was all you could do when your name was in print for trivial matters; Don, because of the absurdity of it all.

They both stood from the swinging bench and looked skyward in awe of the sprinkling of lights. The sky was particularly clear out here in Idaho. There were no neighbouring lights, no steady flow of car lights. It was, as Don put it, a perfect place to see the black blanket with holes in. Karen loved his analogy and told him that the blanket with holes in was made more perfect because he was with her to witness it.

"Well," he said, "I never dreamt that I'd ever be under a blanket with the famous Karen Crawford." She mimicked a punch to his arm and told him to stop it. Don pointed out the Plough to Karen and remarked that he had never seen it in such a position. It wasn't on its side, it was practically upright with the curve at the top reaching up to the heavens.

It was a huge question mark in the sky, just like he had described in his poem all those years ago. Nobody that read it actually understood the question mark analogy though.

"Seven sisters," he whispered in her ear as he snuggled up behind her.

That's when she turned to face him.

"What, what did you just say?" She asked.

"Seven sisters, babe, the Plough. You guys might know it as the saucepan. I like to call it the big question mark in the sky."

"Oh my God, Don!" She exclaimed. "Angie had a vision. She told me it had something to do with a Bible passage and that Bible passage mentioned the seven sisters."

"What was the message?" Don asked.

"I can't remember. Let me send her a text message," Karen told him.

Karen bent down to pick up her bag. Her phone was in the inside pocket.

She pulled the phone out and stood next to Don. She opened her last message from Angie and hit the reply button. She started to type on the keypad.

That's when Lex Brampton pulled the trigger.

# Chapter Forty-Eight
# The Plan

It had been put into action on the 7 January 2001. Don didn't know it, neither did Karen. It was the day Don's wife told him of her lover, the same day he had seen the message. It simply read, *The Beginning*. As cruel and heartless as the message was, particularly because the intention was for Don to see it, it made Don strong. It made him think that the beginning for his wife and her new lover was meant to happen.

The callous, cold-hearted publicising of Dan Pallatt's affair with his wife merely showed how uncaring and devoid of love his wife and Pallatt were. If they could go online and gloat about cheating then that made them look pretty pathetic in most people's eyes.

Don was never meant to be married to his then wife. It was a mistake; he had just missed all the signs. His fate was always with Karen Crawford, just as Karen's fate lay with Don. They just both needed a little helping hand in finding one another. It was their destiny.

It was, indeed, the beginning, but Don had not made the spiritual connection. The message that Dan Pallatt had posted was for Don in more ways than one. The *plan* had been set into motion upon him reading it. It was also a test.

Archangel Gabriel needed to see if Don's heart had room for hate, for vengeance. By Don recognising that it was his wife and Pallatt who had the issues, it showed Archangel Gabriel that Don Williamson wasn't incapable of hate, his heart would just not allow it.

For a wife to dupe you into believing that everything between you is okay and for that same wife to fornicate with another man, and then for that fornication and apparent love for one another to be posted online was a serious test for Don. On briefing Sara and Teresa, Archangel Gabriel likened Don's experience to that of Job.

Like Job, Don was innocent and decent. He suffered because he is among the best, not because he is the worst. Like Job, Don showed that people, no matter what they had done, were always worthy of love. Job was selected as a subject of a firm test of faith, because he was unquestionably the greatest man of faith alive.

God declared that Job's faith was real faith. Okay, Don didn't particularly love his ex-wife or Dan Pallatt but he had not allowed hatred to enter, he had avoided his heart being blackened because, well, hate just wasn't part of Don's make-up.

That was the test on Don, and he passed it. Archangel Gabriel had told Sara and Teresa that trials and suffering provide spiritual development and this was the initial goal in preparing Don.

Without Don's spiritual development, there could be no end goal and without the end goal there could be no beginning.

The start of Don's awakening came from the seven sisters, the Plough. On the very same night, he penned the poem entitled 'God's Thumbprint in the Sky' he began the waking process.

He'd been very proud of his poem, had shown it to friends, and had even entered it into various poetry competitions. He never won anything though—he wasn't meant to—the poem was a personal message. It was a message from his guardian angels, Sara and Teresa. Seek and you will find, ask and you shall receive watch and you shall learn. It was Don who wrote those words.

Just two lines from the poem he wrote, two profound lines—a hidden code that had brought Don to this moment with Karen.

The string of lovers he'd had after his wife, once again, all *planned*. The one night stands, the fuck-buddies, all *planned*. The heartache he'd endured with Katy—*planned*. All part of the itinerary that had been booked from his birth. It was a journey where the final destination was love. His excursions hadn't brought him the love that his heart craved; Sara and Teresa hadn't allowed that to happen.

It was just a test. Push him, prod him, poke him, test him as Job was tested; take him to the limits just to see how he would react, just to see if he would allow darkness to enshroud him and hatred to enter him.

Having sex out of wedlock wasn't frowned upon by either of the angels, they encouraged it, particularly in Don's case. They instigated it in fact. Their sole purpose was to show Don that sex without love is nothing; it gives humans pleasure but it's merely a short-lived pleasure. In time we, as humans, realise that it's companionship and love that make the earth shake.

Don, after his relationship split with Katy, became disinterested in sex. Once again this was all part of the *plan*. They wanted him to go through the motions of heartache so when he found love, true love, he would realise just what he had been missing in his life. His heart was good but Archangel Gabriel wanted it to be great.

By the time he met Karen Crawford on the busy street in London, he had achieved that greatness in his heart. There was just one more level. Archangel Gabriel needed two hearts to beat as one.

This was achieved the moment Karen and Don's eyes met. They both felt it, they both heard it. They thought they were hearing their own hearts, they weren't; they were hearing one another's; they were tuning in to one another because it was their moment, a moment that had been with them from birth. They just both had to endure what life threw at them to appreciate true love.

Don had been handpicked by Archangel Gabriel. He was born on 31 July at precisely 9.21 pm (2121). His mother, Maria, should have died whilst giving birth but Gabriel had intervened. She had to bear another child, a sister for Don and his elder brother, Dan. Her time would only be brief.

Archangel Gabriel gave her 6 years, more importantly he gave Don 6 years of Kim. It was a period where Don grew spiritually. He always, even at such a young and tender age, felt protective of Kim—that was the *plan*.

And now there was danger. Archangel Gabriel had to act fast. The evil one had returned and his plan was to put a halt to the new beginning. He was using Lex Brampton in an effort to stop the one thing that epitomised pure love. The one thing that was the reason the *plan* had been put into action and the reason why Don Williamson and Karen Crawford had been brought together.

Nothing could stand in its way but the evil one was trying so desperately hard.

He had to be stopped.

That's when Archangel Gabriel called upon Archangel Michael.

# Chapter Forty-Nine

They both heard the explosion of gunfire, only one of them felt the bullet. They both saw the figure walking towards them, only one of them knew who it was.

Neither of them saw the crow.

Neither of them anticipated what was about to happen next.

# Chapter Fifty
# Archangel Michael

She knew that Archangel Michael had to be called upon. It was the only way.

Neither Don nor Karen had called upon Archangel Michael, neither of them knew about Lex Brampton hiding in the bushes and aiming his 'Ruger No. 1 Varminter K1-V-BBZ rifle' at them.

Archangel Michael showed himself to Angie when she had been doing a reading for herself.

To be certain, Angie had spread the cards three times. Her gut instinct was that the original spread was a warning, but she needed to be certain. Her second spread showed the same, as did the third.

The *Tower* tarot card had landed in an upright position on all three occasions. It was surrounded by cards that shed light on a sudden crisis, critical event or unseen danger. Angie knew there was a catastrophic influence at work.

That's when Archangel Michael appeared to her. Angie had invited him.

Both Archangel Michael and Angie called upon the white light of pureness to surround Angie in a bubble. This was her level of protection. Immediately, she felt her energy expand as she was enveloped in light. She knew that she was safe because within her shield of light Archangel Michael had told her was his protection.

He had spoken, and this is what he told Angie, "Feel the truth of this as you vibrate at the level of love. You are loved, and you are protected now."

She knew what she had to do, the cards surrounding the *Tower* tarot card had pretty much told her. Spirit had come through too. Odelia, Karen's child, had shown Angie symbols and objects—a telescopic rifle lying in a ditch—the same telescopic rifle that Angie had once held when the Idaho Sherriff's Department had asked her for help in hunting down the sniper who had killed three people, Brett Myers.

Odelia also showed her a blue baby blanket, Angie knew that it was Odelia's blanket. She made the connection of blue for a boy, a male, the father of Odelia.

Finally, Odelia showed Angie a picture of a target, within that target there were five circles joined, five Olympic circles.

This confirmed everything for Angie. Archangel Michael had merely given her a suit of armour in the shape of his protecting light.

She wouldn't need to pack the trunk of her car. What she needed was already packed. She had used it only a few days ago. Angie grabbed her car keys and a pair of wrist slings and was soon pulling out of her drive for the two mile journey.

# Chapter Fifty-One

The force of the bullet had knocked Don to the floor, it took his breath away. The pain was coming from his cracked ribs. He was lucky (*no such thing as luck*) but he didn't know it yet.

Karen held the back of his head as she carefully laid him down on the patio, his quick breathing scared her.

"Well, well, well, if it isn't Miss goody two-shoes attending the sick." Karen recognised the voice immediately. It had been almost 30 years since she heard Lex Brampton speak, back then he was just a 16 year-old. He had told her that it was normal for 13 year-old girls to have sex. She had refused politely but he became violent.

He had held her down, pinning her wrists to the barn floor. She even remembered the stale smell of cigarettes on his breath as he exhaled with every thrust, each exhale a reminder that the act of rape was taking her virginity.

"And what do we have here? Fe-fi-fo-fum I smell the blood of an English 'mun'."

Don looked up. The male figure stood on the top step of the patio. He was dressed in jeans, a lumberjack shirt and a baseball cap. He was holding a rifle and pointing it at Karen. He spat and Don saw missing teeth.

Don managed to control his breathing. "Please, I have money in my wallet, please take it, take it all."

Brampton laughed. "You hear that, baby, he wants me to take it all. Well, isn't he the kind old English 'mun'." It wasn't a question.

He grabbed Karen's arm, she struggled but it was futile. Lex Brampton was strong. Years of sexual abuse had given him an intolerance to pain. He worked out daily and had done so since his release.

He looked down at Don. "Maybe I should start by taking a little piece of your whore, Mr English, what do you have to say about that?" Before Don could answer he felt an almighty thud into the side of his ribs. "You ever been kicked by an

American before, Mr Limey?" The pain was bearable, Don expected it to be much worse given that he had just been shot.

Brampton turned to Karen. "How 'bout you give the father of your child what he wants now, mama?" The stale cigarette smell was identical to that of 28 years ago.

"How bout you fuck off!" Karen told him.

Brampton just laughed and pushed Karen towards the patio door. "C'mon, honey, let's take this inside."

Don struggled to turn his body. He felt the dampness on his shirt from where he thought the blood was seeping. "Wait," he shouted. "Take me instead."

Once again Brampton found this amusing and mocked a laugh.

"Ha-ha-ha, your shining knight in armour is so noble, Karen. Maybe we should bring him in so he can watch the show, hey baby? Maybe if your English mun was around back then, he could have saved your sorry ass or maybe he could have joined in and we could have had ourselves a nice little threesome going on."

"You're a sick bastard, Brampton," Karen said.

"Maybe so, baby, but my daddy was sicker and my granddaddy. I bet you didn't even know that it was my granddaddy who told me about those underground gas pipes on your momma and papa's farm now, did you?"

Karen felt bile rise up her windpipe. She asked Brampton how he knew.

"Well, hot lips, my granddaddy worked the land long before you came into this world. He used to work for Mesa Gas, they were the folks responsible for laying the new pipes. Granddaddy kept the blueprints. Turned out that one of the pipes ran underneath your momma and papa's farm. Didn't take a lot of digging to find it.

"It was a bastard to pull through the earth though but my daddy helped my granddaddy. They headed up there when your folks were away; I believe you paid for them to go on holiday, that's when the deed was done. All they had to do then was cover the exposed pipe with some brush then wait for the firework display."

Brampton started laughing hard.

"Best part about it, daddy and granddaddy wrote to me in prison; they'd told me that there had been an accident up at the farm. Mr and Mrs Crawford had died, oh, it did lift my spirits. Funny cos on the morning of my trial, they both told me that they would get you back for framing me." He laughed again.

160

Karen lunged at Brampton, her weak attempt at retribution was met with a slap to the side of her face. She fell to the floor clutching the side of her reddened face; the signet ring on Brampton's little finger had cut her cheekbone.

Don managed to sit upright. He had a bruise on a bruise on an already cracked rib. He grimaced and then smelt the whiskey from the inside of his coat pocket. The hip flask that Karen had gave him earlier had stopped the bullet from penetrating—that was the *plan.*

It gave Don a new lease of life; a second chance at saving Karen from the clutches of the man with broken teeth; the cocksucker that had raped Karen when she was just a child. The same cocksucker whose father and grandfather had murdered Karen's parents. Don reached inside his coat as if to show Brampton that he was in considerable pain.

He gripped the hip flask and felt the hole, it was slightly down the neck of the flask so he knew that much of the whisky was still inside, giving the flask some weight.

Brampton grabbed Karen by the arm and pulled her up off the floor. Blood trickled down her cheek.

"On your feet, Williamson," Brampton ordered. Don was surprised that he knew his name.

"Yeh, I know who you are; you are famous now, boy. Your face is all over the news. They are saying lots of nice things about you back home in England. Do you think they will still be saying that when you're dead?" Brampton pointed the rifle at Don.

Karen screamed, "No, please, don't kill him, Lex!"

Brampton let go of his grip on Karen, she fell forward towards the patio doors and her head hit the glass. For a brief moment, Brampton seemed concerned, he turned to check to see if she was okay. That's when Don quickly removed the hip flask from his coat pocket, that's when he threw it at Brampton's head. He missed.

Brampton turned and pointed the rifle once again at Don. He was going to put a bullet through his face then he was going to fuck Karen in front of her English corpse. "Say bye-bye, you English cunt," Brampton said. He placed his finger on the trigger then heard the oncoming whooshing sound.

He turned just in time to see the 'Gold Tip Kinetic XT Arrow'. It hit him right between the eyes. Death was instant. Angie Jakobs was standing 20 feet away. Her left hand holding the 'OMP Smoky Mountain Hunter Recurve Bow' vertically.

Tonight, archery had not been a pleasure activity, she had not sought the inner circle for gratification. Lex Brampton had been her target and she, with just one attempt, scored maximum points.

There was a sudden flash of lightning followed by a roll of thunder. No rain came because the night sky was clear. The lightning and thunder was the start of the event. It was the Metro- Goldwyn-Mayer roar of the lion, and it was the Rank Organisation gong man.

Their movie was about to start, the silver screen tonight would be the blackness of the night sky.

That's when Angie Jakobs turned to both Don and Karen, and said, "Watch the sky, something is about to happen."

All three of them looked skyward.

Blackness filled with tiny specs of light and a half circle of light. Don's black blanket full of holes.

Lights.

Camera.

Action.

# Chapter Fifty-Two

His vision was always impaired at night. That's why, tonight, he had perched himself on one of the seven intruder lights that were affixed to Karen Crawford's stable. Each halogen light encased in a black rectangle box trimmed with gold coloured paint around their edges. The stable was empty, save for a few bundles of hay neatly stacked in the corner. The light helped his vision and kept him safe from his nemesis, the Great Horned Owl.

He'd been with Don for some considerable time now, from an early age in fact. He was even with him on the night that he penned the poem. The crow was Don's spirit animal. It supported him in developing the power of sight, transformation, and connection with life's magic.

It had guided Don in getting in touch with life mysteries and had developed his ability to perceive subtle shifts in energy within himself and in his environment. Don had a gift, he just never knew it.

The crow had been outside Don's window back in 2001. Watching Don at the typewriter, watching him conceive the poem. Archangel Gabriel, who was also with Don that night, had acknowledged him. There was a great respect between the two.

There always had been.

Earlier in the day, he'd been over five and a half thousand miles away. He'd been sat on the window ledge. Watching. Listening. Learning.

Cardinals and bishops and Vatican officials from all over the world had recently elected a new Pope. He was announced to the world from the balcony of St Peter's just 2 weeks ago, and now Pope John Paul III was discussing with those same cardinals and bishops and Vatican officials about what they should do next.

They knew when, they just didn't know where. They knew it had something to do with a code hidden in a poem but they didn't know what that code was. Moreover, they didn't know what the poem was or who had wrote it.

He could travel from place to place fast. He didn't just have wings, he had the power to slip through the vortexes present here on earth. Those holes that only their species could see.

Tonight, he was here to witness the astronomical event; an event that Don had, unknowingly, foreseen. The thumbprint. Life. The beginning.

The hidden code inside Don's poem was only known by a few. The crow was one of those few.

The crow looked skyward towards the North Star.

# Chapter Fifty-Three

*After they had heard the king, they went on their way, and the star they had*
*seen when it rose went ahead of them until it stopped over the*
*place where the child was.*
Matthew 2:9

Don knew it was the North Star. He'd been a budding astronomer all those years ago and he knew the position of it. He knew that tonight it was the brightest star underneath the start of the curve of the plough, the start of the question mark if one was drawing it. All three of them had looked up in awe. All three wise to the fact.

The North Star had slowly moved towards the Plough before nesting itself in the curve. The Plough had then slowly rotated clockwise before resting on its side, the North Star still and inside its curve. Inside its womb.

Angie turned to Karen, who then turned to Don.

All three of them knew the significance of what they had just witnessed.

All three wiser than before.

The angels present knew that they knew too.

The beginning had started its second journey; a journey that would take a further nine months to complete. Then its third and final phase would take shape, a phase of love, light and truth.

The stars, the three witnesses, the crow sitting over the stable whilst the seven intruder lights shone brightly and Odelia who had been all of the seven sisters; her male form had been the North Star. All was played out for Karen, Don and Angie— it was an astronomical movie directed by Archangel Gabriel and produced by the angels, Sara, Teresa, Anthony, and Sebastian.

The message was crystal clear. It would be confirmed some four to five weeks later when Karen would see the indicator of two pink lines showing her the beginning.

Angie ran the Bible passage through her head.

*The hidden meaning of the seven stars that you saw in my right hand and the seven gold lamp stands is this: The seven stars are the messengers of the seven churches, and the seven lamp stands are the seven churches.*

That's when they heard the caw of the crow.

The astronomical event was an advance screening for their eyes only. It was the absorbent tip with two pink lines indicating the start of the second journey.

Karen, Don and Angie already knew. Their own personal screening had been their confirmation.

Karen was carrying Don's child. That was the *plan*.

The crow had flown away from the seven bright lights (*seven gold lamp stands*) around the stable. Within 15 metres, he let out a single caw then vanished.

He'd found his vortex and within minutes, he'd be back in Vatican City.

# Chapter Fifty-Four
## Vatican City
## 1 January 2015, 10.15 pm

"We are still working on the three words but I fear we are no closer to deciphering them, Your Holiness. We believe the three words have been translated correctly and are confident they will be deciphered shortly," Cardinal Abandonato had delivered the message to Pope John III.

"And the numbers?" Pope John Paul III asked.

Abandonato shook his head from side to side and said, "No, Your Holiness." It was disappointing news as he had hoped the three words and sequence of numbers would have been deciphered by now.

"Very well, we shall convene the meeting in the morning, just as we planned." Pope John Paul III offered the sign of the cross to Cardinal Abandonato and then headed towards his study and the huge oak table. He reached into the pocket of his full-cut chasuble and pulled out a key.

On reaching the desk, he placed the key in the lock on the drawer and turned it once to the left. He slid the drawer open and pulled out the scroll. It was a copy of the original; the original had been locked away from light, from the air. A red bow was tied loosely around the copy. He unfastened the bow and rolled the scroll before laying it on the table.

He placed his left hand to the top of the scroll and his right to the bottom. He then read the text, it had been translated from Hebrew to English. Numbers appeared in brackets at the end of each paragraph, none of which made any sense at all. He read about the astronomical event and also what needed to be done.

He paused at the three words at the end of the sacred text. Three words that had baffled everyone, including those hired to decipher the sacred text.

The scroll translated read:

*The son from the north will join the seven sisters on the eve of the New Year twenty thousand plus fourteen and there will be three wise to the event. Two of the three are the chosen ones. The mother who will bear the child will be adored by the masses and there will be much interest in the pregnancy and birth.*

*The father will be rich with information and will have carried the code in his heart as it was written by his hand in the form of a verse that the stars would align and then unite. The third will be the protector and will keep the chosen ones safe from harm. (68061)*

*The church will have ownership over the son of the code bearer. He must be offered the protection for the sake of humanity. (1434)*

*The church shall wait for seven months until it makes contact. The fifteenth day of the fourth month in the year of twenty thousand plus fifteen. The child shall be known as Gavri'el and he will be removed and taken to the Holy place of worship. (43)*

*He must be anointed as Satan follows Gavri'el in the city. Satan is not welcome. (28)*

*All Envy Us.*

# The Beginning

# Chapter Fifty-Five
# Friday, 31 July 2015
# Crawford Ranch, Sun Valley, Idaho

"Firstly, I've been warned to keep this speech quick. They say that a best man's speech shouldn't take longer than what it does for the groom to make love. So, goodnight." Jake McNulty sat down in his chair to laughter.

He stood again.

"That's the second time today I've had to stand up from a warm seat with a piece of paper in my hand." More laughter.

"Firstly, I'd just like to say to you all what a privilege and an honour it is to be given this opportunity to be present with you all today. It all seems to have happened so quickly. One minute I'm out drinking with Don in the Lyndon Poacher, his local pub back home in England, the next minute I'm picking up a newspaper and reading how my friend of 25 years is the envy, and more than likely enemy, of the majority of the male population that have posters of his wife on their bedroom walls or secretly hidden on their home computers." Karen was blushing.

"I'm sure you all agree that the bridesmaids today, Angie and Bella, look positively stunning, being outshone only by the beautiful bride." It was clichéd but the guests rolled with it by applauding.

"Don has been a great friend down the years. He's been always someone that both me and my wife, Jade, can rely on and I hope he feels the same about us.

"Although, if Don had taken my advice of settling down with a woman in England, we all wouldn't be here today celebrating his marriage to Karen. A quick word about Karen. She gorgeous, she's smart, she's witty, so I guess it must be true when they say opposites attract." The guests were laughing again, along with Karen and Don.

"About 10 years ago, Don and I arrived back at his new place in Olton, Solihull. For those of you that don't know, Solihull is just outside of Birmingham in England and Don wanted to show me his new flat, that's apartment to the American's here

171

today. It was about 3 in the morning and we were both pretty drunk, well, that's kind of an understatement. We were both paralytic and could barely stand.

"On approaching his front door to his new place that he wanted desperately to show off to me, Don realised that he had forgotten to put the keys in his trouser pocket when he left earlier that night. Don, being the forgetful person that he is, had left them on the table inside his flat. It was a cold night and I didn't want to have to wake my wife up to ask her to drive out the 5 miles to Don's place.

"Don then hit on a brainwave. He stood on the bin and lifted himself up to a small window. He told me that he could reach inside the small window and grab the bigger window handle and we'd be inside within seconds. Once he hoisted himself into position he reached inside the smaller window. It was at this point that I learned that Don had gone and got himself a dog.

"A big German Shepard was obviously happy to see him as he was barking excitedly and jumping up Don's outstretched arm which was through the window. Next thing I see is Don jumping down from where he had climbed. Just three words came out of his mouth. 'Shit, wrong house'."

Don and Karen had tears of laughter rolling down their cheeks. The rest of the guests were laughing hysterically before Jake made them laugh again with, "The thing is, ladies and gentlemen, not only had Don tried to break into the wrong flat, he'd actually turned down the wrong road. His road was a further 50 yards away."

Jake upped the ante.

"It's nice to know that Don has taken up DIY, although I doubt very much if he can put his DIY skills to this beautiful home Karen has here. He did tell me earlier though that when we have all left tonight he intends to be banging and screwing all night long." Jake McNulty really had the guests at Karen and Don's wedding reception eating out of his hands.

"Now, it would be wrong of me, as a married man, not to pass on some useful tips to Don regarding the better half. Firstly, Don, set the ground rules and establish whose boss. Then do everything Karen says." Jake waited for the laughter to die down.

"Don, remember that marriage is a relationship in which one person is always right and the other is a husband." Once the laughter had died down, Jake lifted his glass. A glass that had been filled with Salon Blanc de Blancs Le Mesnil-sur-Oger champagne by the hired waiters.

"Ladies and gentlemen, I'd like you all to raise your glasses to toast two people who, one day on a busy street in London found one another; more importantly than that, they found true love. It's a story that dreams are made of and it happened to one of the most kind-hearted human beings I have ever met. Don, you deserve this happiness, my friend.

"You deserve to be loved and you deserve to have the love that you hold in your heart to be enjoyed by someone else, and that someone else is now your wife. To Mr and Mrs Karen and Don Williamson." Jake raised his glass along with the guests before taking a well-deserved drink and rapturous round of applause.

Karen joined in by drinking her freshly squeezed orange juice. She was 7 months pregnant.

A pregnant Karen Crawford married Don Williamson on 31 July 2015,

Don's birthday, and exactly 2 years after she had received an email from her best friend, and bridesmaid, Angie Jakobs. The email had explained the message of Archangel Gabriel, the premise of which was to love others in their own chosen path so you could set the energy you want in your world.

The wedding ceremony was held on the ranch and the guest list had been kept to the bare minimum. Dan and Tayla were present; Karen had flown them over from Australia. Jake was Don's best man. Don managed to build some bridges with his brother. They embraced and spoke about how each of them felt sad that their dad couldn't be at Don's wedding today.

Neither of them raised the issue that had drove a wedge between them years ago. Bella flew over; she brought Tony Turner with her. She had decided that she had treated him harshly last year when he had asked if they could see each other again. Bella jumped at the chance of being Karen's other bridesmaid but was secretly disappointed that it wasn't a more lavish wedding reception paid for by one of the higher class magazines.

Karen didn't want that though. She just wanted close friends to share her experience of marrying the man she had always known was out there.

The man she had waited so long for. The man her best friend had assured her that she would meet.

In all, there were twenty four guests present that day. Jake and his wife, Jade, had flown over from England with Don's other friends, Satnam and Guppy, and their Indian wives, Supria and Padma. Don's two bosses, Torsten Cederquist and Bengt Linklaters, from the Swedish law firm he had worked so tirelessly for also flew over.

Karen's guests included her two bridesmaids, Angie and Bella, and her new partner, Tony Turner. She also invited *Washington Post* editor Richard Grantham and his lovely wife, Sadie. Her ever-faithful agent Melissa and her husband, Marc, were also present. Four of her closest model friends, all single women looking for love—Kristy Jameson, Debra Ritchins, Nicole Robins, and Amber Stone.

Karen and Don, when drawing up their wedding invitations, also thought it fitting to include the one man that was around during the time they both spent together in London.

Luigi Zoccolitto. Luigi travelled over alone. He'd lost his wife, Betty, some years ago. She had died from a massive stroke and Luigi had remained faithful to her memory.

Karen and Don's other guests did not make the start of the reception. They had been there for the ceremony though and had each shared tears of happiness. Their happiness was, however, short lived as Teresa, Sara, Sebastian and Anthony were pulled back by Archangel Gabriel and told of the warning.

# Chapter Fifty-Six

"Behold, I am the bearer of bad news on this day of celebration," Archangel Gabriel told them.

"The evil one is returning soon and is bringing with him some support in the shape of Tommy McGinty, Haskin Bruette and Clément Dubois."

All four angels looked at one another. They each shared an expression of shock and horror. McGinty, Bruette and Dubois had already met their fate and now they were joining forces with the evil one.

"Arrangements are being made for you all as we speak. You are not in any immediate danger. This will not happen before the child is born, it will happen after. I will be showing you each a higher level of security over the coming months. We will all be working with Archangel Michael and his protective light.

"It will protect you from any harm and, hopefully, protect the chosen ones and their child too." Archangel Gabriel's words offered a small amount of comfort to the four.

"We are also facing opposition from one of the Holy religions on earth. They have in their possession a sacred scroll that spoke of the event. We have time on our side though, for they cannot act until 7 months after the child is born. This gives us much needed time to prepare."

"Where does the scroll come from?" Anthony asked.

"It was buried in code on one of the Dead Sea Scrolls found in the Qumran caves over 70 years ago. Only the Holy One and his cardinals know of its existence. The archaeologist who found it buried in the manuscript was recently killed," Archangel Gabriel told them.

Next, it was Sara to ask about the scroll.

"And what does the scroll say?"

"It tells of the astronomical event and of the child. It also gives clues as to who the chosen ones are and the whereabouts of where the event took place."

Sara pressed for more. "But if the scroll told them of the whereabouts, then why didn't they see them?"

Archangel Gabriel smiled at Sara.

"Dear Sara, they could not decipher the hidden message in time. There were a series of numbers throughout the message and a strange line of text at the end that made no sense. The archaeologist who was killed in an accident last week, Dr Henry Mattheson, knew what the numbers meant. Once he knew what they meant he then figured out what the strange line of text meant."

Sebastian then asked the obvious. "The hidden code, what is it?"

Once again Gabriel smiled.

"My dear Sebastian, all in good time," he told him.

"Now, go back and be amongst the love that surrounds the chosen ones."

In an instant Teresa, Sara, Sebastian and Anthony were pulled back to Idaho, just in time to see Don and Karen embrace on the makeshift dance floor that had been erected in her garden.

Love was, indeed, surrounding them both. It was a love so pure that the angels could see it.

Beautiful butterflies fluttered around Karen and Don as they took to the floor for the traditional first dance.

Donny Osmond's *Puppy Love* was playing.

# Chapter Fifty-Seven

Tommy McGinty and Clément Dubois had each attended their own funerals. The evil one had put his arm around each of them. Haskin Bruette met the evil one at his execution.

McGinty was found guilty and sentenced to 21 years in prison in 1958.

He was released 13 years later, in 1971. The parole board had all agreed that he had been the model prisoner and they also took into account that he was just a boy when he had strangled Teresa O'Brien to death. The board set restrictions telling McGinty that he could not return to County Clare nor have any contact with the O'Brien family. He moved, instead, to County Wicklow.

In 1985, at the age of 43, McGinty succumbed to cancer. It started in his colon then spread to his lungs, once there it spread to his brain. It was inoperable and McGinty died at Newcastle Hospital in County Wicklow on the 8 of November 1985.

He saw them lower his casket; he saw his brother, Brendan, crying. It was a sunny day and he saw the crow watching from the oak tree, every now and again it would caw.

The evil one had joined him. He was dressed in black robes and his face, as always, was hidden.

*I am your maker, Tommy McGinty, I am the voice you heard. Now you belong to me.*

Haskin Bruette died at the Nebraska State Penitentiary on 12 October 1959. 2500 volts of electricity from 'Old Sparky' passed through the skull electrodes and saline-soaked sponges then to the ground. The circuit went through Bruette's muscles and veins then into his brain, eye sockets, sinuses, and finally out the leg electrodes.

The evil one was with him all the way. It took just 30 seconds for Bruette's heart to stop beating.

*Take it like a man, Bruette, suck it up. You're mine now.*

Haskin Bruette was cremated on Tuesday, 13 October 1959. Nobody came to say goodbye.

Whilst awaiting trial at a Toulouse prison in 1970, Clément Dubois committed suicide. He was buried at La Chartreuse Cemetery in Lacourt, Midi-Pyrénées. He watched as his casket was lowered. He watched as a crow landed on a headstone nearby. He listened as the evil one spoke.

*Come with me, Dubois. There's more fun over here. More titillation for you. Lots of children to play with where I come from, Dubois. There's one child in particular that you should meet. I'll introduce you to him. But first you must sleep. I will wake you with the other two when it's time.*

McGinty, Dubois and Bruette were all entered into a state of suspended animation. They were back-up in case others did not succeed.

On 1 January 2015, they were all awakened. They, *He* thought, would succeed where Katy Johansson and Lex Brampton had failed. It was his master *plan. He* knew that they each had a connection with the chosen angels who guarded Crawford and Williamson.

*He* didn't yet know who was guarding the boy child.

# Chapter Fifty-Eight

*Washington Post*
16 September 2015

**Breaking News: Model Karen Crawford Gives Birth to Baby Boy.**

*KETCHUM, IDAHO. Earlier today at 3.15 in the afternoon, a son was born to Karen Crawford, 41, and her husband, Don Williamson, 51. The baby boy, who weighed in at 8 lbs., 6 oz. was delivered by a senior obstetrician at an unspecified hospital in Ketchum, Idaho. It's unknown if the boy has been named yet but sources close to the couple claim that a name has already been chosen.*

*Long-time friend to Crawford, TV psychic Angie Jakobs, was asked at her ranch in Sun Valley if she knew what name Crawford and Williamson had decided upon. She told the Washington Post, 'I know they have chosen a name but they are keeping it secret. They do plan on having him christened within the month though'. Jakobs, wearing a pair of jeans and a t-shirt (see photo), also told the Washington Post that both Karen and Don Williamson were delighted with their new arrival.*

*Stay with The Washington Post for updates.*

\*\*\*

A large photograph of Karen Crawford appeared just underneath the headline. It was a few years old and was less than conservative. It showed Karen in a slinky dress, sitting on a chair and looking at the camera seductively.

No photo of Don had been printed in the article.

The headline ran with *Model Karen Crawford Gives Birth to Baby Boy.* Karen had, in fact, announced her retirement from modelling a week after her marriage to Don. Both she and Don had laughed hysterically at the newspaper reports that had suggested Don was the jealous type and had made Karen break the hearts of millions of adoring fans across the globe.

The British press had had a field day. It was payday for a lot of Don Williamson's one-night stands. They spoke of his love-making as if they were discussing it over breakfast with their close friends.

Some of the tabloids had even given him the nickname 'Willy' Williamson after barmaid, Annette Roach, had told a warts n' all story about how she had given oral sex to Don in the cellar of his local pub, 'The Lyndon Poacher'. Annette was paid £5,000 for her story and, for a while at least, The Lyndon Poacher had more customers through the door. Hot blooded males and perverts wanted to see the barmaid who had taken Don Williamson in her mouth.

When the customers dropped off, Annette was fired by her boss. The brewery didn't want The Lyndon Poacher associated with promiscuity. Annette filed an unfair dismissal claim and even went back to the press with her story. Sadly, for her at least, the press wasn't interested in a barmaid losing her job. Annette now works in a supermarket, stacking shelves.

A small photo of Angie Jakobs had made it on to the Washington Post article. It was taken at her ranch that very day. Just as the article suggested, she was wearing jeans and a t-shirt.

On the t-shirt were the words, 'All Envy Us.'

# Chapter Fifty-Nine
## Vatican City
## 17 September 2015

"Her name is Angie Jakobs, Your Holiness. She is a heretic who believes she has the gift of seeing the dead." Cardinal Abandonato was the bearer of good news.

Pope John Paul III was sitting in the roof garden of the Vatican. It was early morning and he was sipping tea and enjoying the sun on his face. He offered Abandonato a seat opposite and then poured tea into a cup for him.

"Please continue," he said.

"The photo you see was taken yesterday outside her home. The article is about a new born boy and mentions the mother and father. Once we saw the photo and read the article, we quickly deciphered the hidden code from the sacred scroll," Abandonato told him.

"Continue," Pope John Paul III politely prompted.

"It was quite simple once we were alerted to the Washington Post story, Your Holiness. The heretic wears the clothing with the words 'All Envy Us'. The child was born to a famous woman who is adored around the world. The sacred text speaks of her with the line, 'The mother who will bear the child will be adored by the masses'.

"We don't know too much about the father, Don Williamson, other than he is an Englishman who met the American woman in London. It was a relatively quick marriage. They, it seems, met in December of last year and were married some 7 months later. We did some digging on the heretic too. She killed a man on New Year's Eve, the night of the event.

"The man had shot at Williamson and, according to reports, was going to kill both Williamson and Crawford. The heretic shot him with an archer's arrow before he could do that. The sacred test speaks of a third person, Your Holiness, the protector. The man she shot had served time in prison.

"He had raped Karen Crawford when she was just a child. We managed to get our hands on the original court documents. Because she was just a minor at the time, her name was suppressed but we managed to trace it down by lifting the document that the judge had signed upon handing down his sentence. The file was sealed but we pulled a few strings. The man the heretic shot was Lex Brampton.

"She had told investigators that she was at the ranch that night because she had a vision that Karen's life was in danger. She's worked with the police a lot and they have been duped by her beliefs, Your Holiness."

Pope John Paul III never acknowledged Abandonato's assumption regarding her beliefs. He knew that there were many people who walked the earth that had been blessed with the gift of clairvoyance.

"There are a total of thirteen numbers hidden in the message, each of them appearing in sequence at the end of the paragraphs. We missed something else in the text too, Your Holiness. The line 'Satan is not welcome' is significant. The heretic's photograph that appeared in the Washington Post was taken on her ranch in Idaho. The mother and father of the newborn also live in Idaho." Pope John Paul III felt that Abandonato was dragging out the story for his own pleasure.

"Get to the point Abandonato," Pope John Paul III ordered.

"Your Holiness, they, all three of them, along with the boy child, live in a place called Sun Valley." Abandonato looked at Pope John Paul III. There was no reaction.

"All Envy Us, Your Holiness."

That's when the penny dropped for Pope John Paul III. A smile of recognition appeared followed by a question.

"And the numbers, what do they signify?" Pope John Paul III asked Abandonato.

"We struggled at first to find a connection but we then hired a statistician. He played around with the thirteen numbers then broke them down into groups. Once we had the Sun Valley link and gave it to him, he was able to break the thirteen numbers down into just two groups, each with a sequence of numbers. The first group having six numbers whilst the second group contained seven numbers.

"We then looked at the text again and saw the line 'Satan is not welcome'. It seemed out of place so we threw it into the mix with the numbers and the photograph of the heretic. They are, Your Holiness, coordinates." Pope John Paul III raised an eyebrow.

"Coordinates for Sun Valley, right?" He asked Abandonato.

"Yes, Your Holiness."

Abandonato then explained about the 'Satan is not welcome' line in the sacred scroll. He told him that they took the first letter of the word 'Not' and the first letter of the word 'Welcome'.

"North and West, Your Holiness, with the two sequence of numbers being, 436806 and 1143428. In coordinate terms, it shows as 43.6806° N, 114.3428° W. The exact coordinates of Sun Valley in Idaho."

Pope John Paul III offered himself a smile as he gave Abandonato his blessing with a sign of the cross.

"Before I go, Your Holiness, there is one more thing. There's a man, an archaeologist by the name of Dr Henry Mattheson. He worked out the code and may talk. We are having him followed by Papal security and he's currently in Darwin, Australia giving lectures to students."

This annoyed Pope John Paul III.

"Well, if he knows the code, he will know by now who the parents are. Do we know if he has talked?"

"I took the liberty of bugging him, Your Holiness. Agents Onorati and Evangelista have been following him for a week. They bugged his hotel room and his clothing. He has not spoken to anyone regarding the code."

"How can we be sure he hasn't talked to anyone prior to you following him?" Pope John Paul III asked.

"Well, Your Holiness, he already did tell someone, that's how we learned that he knew."

"Who, who has he told?"

"Monsignor Fioravanti, apparently they go back a long way when they were on an archaeological dig in Egypt. It was Monsignor Fioravanti who tipped us off. We told him to call back Mattheson immediately and to tell him that he could tell nobody else as he may put his own life in danger."

"And did he?"

"Yes, Your Holiness. Not only that, he also had assurances from Mattheson that he had not told a soul. Once we found his location, we sent out Onorati and Evangelista to Australia. Technically speaking, the only time Mattheson would have had a chance to tell anyone about the code would have been from the time Fioravanti had told him not to tell anyone to the time both our agents were able to bug his room and clothes. He's an honourable man and Monsignor Fioravanti believes he was telling him the truth that he had not told a soul."

"Okay, good work."

Abandonato left the table and Pope John Paul III folded his breakfast napkin then took a sip of tea from his cup. He picked up his personal organiser and looked for Alonso Ferra, a former Sicilian priest who had recently moved to Cairns, Australia. Pope John Paul III lifted the biro and notepad that had been placed there, as it was each morning, by his aide.

That's when he wrote down Ferra's phone number. Ferra could be trusted, Monsignor Fioravanti could not. Pope John Paul III knew of Fioravanti's background, it was unsavoury to say the least but the Catholic Church had, as they had on many occasions, covered it up. He then looked skyward, to the heavens, to his God, and silently offered thanks. If only he had known before the event occurred that 'All Envy Us' was merely an anagram of Sun Valley.

A crow cawed in the distance as Pope John Paul III picked up the phone receiver on his table.

"Papal vault room, your Holiness, how can I help you?" Head of Security Brianna Esposito asked.

"I would like you to pull the Mankind Documents for me and send to my study in 15 minutes, I would like them all and also the correspondence between us and Majestic-12," he told her before replacing the receiver in its cradle.

He took one final sip of his tea before rising from his chair and heading to the balcony elevator that would take him straight to his study. He'd been briefed many years ago about the *Mankind Documents* and, indeed the correspondence between former Pope's and *Majestic-12*, a top secret group within the US Defence Department. He strongly felt the poem was connected to the *Mankind Documents* as stars don't move, particularly whole constellations like Ursa Major.

If there was an impending astronomical invent then it had more to do with the vehicles that had been visiting earth long before Christ was born. After all, he thought, Christ's birth was not the only time they'd had to change the text from 'tic-tac vehicle in the night sky' to 'Star of Bethlehem'. The original text in the book of Matthew was far different to how people viewed it today.

It wasn't a star, in fact it was a tic-tac shaped vehicle that appeared from a huge circular-craft, the same craft that Ezekiel had described, 'a wheel within a wheel', another text that had been watered down by Bible scholars. Everything had to appear as if it were from God, when in actual fact the whole of the original texts were played with, altered and dramatised.

It was easier to inform the people that there was a loving man in the sky watching over them, then it was to tell them that metallic craft were being flown across the earth by civilizations far more advanced than we. He'd been told by many that the people were not ready for the truth; he knew the truth was approaching fast.

The elevator doors opened and he stepped out and into his study. As promised, on his table were three large boxes, all were marked 'FOR YOUR EYES ONLY'.

# Chapter Sixty
# Washington Post 27 October 2015

### American Archaeologist, Dr Henry Mattheson, Found Dead in Litchfield National Park.

Darwin, NT, Australia: American archaeologist Dr Henry Mattheson has been found dead more than a month after he went missing in Australia's Northern Territory outback.

It's believed that Mattheson became disorientated when he ran into car trouble.

His body was found in scrub 3 days ago in Litchfield National Park, about 116 km from Darwin.

Darwin police say the body is that of Dr Henry Mattheson, after a post-mortem examination was carried out.

"While investigations will be continuing, there appears to be no suspicious circumstances at this time," a police statement said.

Detective Inspector Brian Williams said it appeared Henry Mattheson walked off after his car was damaged in the rough terrain.

"It appears that the vehicle, that Mattheson had hired when he arrived in Australia in August, had been driven to that location over rough terrain and the vehicle sustained front-end damage and a shredded left front tyre and was most likely undriveable," he added that there were no signs of violence in the car.

"It appears that he's become disorientated and the vehicle's not working, so he's decided to walk," he said.

Earlier this week, police described the search as looking for a needle in a haystack after covering 4300 square kilometres by air and land without any sign of the man or his car.

Mr Mattheson was carrying enough fuel to travel about 4000km and a quantity of food when he left Darwin last week.

The father of two last contacted his wife, Beatrice, by telephone, on Friday, 18 September, from his hotel in Darwin to say he would be arriving home in America the following Tuesday.

When this didn't happen, Beatrice contacted the Darwin Police.

The last confirmed sighting was on the afternoon of 18 September outside the Darwin Convention Centre, just yards from the hotel where he was staying.

Eyewitnesses said that Mattheson seemed to be agitated whilst speaking into his mobile phone.

The 71-year-old had been in Darwin since 13 August lecturing students.

**2016**

# Chapter Sixty-One

It was Thursday, 4 April 2016, 3 days shy of being Gabriel's 7th month on earth.

It seemed only fitting that they would call their son Gabriel. They had also both agreed to give him two extra names, Odelia, which is a gender-neutral name, and Don.

Their child was born on 15 September 2015. Martha and Jon were present, they both had wings. He was christened 4 weeks after his birth.

Karen sold her property in England and added extra security to her ranch in Sun Valley.

There were seven spotlights situated on top of the wrought iron entrance gates. Fourteen lights lined the driveway (seven on each side) and, of course, seven intruder lights over the stable.

Angie had gave her a few personal readings over the past week or so. She'd been having visions again, unpleasant ones. Kids being murdered, all different ages, all from different parts of the world. She knew the children were at peace as she felt them in her dreams. She even told Karen the names.

There was the youngest of the four, Teresa. She had an Irish accent. Then there were three others, two males, Sebastian and Anthony. They spoke in two languages, French and English. Then there was one other female, Sara, an American, a teenager. Angie's dreams were becoming more frequent and more graphic.

She saw the killers in her dreams, all men. She felt darkness around each of them and also felt the blackness in their hearts. At the end of each recurring dream, she would see the three men sleeping. She would then see her own mother, blowing out candles on a birthday cake.

Angie's mother, Julie-Ann, celebrated her birthday on the 15 of April so Angie knew that this date was significant and that it somehow tied in with the visions of the four children and their three killers.

At their home in Sun Valley, Idaho, Gabriel slept soundly in his crib. A blue blanket was over him, it had been given to him by his Godmother, Angie. A fabric mobile was above him, it had seven arms with seven yellow stars. When wound, it would play the tune *Twinkle, Twinkle Little Star.* Above his crib was a golden plaque that Karen and Don had had made especially, on it the two lines from Don's poem.

They read:

*There's a question mark tilted. Maybe it holds all the answers?*

A crow was outside Gabriel's window. It cawed loudly as it surveyed the grounds of the ranch. He was the only living creature, outside of the Vatican, who knew that Pope John Paul III would be arriving next week with his entourage to lay claim to Gabriel.

# Chapter Sixty-Two
# Karen's Parents

They both attended their own funerals back in 1995. It had been a great turnout they had thought. Their caskets were white and they had never ever seen so many flowers. Martha's wreath contained lavender gladiolus, pink Asiatic lilies, lavender chrysanthemums, pink mini carnations and lush greens, all formed together neatly on a wire easel that formed the word 'MOM'.

Jon's wreath was made up of white roses, carnations, gladiolus, stock and Oriental lilies, all formed the word 'DAD'. All their friends were there too. All with their heads bowed as the caskets were lowered. It seemed that every Tom, Dick and Harry had turned out.

Farmers, shopkeepers, even people whose names they didn't know. They were buried outside the church that they went to every Sunday, St Matthews on Ridge Street.

Martha and Jon had been dead for almost a week now. They'd been sleeping but had woke for their own funerals. They slept together, as normal. It felt surreal but there was no need to set alarm clocks, no need to take out their dentures, no need to check that all the lights were switched off. All those rituals didn't exist in limbo. They didn't even sleep in their own bed, didn't even sleep on their own farm.

They just followed the light that guided them to a safe place. It was a light at the end of a corridor where there was one single door slightly ajar. Here they would sleep until the day of their own burial. Time was suspended, it didn't exist. They didn't even know that they had slept for an earth week.

They had none of the burns on their skin anymore, in fact their skin felt different than it did during their time on earth, it felt vibrant and young. The one thing they both felt, however, was an overwhelming feeling of love; they felt it for one another and they felt it all around them. They had never felt the power of love, not the true power of love. The light had shown them love and it felt so pure and clean.

There was no fear, no questions. They both just opened the door and rested their heads side by side on the Queen sized bed. They kissed and held hands, then they drifted, then they woke. That's how it was in limbo.

They didn't like to see their daughter weeping as the pall bearers lowered their caskets into the ground but they both knew that her grief would subside eventually.

Martha and Jon had raised their daughter well and, according to the two angels that were standing next to them, they were going to play a major role in the future with their daughter. For now, at least, they had to cross over to the other side.

Their time in limbo had come to an end. Most people spend just a week in limbo, it all depends on the circumstances. Tragic accidents, which was the way Martha and Jon died, slept for the duration between their death and their funeral. When couples die together, they can walk together on the other side, it all depends if they want to.

After waking from limbo, they are told to imagine a beach and then to imagine a person they would like to walk with down that beach. The companion has to have crossed over to the other side. They can be family members, pets, famous people. Just you and that person or animal can walk from sun-up to sundown.

You can hug, reminisce, ask questions. Animals, after the walk is finished, will turn into their human form and, usually, thank it's owners for its time on earth.

Only two can walk together, the newly dead and the 'beach person'. Many who wake from limbo pick icons of their past, Elvis, Monroe, Jackson. Others pick sports personalities who were taken before their time. In the main, the newly dead pick family members who have crossed over to the other side.

Martha and John asked to walk with Odelia, their granddaughter. Sadly, for Martha and Jon at least, Odelia was not an option, she was away, being prepared. Instead, they chose Benn, their faithful four-legged companion on earth who had been euthanised 2 years prior to Martha and Jon's own death.

Benn was a Rhodesian Ridgeback crossed with a Boxer. He had been happy to see them. All three walked from dusk til dawn against the backdrop of a quiet, beautiful beach, save for a spattering of small children playing and building sandcastles, after which Benn metamorphosed into his human form to thank his owners for the life they gave him on earth. He became a boy of teenage years and then walked into the calm sea before swimming out of sight. That was how things happened on the other side.

Those who succumb to long term illnesses are usually met by their loved ones the moment they die. When they walk the beach they have no illness.

Those who die by suicide are wrapped immediately in love. The light enshrouds them the moment their hearts stop beating. Their hearts are then filled with unconditional love. Quite often suicide victims feel unloved, unwanted. That all changes when the light greets them.

Children are met inside the light, usually by family members who have crossed over before them. If none have passed before them then angels are sent. They meet other children and are taken to the beach to play and build sandcastles.

Death as a foetus, be it by abortion, natural causes or drug induced death is treated as a high priority. Each foetus is attached to an umbilical cord where they continue to grow until their birth day. Each chord picks up their mother's heartbeat, it's as if they have never left the womb. When fully formed, the umbilical cord is cut and they are adopted and raised by angels.

They will know only of love. There are no negative emotions on the other side. Light is everywhere, there is no darkness, no night. No judgments are made, there is no wrath of any God, no turning away from pearly gates.

Those that kill are treated the same. They have two doors to choose from down the corridor of light. Their heart, if still blackened after their death, will choose the door which leads to permanent limbo, a place where everything is dark and one where you wait until you are woken by the fallen one. Killers don't have the option of the beach walk.

*** 

The beautiful winged creatures standing next to Martha and Jon had told them that they needed preparing for what lay ahead. They were both male, both were equally handsome, both had striking blue eyes and smiles that spoke of peace and happiness.

"My name is Michael, you may know me as Archangel Michael."

"And I'm Archangel Gabriel."

The two angels introduced themselves to Martha and John. They each put a hand on their shoulders and reassured them both that their daughter would be okay.

"We know the pain you are feeling and we both know the pain and emptiness your daughter is feeling too. This will pass. Death is not final, it's merely a short vacation without family members. Just as you journey to a far distant place on earth to visit loved ones or to be reunited with loved ones, same thing happens over the other side.

"You are both merely on vacation, your daughter will be visiting you in the future. She is well protected and has been from birth, so do not weep for her. 20 years from now it will be your turn to become guardians once more," Archangel Michael told them.

He smiled at them and then said something that they had, both as devout Catholics, often struggled with. They'd often wondered if, they would ever get to see their granddaughter, Odelia, again. Archangel Gabriel made their hearts sing.

"Come with us, we want you to meet someone. We want you to meet your granddaughter, Odelia. She's been waiting to reunite with you."

That was back in 1995. They were told that Odelia was not a child anymore but, to Martha and Jon, at least, she would still look like and act like a child. They told them that Odelia was in training and that they would be with her for 20 years on the other side.

"Why just 20 or so years?" Martha had asked.

Archangels Michael and Gabriel looked at one another, smiled, and then told Martha, "Because we are sending her back and both you and Jon will be going with her, but first you need to spend time with her and prepare."

"Granny, Papa." Odelia entered the room. Martha and Jon began to weep. Archangels Gabriel and Michael smiled.

She was in her teenage years and looked just like their daughter, Karen. She held out her arms and Martha and Jon allowed her to embrace them, as she did a flashing light filled the room, and in an instant all three were gone. Only Archangels Gabriel and Michael knew where to.

# Chapter Sixty-Three

"So, this is why we all must leave immediately," Angie told them.

It was mid-afternoon in Idaho and Angie Jakobs had turned up at the Crawford ranch unannounced. She'd explained about the dreams, the ones where she saw children being murdered. She explained that these four children were Karen and Don's guardian angels and that they were around them right now. Angie also told them about the threat to Gabriel.

"We all know about the story of Mary and Joseph, the star of Bethlehem, the three wise men and the birth of Jesus. Let's not kid ourselves here. We all recognised and understood the astronomical event that night, each of us knew the significance. We now know that Don had somehow predicted this event, thus predicting his own future." Angie turned to Don.

"Don, you have what is known as Astrological Divination. It's an ability that is rare. You basically have an insight into future outcomes and you are going to need to nurture this ability."

"Look, Angie, I wrote a poem 15 years ago. I don't know why I chose the two lines that I did, I just did," Don told her.

Angie let out a small sigh then smiled at Don.

"Don, you spoke with your heart. You allowed your heart to be ruler thus eliminating outside influences such as thought. When we listen to our hearts, we listen to the spiritual messages of those around us. You have had this ability from birth, Don, we all have an ability to tune in; for some, realisation comes after an event that affects the heart.

"In your case, Don, your heart had been broken by your wife. Her infidelity and deceit left you with a couple of reactionary choices. You chose the pure one. You forgave despite all of the odds stacked against you."

Don looked at Angie with a surprised look on his face.

"Odds, what odds?"

"Okay, let me explain," Angie told him. "When people hurt us, our natural human reaction is to defend ourselves or to seek retribution. It stems from our built

197

in survival system. I throw you from a boat into an ocean and your natural reaction is to stay afloat. You fight against it because your life depends on it, Don.

"When mothers give birth to children in water, they, once they are born, do the same. They enter into water and their natural reaction is to swim to the surface. That's survival instinct at play, Don. Same way a child knows that the nipple or teat being offered, although completely alien to them, is something they must suckle on to survive.

We are born with it, Don, just as we are born with love. The moment a child is born, he or she have hearts pure and full of love. They have a survival instinct and no fear. The emotion of fear comes later, as they grow, as they look, listen and learn. You, Don, had a number of choices when you learned that your wife was cheating on you.

"You chose the righteous path. Despite all the pain and misery you were suffering, you were able to keep away those dark thoughts that appear when we are at our most vulnerable. Jealousy, anger, hatred, all of which lead us to retribution, or, at the very least, a need to seek revenge. Karma is the only revenge that is needed and that, Don, is a law that is out of our control.

"We can prevent karma but we cannot stop it once the wheels have been set in motion. Tell me, Don, what happened to your wife?"

"Well, she left Pallatt after she caught him in bed with her boss."

"And Pallatt, what became of him, Don?"

"He, as far as I know, lost his job at the bakery. His boss, the woman he was caught with by my ex, learned that he was talking to women online and arranging to meet them. She was sickened by it by all accounts as Pallatt was arranging to meet up with girls in their early 20s. His boss finished with him as soon as she learned then fired him."

"You see, Don, the law of karma could not be stopped. Your ex-wife finds her lover in bed with someone else and she leaves the relationship. Your ex-wife's lover is caught cheating by his new lover, his boss. She leaves and as a result then fires the Pallatt guy from his job.

"Her retribution was guided by karma. You cannot stop it. Now, Don, tell me how you felt upon hearing the news that your ex-wife and Pallatt had ended their relationship?"

"I felt bad for her. She had to move into an unfurnished council flat because she walked away from her job. My old neighbour, Bridgette, told me that she had seen her and she looked awful. She left her job because she couldn't bear to see her boss and ex-lover together."

"So, even after what she had put you through, you still felt kindness in your heart. Most people would have been positively gloating but not you, Don. You see, you have a heart that does not allow outside influences in. Just as that child taking his first swim for survival when he is born into a water world, you, or your heart, has remained in a state of love, and instinctively you knew that the love you carried needed to be shared with someone else.

"Those you were in relationships with before Karen were vessels that you wished to fill but, for one reason or another, that did not happen. You met Karen who was that empty vessel. She wanted to be loved and she wanted to reciprocate that love. The rest, as they say, is history. Now, the two of you have a child.

"His heart has a combination of his own love, Karen's love and your love, Don. I feel it when I am around him, Don. Gabriel is pure love. He is light. He is truth."

"Are you saying what I think you're saying?" Karen asked.

Angie then reached into her bag and pulled out a Bible. There were three small bookmarks sticking out of the pages.

"Read these passages. I've highlighted the bookmarks with numbers for relevance," she told them both.

Don joined Karen on the sofa. Highlighted in yellow were a series of sentences. This is what they read.

*Matthew 2:1-11:*

*For we have seen his star in the east, and are come to worship him.*

*Then Herod...inquired of them diligently what time the star appeared.*

*When they had heard the king, they departed; and, lo, the star, which they saw in the east, went before them, till it came and stood over where the young child was.*

Karen turned to the next bookmarked page highlighted '2'. She opened the page at Acts 1:11.

*"Men of Galilee," they said. "Why do you stand here looking into the sky? This same Jesus, who has been taken from you into heaven, will come back in the same way you have seen him go into heaven."*

Karen looked at Angie.

"1.11?" Karen asked. Angie smiled.

"Read the third," she prompted.

Amos 5:8:

*Seek him that maketh the seven stars and Orion, and turneth the shadow of death into the morning, and maketh the day dark with night: that calleth for the waters of the sea, and poureth them out upon the face of the earth: The LORD is his name.*

Karen once again looked at Angie, this time her face was the picture of total disbelief.

"Are you saying that…"

Angie signalled Karen to remain quiet, it was a signal using her eyes. They widened and expressed silence. Don saw the signal too and then looked towards Karen to see her reaction. She said nothing.

"What's going on?" He asked.

The tune of *Twinkle, twinkle, little star* came out of the speaker of the electronic baby monitor on the table in front of them.

Sebastian, Anthony, Teresa, and Sara, smiled together. Archangel Gabriel then pulled them back.

Don, Karen and Angie headed for the stairs.

Upstairs, Martha and Jon were watching over Gabriel. Guarding him.

The crow had been outside Gabriel's window. He saw the winged female turn the winder on the fabric mobile above the child's crib. They knew it was close to the time. They knew that they had to get the attention of Karen, Don and Angie. The window in Gabriel's bedroom looked over Sun Valley and they'd get a much better view from there of the Holy One approaching.

The crow flew from the ledge and rested on the same light above the stable that he had rested on for the astronomical event. He looked across Sun Valley and, on the downward slope of a hill, saw five black cars in a line. The April sun had caused a mirage effect in the distance making the five cars appear as boats skimming across the water. All five were heading towards the Crawford ranch.

It was time.

# Chapter Sixty-Four

"Clever, so fucking clever. The twist of all twists, huh? You had me completely fooled, I'll give you that. You disguised yourself well, I applaud you. You schemed and hoodwinked and fooled all those involved, fucking fooled me too, the master of manipulation. So, this is why they say you have great wisdom, huh?

"You may have thrown a spanner in the works of my plan but I'll still use the three; we will still join forces. Let's see if you can be oh so fucking powerful with four of us. The Holy one will take care of the child; they can have him. We will take care of the rest.

"Repeating history was a great touch, the stars, three being present, each of them believing what you wanted them to. So fucking clever. And the sacred scroll, fucking genius. You duped your own kind because you knew they were desperate for ownership of your son. That's going to take some explaining to them. Whatever happened to the ninth fucking commandment, 'thou shalt not lie?' And lie you did, on a monumental scale.

"I fucking bow down before your deceitfulness. I applaud your capabilities to write the script of all scripts, the plot of all plots, and the trick of all tricks. And we all fell for it. We all became your puppet instruments and fell right into your trap. Very fucking clever. I acknowledge your fucking greatness and your mastery and now, God, you will witness mine."

The evil one turned to Tommy McGinty, Clément Dubois, and Haskin Bruette.

"We need to rethink our strategy. He has deceived us," he told them.

# Chapter Sixty-Five

They were already a mile away by the time the five car convoy had pulled up outside the gates of Karen Crawford's ranch. Martha and Jon had done well. The distraction brought the three into the room. None of them looked outside the window at first, not until they heard the flapping of wings against the glass and the cawing of a crow.

It was Angie who threw back the curtains, just in time to see the crow heading off in to the distance, towards a hill where, at the bottom, were five black cars heading towards the Crawford ranch. The crow flew towards them then, as if by magic, disappeared. Angie turned to Karen and Don.

"We need to get out of here, right fucking now."

Both Karen and Don were shocked. Karen more so as in all the years she had known Angie, she had never once heard her swear.

"Quick," Angie said, "grab Gabriel. We can use my car."

Angie had a four wheel drive, a Cadillac Escalade ESV that could comfortably accommodate an extra two adults and small child. She had parked it around the back of the house when she had arrived earlier for no other reason than convenience. Don and Karen had been out in the sun eating brunch. Angie had joined them.

There was another entrance and exit from Karen's ranch. It was to the right of the stables and was only ever used for hay delivery for when Karen had horses. The driveway towards the exit was overgrown, thought Don, as Angie steadily drove. Karen was cradling Gabriel, she'd grabbed four of his bottle feeds that she had made earlier.

"I will drop you at my place and then head out to the stores to get some provisions," Angie said. In truth, she needed her space, she needed to speak with Archangel Michael.

"Who are they and what do they want?" Karen asked.

"I'm not sure who they are, Karen, but the cars looked official and I felt danger."

Don, not wanting to feel left out, piped in.

"Official, how do you mean?"

"They had small flags on the cars. I could see them but couldn't quite make out what the insignia on them was," Angie told him.

Confused by it all Don asked, "But what do they want with us?"

"I don't know, Don, I need to tune in to spirit. Something ain't right and it has to do with the astronomical event we all witnessed. I think we may have all jumped to the wrong conclusion about Gabriel and I think, Don, that you hold the key to all of this." Angie broke off the conversation as she turned into her driveway.

"Me?"

"We'll talk when I get back," Angie told him.

"Are they keys in the usual place?" Karen asked Angie.

"Yes. We don't have long. Go to the basement and double lock the door. I will go get some provisions and we can talk about all of this when I get back. We need to move fast and we need to get out of Idaho."

Karen, with Gabriel in her arms, and Don, stood and watched Angie pull away. They then headed inside Angie's house and to her basement.

"Do you know what's going on?" Don asked Karen.

Karen looked at him. "I'm not sure, Don, but Angie is right. I think we are in danger."

"What makes you say that?"

"Because you told me about it, Don."

"Huh, what do you mean I told you about it?"

"In your sleep, Don, you talk a lot in your sleep."

"When, what did I say?"

"You've always talked in your sleep, it's usually incoherent stuff but this past week it's been clearer."

"What have I been saying?"

"You've been having a conversation with someone in your dreams. You told them..." Karen paused.

"I told them what?"

"You told them that Gabriel was not the son of God. You told them that you are."

# Chapter Sixty-Six

Archangel Gabriel pulled all six back.

"The time is near. Archangel Michael is with Angie as I speak. He is giving her his light and protection. Everything is being explained to her in a way that she will understand. It is imperative that you each be vigilant over the next few earth hours. The dark one is returning and will be using forces of great evil via an innocent."

"Might we know who this innocent is?" Sebastian asked.

"It will be someone you least expect. The evil one will gamble everything so he can get close to the child and father. I do know that he has not yet entered into the body of an innocent. He is biding his time, trying to second guess God. This is why we must keep him awake at all times.

"The only way he can communicate is when Don sleeps. Don has not had time to nurture his ability but Archangel Michael will show Angie how this can be done quickly."

"You say the evil one will gamble everything; what do you mean by this?" Sara asked.

"Well, Sara, he has to enter the arena where he is least comfortable. We have six of you and also an entourage of Holy men in the vicinity. Then, of course, we have Don. We know that the evil one is a coward and will not face Don whilst he is in the presence of you all, in this instance he has to. He is entering into a field of battle where all the odds are stacked against him, so he will disguise himself as to blend in.

"By entering into such a field of play, he is taking a huge risk. The Holy one has protection and the evil one will steer clear of him. Angie will have protection when she returns so he won't be able to possess her. He will, however, use someone as his tool and that person will try to entice Don to a place where he will have him alone, away from those that are trying to protect him."

"But if Don has the wisdom then why should he fear the evil one?" Martha asked.

"Don only has the wisdom when he sleeps or when he is able to focus on one thing. He focused on the star formation 15 years ago. He put into words what he felt. We knew what those words meant but he didn't because he did not know who or what he was back then. He surveyed the night sky because his heart was searching for an answer. He wrote the verse and hidden within it was the answer.

"The question mark tilted held the answers for him but, to him at least, it was just a question and not an answer; a never-ending question regarding his faith. Our Lord had to go back without knowledge, he had to go back as man, just as he did over two thousand earth years ago. It's now almost 52 years since Don Williamson was born. He was born on exactly the same day that humanity had their first glimpse of their nearest star.

"On 31 July 1964, the date of Don's birth, Ranger 7 transmitted pictures of the lunar surface back to earth. It was the turning point for space exploration. Don unknowingly made this connection when he wrote the verse. A verse that he gave the title, 'God's Thumbprint in the Sky'. The thumbprint being the moon.

"He was right; the moon is a type of fingerprint, and it reminds everyone on earth that, even in times of darkness they will have a light to guide them. Don's verse was prophetic because it was created and penned by a prophet. Let me take you all through it step-by-step."

Archangel Gabriel then showed the six the last seven lines of Don's prophetic message.

"The number seven, my sweet angels. It's been with Don since he was born. Ranger 7, the seven sisters, even the birth of his son, Gabriel, has the seven connection when we take the date, the 16 of September, one plus six. And now the last seven lines of his message.

"Line one, 'There's only one colour beyond the duvet'. Line two, 'Where there is no night, no darkness'. The third line, 'Light beyond the realms of understanding'. And the fourth, 'The holes giving us hope'. The fifth line, 'God's thumbprint a constant reminder'. And sixth, 'Of what we are'. And finally, the seventh line, 'And where we are going'.

"Don's message was to humanity. It is, in fact, the sacred message, a 21st century message. He is speaking about light and reminding everyone that they should remember who they are and what they are about. It's also a message to us."

All six looked at Archangel Gabriel in surprise. None of them needed to ask the next question.

"I'll explain. Don gave us all a clue about the evil one. Let's look at the following lines. 'Shoots bullets across the sky, I see them flash by. There's only one colour beyond the duvet where there is no night, no darkness. Light beyond the realms of understanding'. It's not apparent at first, not until we understand what Don was saying, or writing.

"Archangel Michael and I worked on it and what we revealed was startling. It's another message, a message within a message."

"So, those lines are a prediction, a premonition of something that will take place in the future?" Sebastian asked.

"Yes, Sebastian, exactly that. Let's take the first line, 'Shoots bullets across the sky'. Now, keeping in context of what Don wrote back then we can take it that he was referring to shooting stars or maybe comets? The line is followed with, 'I see them flash by'. Again, he is just bearing witness to seeing shooting stars or comets. 'There's only one colour beyond the duvet'. We initially struggled with this. Don, it seems was using a duvet as an analogy for the night sky, a blanket, a cover.

"He followed this up with, 'Where there is no night, no darkness'. Once again, he was writing about what was behind the duvet, he answered his own question when he said there is no night or no darkness. In other words there is no evil. Finally, 'Light beyond the realms of understanding'. Here we see Don asking about the light beyond, the light being the truth.

"Now, here's the interesting part. There's a hidden message in all of those lines. We started at the first word in the sequence, 'Shoots', we took the last letter then counted thirty letters forward."

Archangel Gabriel had already prepared the sequence of letters and wrote them down. He held a glossy card in his hand, it was about as big as your average newspaper.

"Now, before I show you this, you need to understand that Don was unknowingly using a basic form of mathematics. It's an equidistant letter sequence that Archangel Michael and I used within the lines I just read to you all. Starting with the last letter of the word 'Shoots' and then continuing forward thirty letters in the sequence and then another thirty letters after that, and so on. I guess it would be easier if I showed you all."

Archangel Gabriel, grabbed the glossy card with both hands.

"I have put each letter in sequence in brackets."

He then turned the glossy card towards the six.

Shoot(**S**) bullets across the sky; I see them fl(**A**)sh by; there's only one colour beyond (**T**)he duvet where there is no night, no d(**A**)rkness; light beyond the realms of understa(**N**)ding.

"What we now know is that Don has predicted a showdown with Satan himself. Your job is to guard over Karen, Don and Gabriel and watch out for anything that resembles the lines on this card. Memorise them. Angie has been told everything by Archangel Michael, everything that I have just told you. Now go back my sweet angels and watch over them."

"Before we go, can I just ask why you used a sequence of thirty?" Jon asked.

"Absolutely, Jon, and it's a very good question. Go back now and you will hear Angie explain."

In an instant, they left Archangel Gabriel and were back with Angie, Don, Karen and Gabriel.

# Chapter Sixty-Seven

By the time Pope John Paul III and his entourage had arrived at the Crawford ranch, the occupants had vacated. It seemed to make sense to next check the Angie Jakobs' ranch. Once again, upon arrival, they learned that the Jakobs woman was nowhere to be seen.

Pope John Paul III had travelled under his given name, Angelo Landro.

There had been no pomp, only the twelve undercover papal security that travelled with him. The Catholic Church had arranged the five black Chevrolet Tahoe's.

Again, it was all done discreetly. Angelo was picked up and chauffeured out of Boise Airport. He just looked like any old Italian businessman and nobody really took any notice of him as he sipped his orange juice and read his newspapers in the business class section on the US Airways flight.

Landro came from a modest background. He was born and raised in Catania, Sicily. He travelled to Rome at the age of 18 where he became a Benedictine monk, shortly after he was ordained a priest. He was elected as pope at the age of 62 and had vowed to travel far and wide to spread the Catholic message. Today, however, he was incognito, albeit using his real identity.

Monsignor Fioravanti had travelled a day ahead from Australia and was now sitting in the back of one of the five Chevrolet Tahoe's with Pope John Paul III as it pulled out of Angie Jakobs' driveway.

"We must head back to the hotel, Your Holiness. The more you are exposed, the more you are under threat," Fioravanti told the Pope.

Pope John Paul III waved his right hand in dismissal of Fioravanti's concerns.

"It appears that the Jakobs' woman is one step ahead of us. We underestimated her ability, and we seriously underestimated her connections to the afterlife," Pope John Paul III told Fioravanti, then added, "Tell me, did you not feel it when we were outside both ranches, Monsignor Fioravanti, did you not feel their presence?"

Monsignor Fioravanti had felt the presence, it was the residue presence of angels. He knew, at that moment, that taking the child was never going to be an option. Angels were not in opposition to the Catholic religion, or indeed any organised religion.

Both he and Pope John Paul III knew, however, that angels attached themselves to every single human, even those without faith. He felt the residue of all of them and also knew of what Pope John Paul III was speaking of. It wasn't just the angelic presence.

"Yes, Your Holiness, I felt it. I felt the protection that they have, particularly the heretic woman. What do you suggest we do, Your Holiness?"

"I think we only have one option. We need to call upon Archangel Gabriel."

"But, Your Holiness, he will not show himself."

"Then we will have to make sure that he does." Pope John Paul III tapped the divider in the Chevrolet Tahoe. The driver, one of his own security, lowered the glass and awaited the Pope's instruction.

"Find me a Catholic Church," he told the driver.

# Chapter Sixty-Eight

"In 1858," Angie began, "Saint Bernadette, who was, at the time, just a 14-year-old French peasant girl, claimed to have seen the Virgin Mary. The apparitions, which totalled 18 before the end of the year, occurred near Lourdes, France. Saint Bernadette asked the Virgin Mary who she was and she replied, 'Che soy era immaculada counceptiou'.

"Translated it means, 'I am the immaculate conception'. Saint Bernadette died of ill health at the age of 35."

Don and Karen looked at Angie somewhat surprisingly. They felt they were being given a lecture at Sunday school.

"So, what does this have to do with anything?" Don finally blurted.

"I'm getting to it, Don, please don't rush me. It needs to be explained as slowly and concisely as possible."

"I'm sorry, Angie, please continue," Karen told her.

"Don," Angie asked, "What was your mother's name?"

"Marie; why do you ask?"

Angie just smiled.

"And when did you first see the message. Don, the message that your ex-wife's lover published on the Internet?"

The date was engraved into Don's mind.

"It was the 7 of January. Why?"

Angie smiled again, much to Don's annoyance.

"And tell me what you saw, Don, tell me again."

"It was just an image of a heart with two words, 'The Beginning'."

Angie was now smiling from ear to ear.

"Have you ever felt that you have a special gift, Don?" Angie asked.

"No, not at all," he answered.

"Your poem, do you not think it is strange that the events you described in a poem that you wrote actually came true? Do you not think that what you described in words all those years ago happened on New Year's Eve 2014? What are the two lines you had inscribed on the plaque for Gabriel?"

"You know I can't explain that, Angie. Look, I know that you have this ability to tune in to the other side and I know you have predicted things that have come true; Karen and I meeting being just one example. I don't have that ability, Angie, so I can only put it down to coincidence that we witnessed an astronomical event that night. Yes, it was weird, yes even more weird is that we were the only three people to witness it but I didn't predict it, Angie. That's just impossible."

"What if I were to show you other lines from your poem, Don, do you think you could tell me what you were thinking at the time you wrote it?" Angie asked.

"Yes, absolutely."

Angie took the folded paper from the back pocket of her jeans, she had made notes just like Archangel Michael had told her to. She read the following lines to Don.

"Shoots bullets across the sky, I see them flash by. There's only one colour beyond the duvet where there is no night, no darkness. Light beyond the realms of understanding. What did you mean when you wrote this, Don?"

"Well, shoots bullets across the sky, I see them flash by, is me explaining about shooting stars. There's only one colour beyond the duvet where there is no night, no darkness, is me saying that the sky is basically a big black blanket with holes in it and the stars are merely holes in that blanket allowing light through from the other side. Light beyond the realms of understanding is me, in essence, asking what it all means," he told her.

"Are you familiar with the term equidistant letter sequence, Don?"

"Hasn't that got something to do with putting codes into messages? He asked.

"Yes, Don, it's exactly that. And did you write any code into your poem, particularly the lines I just read to you?"

Don laughed. "Not to my knowledge, no."

"Don, do you know who Saint Bernadette was?"

"Well, I've heard of her name and knew that she had something to do with seeing a vision of the Virgin Mary, but it's not something I've really researched or ever really been interested in."

"Saint Bernadette, Don, was born Marie Bernarde Soubirous in 1844. Do you think it coincidental that she shared the same name as your mother, Don?"

211

Don laughed again. "Well, there's lots of women called Marie, Maria, Mary, whatever you want to call them."

Even Karen didn't know where Angie was going with this.

"There is a message in your lines, Don. A hidden message."

"What?"

Angie then showed them the lines she had wrote earlier. She asked them both to start counting after the final 's' on the word 'shoots'. It took them under a minute before they spelled out the word SATAN.

"I expect you are wondering why it's every 30th letter?"

"Well, yes, that had crossed my mind," Don told her.

Karen, holding Gabriel in her arms, along with the six angels present, leaned in closer. They each wanted to hear the result of the cliff-hanger.

"Che soy era immaculada counceptiou," Angie said.

Both Don and Karen had blank expressions on their faces. The six angels were also bemused.

"Count the letters," Angie said, handing Don and Karen a slip of paper with the phrase.

The angels, looking over the shoulder of Don, were the first to finish counting. There were *thirty letters.* They smiled.

"Angie, I hate to be dismissive of your psychic ability but don't you think you are just trying to make things appear to be something more than just a coincidence?"

Angie wasn't offended by Don's remark in the slightest, she'd had many critics in the past.

"Don, tell me again the exact date you saw the words 'The Beginning'." She asked.

Don let out a sigh before adding, "7 January."

"Marie Bernarde Soubirous, who later became Saint Bernadette, was born in 1844 Don. 7 January 1844 to be precise."

The church bell gave them all a fright. They had sought solace in there after they had left Angie's ranch and while she explained things to them.

As the sound of the last 3 pm chime echoed out, they each turned to the entrance of the church. Standing at the doors was Angelo Landro. He'd been standing there for some considerable time.

He'd heard everything.

# Chapter Sixty-Nine

*Be sober-minded; be watchful. Your adversary the devil prowls around like a roaring lion, seeking someone to devour.*
1 Peter 5:8

*Get him out of the church now or he will stay in there all fucking day and you won't be able to make contact with Williamson. Go on, try it. Approach the church door and see what happens. If you manage to make it up the path you will have achieved something. Hey, enter the church, look to your right and you will see water.*

*Put your hand in the water and see what happens. Did you feel like throwing up when he mentioned that he wanted to go to church? Why didn't you enter with him, why did you stay in the car? Why are you sweating and why has your face skin turned a shade of ashen?*

*You know what's in the briefcase, open it and take it. Put it inside your pocket. You know that you are no better than the people I am with right now. So, you never had the guts back then to kill, but you still scarred those poor children. They would have been better off dead rather than carry around those images of you throughout their lives.*

*Remember when they came to your confessional and confessed their sins to you? Mi benedica, padre, perché ho molto peccato. Those same kids you sinned against were now coming back to you and asking you for your blessing.*

*Did that turn you on? Without so much of a flutter of your eyelids, you told them each to say ten Hail Mary's. What about you, did you repent for your sins?*

*Ave, o Maria, piena di grazia, il Signore è con te. Tu sei benedetta fra le donne e benedetto è il frutto del tuo seno, Gesù Santa Maria, Madre di Dio, prega per noi peccatoti, adesso e nell'ora della nostra morte. Amen. How many times did you repeat it? Open the briefcase. Take it. Do what you have to do then come and join us.*

He gave himself the sign of the cross. The dark one along with McGinty Dubois and Bruette laughed then each mimicked him.

*Nel nome del Padre, e del Figlio, e dello Spirito Santo. Amen. We can say it in English for you now.* And they did.

*In the name of the Father, and of the Son, and of the Holy Spirit. Amen.*

The dark one continued.

*You think the Holy Trinity is going to forgive you, you really do think that by saying sorry everything will be forgotten about? You Holy people are all the same. You dedicate your whole fucking lives to a God that you believe is all forgiving. Will he forgive you for touching the little girl, Francesca.*

*How old was she when she came to you, seven, eight? Or what about the three boys, Filberto, Manlio, and Salvatore? You do know that as a consequence of your actions, Salvatore now abuses his own children, don't you? Open the fucking briefcase and get that cunt out of the church.*

Monsignor Fioravanti knocked the glass on the divider.

"I'm going in to get him, he's been in there far too long."

He opened the briefcase and removed the 9 inch silver letter opener. He then wiped his brow with a handkerchief before opening the door. As his feet touched the ground, he felt the bile rise, he felt his heart race and he heard the voices once more.

*Suck it up, Fioravanti. Go do what you have to do and you will never need to repent again. You can join us. Ucciderlo, Uccidete la trinità, Monsignor Fioravanti."*

# Chapter Seventy

*It's the Holy One.* Archangel Michael whispered in Angie Jakobs ear. *He is here in good faith. Remember, do not leave the safety of the church and do what I told you to do.*

Angie walked towards the man at the door. She smiled as she approached him.

He smiled back.

"Please, come and join us," she told him.

Pope John Paul III started to walk towards the front of the church. He expected the Jakobs' woman to follow him. She didn't. He stopped and waited for her to rejoin him.

Angie walked towards the font and dipped both her hands in the water.

Cupping them together, she filled them with the Holy water then, in one quick movement, threw the water on to gothic looking church doors. She repeated this until the font was empty, then walked back to where the Holy man was standing.

"*Grazie per essere venuto,*" she told him.

Pope John Paul III raised his hand then said, "Please, in English. We cannot lose anything in translation today, even if you are only thanking me for coming."

Angie smiled and they walked towards Karen, Don and Gabriel.

"Karen, Don, this is..." Angie was interrupted.

"I am Angelo Landro but my official title is Pope John Paul III. I am not one to stand on ceremony so please just refer to me as Angelo." He smiled at Karen and Don; it was a sincere smile and warmed them both to him.

"And this must be your son." Karen held on tight to Gabriel as Angelo held out his arms in a gesture to cradle Gabriel.

"It's okay, Karen," Angie said, reassuringly.

Angelo felt Karen's reluctance to hand him the child.

"It's okay, Miss Crawford, we don't really have much time anyhow. We need to move closer to the altar, preferably on it. We will be safe there," he told them.

Karen felt it wrong to correct him.

She was, and had been, Mrs Williamson for some time now but she understood being in the public eye as Crawford for so long meant that many would still refer to her by her maiden name.

They each turned to walk to the altar where high above was a crucifix with Jesus Christ, complete with red dye on his palms and feet depicting his sacrifice for humanity. That's when they each heard the turning of metal onto wood; the mechanical sound of a handle turning, the handle on the church door. All but one of them looked down the aisle, only one knew that the noise was coming from the doors of the vestry, to the right of the altar. The acoustics of the church playing havoc to all but Angie Jakobs.

"Can I help you?" Father Louis Burley asked them all. All three turned to where Angie was staring. Father Burley recognised Angelo Landro immediately.

Wide eyed, Burley gave himself the sign of the cross and bowed.

"Your Holiness!" He said.

"Can you get us to a safe place quickly?" Pope John Paul III asked him without even acknowledging his bow.

Burley knew just the place. Underneath the church were a series of tunnels that had been painstakingly excavated by Chinese immigrants in the 1850's, at least that's what Father Louis Burley had been told when he took residency at St Bartholomew Catholic Church back in 2006.

The tunnels ran under the courtyard and underneath the adjacent road; the same road where five black Chevrolet Tahoe's were now parked. Each tunnel was different in size. Three of them only big enough for a small child to crawl through, basically they were crawlspace tunnels. The other two being much bigger.

One of those two, however, was being used by the church for storage purposes. Over the years, the tunnels had been reinforced with brick; two of the five, the 'adult' ones, even had lights installed. The other, the one church officials called the 'main tunnel', led out into the street, two hundred yards away from the church.

"I know just the place. Please, come with me," Father Burley told them. Don took Gabriel from Karen, she seemed relieved.

"Here, let me hold him. In the craziness of all of this, I forgot my parenting duties. I also forgot to tell you, Mrs Williamson, how much I love you." They kissed and were soon heading to the vestry door with Karen and Angelo in tow.

Teresa, Sara, Sebastian, Anthony, Martha and Jon were all pulled back.

Their powers were lost underground, anything that exceeded 7 feet meant they could not see, therefore could not guard. Just as well then that Archangel Gabriel needed them at the other side of the tunnel.

Archangel Michael spoke to Angie once again.

*Remember, don't leave the safety of the church.*

She didn't realise that this included the series of tunnels that ran underneath the old church.

It was 3.15 pm (1515).

# Chapter Seventy-One

*Pathetic. Look at you. You couldn't even make it to the door without collapsing in a heap. Is your throat closing, do you feel a tightness around your neck. Baboom, baboom, listen to that old ticker of yours. You'll be joining us soon, Fioravanti. We are done with you for now. You've served your purpose. You've served me.*

The tightness around Monsignor Fioravanti's throat loosened, his breathing slowed and his pounding heart stopped rattling against his chest. He felt the darkness leave him and was able to pull himself out of the bramble bush that had been his resting place for the past 5 minutes or so.

He held on to the Rosary beads that were hanging around his neck and started to pray, to beg for mercy. He was submerged in guilt, a guilt that he had tried desperately hard to bury all those years ago. He knew he had done wrong back when he was a priest; he knew that desiring those children had been a sign of weakness.

He knew. He reached into his pocket and pulled out the silver letter opener. He touched the tip, it was sharp and would do the job. He looked skyward and begged once again for forgiveness.

*"Mi benedica padre perché ho peccato."* (Bless me father for I have sinned).

That's when he plunged the 9 inch silver letter opener into the right side of his neck, below the lower jaw angle. His aim was perfect. The blow cut the right jugular external vein and damaged the right carotid commune artery, causing severe soft tissue damage. His legs were first to give then, as he fell backwards into the bramble bush again, he heard the dark one once more.

*Questo è dove inizia la tua vita. (This is where you start your life)* The dark one continued to goad.

*The penchant you have for children will be rewarded when I next see you, Fioravanti, as will the murder of Dr Mattheson. You did well driving him out to that quiet spot. Clever that you drove out there the day before in your own car. Well fucking planned. Quite the devious cunt, aren't you, Fioravanti?*

He heard the gurgling sound of the blood. He didn't really feel the pain. He had no regrets.

Death would be a blessing. It would free him from guilt and now, at last, he could be judged by the only being that really mattered. His maker. His God.

Monsignor Fioravanti's lights went out.

McGinty Dubois and Bruette left his side and drifted back to the dark side. They still had work to do and they knew exactly who their next target would be. The odds were turning, very much in their favour.

# Chapter Seventy-Two

The tunnel was surprisingly large, thought Don. It was about 10 feet in height and roughly 6 feet wide, he estimated. He walked side by side next to Karen. In front of him was Father Burley and Angelo. Angie took up the rear. The floor beneath them was soft, not muddy but soft enough to leave footprints.

The tunnel was well-lit and had a musty smell about it, the kind you find in second-hand bookstores, thought Don. Angelo and Father Burley were deep in conversation whilst Angie remained vigilant, turning around every now and again to make sure they weren't being followed.

"I promise, when all this is over, we can go on holiday somewhere and just get away from it all. Just us two and Gabe. Here, let me have him." Don handed Gabriel to Karen. He was awake and mesmerised by the bright lights that lined the tunnel every ten yards or so.

"Yeh, a holiday would be good. Maybe somewhere warm and away from the public eye. India perhaps?"

"India sounds just perfect, lover," Angie told him as she cradled Gabriel and made baby noises to him.

"Okay, things get a little tricky here." Father Burley had turned to face Karen, Don and Angie.

"It may be best if we go single-file."

Don looked ahead and could see how the width of the tunnel narrowed. Its height remained the same. About 40 yards ahead, Don could make out a door, hopefully a door that would lead them all to the outside world, he thought.

Gabriel was now responding to Karen's baby sounds. He was wide awake which, thought Don meant he'd be hungry.

Father Burley was stood in front of the twin doors, they ran from the ceiling of the tunnel to the floor and were made of a strong wood.

"I may need some help here opening them," Father Burley said, turning towards Don. He seemed the obvious choice given that he fit the bill, being male and not in a high position of power such as Angelo.

"Okay, I'm coming," Don said as Angelo leaned back against the wall so Don could pass.

That's when all the lights went out in the tunnel.

# Chapter Seventy-Three
# The Tunnel

Working on the railroads and mines back in the 1850's was tough going. The back-breaking work put food on the table for many families and brought together men from different backgrounds. Around the time, Chinese immigrants arrived in Idaho and it wasn't long until they began to dig underground tunnels to smuggle merchandise between buildings, gamble, and create even a few drug dens where opium was smoked and money was exchanged.

Work had started on St Bartholomew's Church in 1855. Dingbang Guō led a team of twelve workers. He hired family member, Shaozu Xióng, as his foreman and blueprints were modified by an architect friend of theirs, Qian Yè. They, along with their co-workers, worked 12 hour days and when the sun went down they each returned and worked at excavating the tunnels under darkness.

The longest of the tunnels was where a secret chamber was built, a small box-like room that could house up to five adults. Building underneath a place of worship meant they could visit after the church had closed its doors. They would make their way via a manhole some 200 yards away from the church, and once in the small box room, they would gamble, drink and smoke into the small hours.

As the years rolled by, the Chinese would use the room to stash their opium and also nuggets of gold stolen by fellow Chinese immigrants who were working the mines. In 1869, some 14 years after they had helped build the local Catholic Church, Guō, Xióng and Yè were arrested and charged and, subsequently, hanged for their part in the massive smuggling ring.

The Catholic Church laid claim to the tunnels and had them reinforced with brick some years later. And here they still remained to this day. Five tunnels, one of which housed the secret box room. A room that was only known to a few. The original blueprint was framed and hung on the wall inside the room. Pencil marks drawn by the hand of Qian Yè highlighted the genius plan.

Father Burley knew where the secret chamber was. The dark one had shown him in his dreams. Those same dreams where he told him about the Antichrist who would be making an appearance soon. Those same dreams where he was told that he had a duty to kill the Antichrist.

The one they called Don.

# Chapter Seventy-Four

Don felt his shirt collar being pulled as the lights went off. He heard the mechanical sound and the sliding of brick on brick. He felt the pain on his nose immediately and, for a brief moment, the darkness that had enveloped him was painted with flashing stars. He felt himself being thrown and the fear of falling in darkness intensified as he heard the voice for the first time.

It was a raspy, phlegmy type of voice that was, it appeared, taking great pleasure. Its accent would change but the sound of its voice remained the same. Irish, American and European, French, Don thought. At times all three would become one; all laughing and all repeating the same words over and over as Don lay on the floor trying to come to terms with the pain on the bridge of his nose and the fact that he had been taken away from Karen and Gabriel.

The pain subsided quickly when he thought of Karen and Gabe. Nothing else seemed to matter, least of all a bloodied, broken nose.

"You will never see them again. First, I will kill you then I will kill your child in front of your whore. I will bury her under the floorboards with Bettie Page, the bitch that made me kill"

Tommy McGinty had taken over Father Burley, albeit for less than a minute. Next it was the turn of Clément Dubois.

*"Nous devons tuer la trinité et vous êtes la trinité."*

"He does not understand, Dubois. Let me interject." The dark one was back.

*"Vi måste döda treenigheten och du är treenigheten."*

Don recognised the language straight away. It was a language that he had to learn as part of his former role working for the Swedish law firm. Translated it meant, 'We must kill the trinity and you are the trinity'. So, Don did what he felt compelled to do. He recited the Lord's Prayer.

*"Vår fader som är i Himmelen. Helgat varde Ditt namn. Tillkomme Ditt Rike. Ske Din vilja, såsom i Himmelen så ock på Jorden. Vårt dagliga bröd giv oss idag Och förlåt oss våra skulder såsom ock vi förlåta dem oss skyldiga äro och inled*

*oss icke i frestelse utan fräls oss ifrån ondo. Ty Riket är Ditt och Makten och Härligheten i Evighet.* Amen."

"Praying to yourself is not going to help you."

Don repeated the prayer. The dark one continued to talk over him.

*"Döda dig själv, livet av dig, döda dig själv. Ucciderti.* Kill yourself."

Still repeating, still being talked over. Don was then pulled from the floor, once again by his shirt collar. He was held against the cold brick wall, nothing in front of him but darkness. He felt the breathing on his face first then he smelled the breath. A putrid stench of excrement and rotting flesh. That's when the dark one spoke in the voice of Katy.

*"Jag älskar dig, Don. Ta mig tillbaka."*

He repeated the words in Katy's voice, this time in English.

"I love you, Don. Take me back."

Don then felt a hand on his groin. The hand rubbed him and Katy's voice returned.

"You want it don't you, baby. You want your baby's lips wrapped around you."

Don was pinned against the wall. His muscles were stiff and cramp was setting in. The voice of Katy continued. The hand on his groin pulled down his zipper.

"In my mouth, baby. Just like you used to."

Don was the only one to witness the light in the corner of the room. It formed from a small pinprick of light to an orb about the size of a melon. It was translucent and inside it words were appearing. They said, *The verse, recite.*

"Shoots bullets across the sky," Don said

Katy's voice became weaker.

"I see them flash by."

The smell faded. Don continued.

"There's only one colour beyond the duvet where there is no night, no darkness. Light beyond the realms of understanding."

The grip on him loosened and he slid down the wall.

Katy came back.

"Shoots bullets across the sky, I see them flash by. There's only one colour beyond the duvet where there is no night, no darkness. Light beyond the realms of understanding."

Katy was moaning. She was crying. She was shouting.

"No, no, no."

The rasping of phlegm in the throat was back.

"You will cease and you will cease now."

Don could sense the dark one was trembling. He could hear it in the voice so he continued to recite. Each time the translucent ball would grow and offer light that would take away the darkness. Each time the dark one would weaken. As he weakened, Don gained in strength, in wisdom. Don looked towards the orb again and saw the scrolling text. He knew he had to read it aloud.

"Most glorious Prince of the Heavenly Armies, Saint Michael the Archangel, defend us in our battle against principalities and powers, against the rulers of this world of darkness, against the spirits of wickedness in the high places. In the Name of Jesus Christ, our God and Lord, strengthened by the intercession of the Immaculate Virgin Mary, Mother of God, of Blessed Michael the Archangel, of the Blessed Apostles Peter and Paul and all the Saints and powerful in the holy authority of our ministry, we confidently undertake to repulse the attacks and deceits of the devil.

"God arises. His enemies are scattered and those who hate Him flee before Him. As smoke is driven away, so are they driven as wax melts before the fire, so the wicked perish at the presence of God. We drive you from us, whoever you may be, unclean spirits, all satanic powers, all infernal invaders, all wicked legions, assemblies and sects.

"In the Name and by the power of Our Lord Jesus Christ, may you be snatched away and driven from the Church of God and from the souls made to the image and likeness of God and redeemed by the Precious Blood of the Divine Lamb. God, the Father commands you. God, the Son commands you. God, the Holy Ghost commands you."

Light filled the room and Don caught a glimpse of the evil one. He had the faces of many and the accents too. He saw Katy in the dark one. She looked at Don and briefly opened her mouth before fading into the face of McGinty, Dubois, Bruette, Fioravanti and then, finally, the Devil himself.

"Christ, God's Word made flesh, commands you. He who to save our race outdone through your envy, humbled Himself, becoming obedient even unto death. He who has built His Church on the firm rock and declared that the gates of hell shall not prevail against Her, because He will dwell with Her all days even to the end of the world. The sacred Sign of the Cross commands you, as does also the power of the mysteries of the Christian Faith.

"The glorious Mother of God, the Virgin Mary, commands you. She who by her humility and from the first moment of her Immaculate Conception crushed your proud head. The faith of the holy Apostles Peter and Paul, and of the other Apostles commands you. I command you. Be gone."

The light exploded and the Devil made one last attempt at defeating Don.

Scratches appeared on Don's neck. His head felt the crown of thorns being pushed down hard and the palms of his hands started to bleed.

"What sort of father are you to leave your son dying?" It was a weak voice from the Devil.

"I am the light beyond the realms of understanding. I am the stars that shine, that give hope. I am the seven sisters. I am the thumbprint in the sky and I am the answer. I am the mirror and I reflect His light. Be gone."

The crown of thorns loosened then crumbled to the floor and the Devil screamed one last time.

"I will be back and I will claim what is mine. I will be born again and you will kneel before me. All will kneel before me."

Then, he was gone.

Then, Father Burley coughed.

Then the sliding brick door opened.

# Chapter Seventy-Five
# The Signs

"From the 7 of January you had been shown the signs. Don," Angie Jakobs told him. She continued.

"Every single sign you were shown led to the present. You missed a lot of them and they knew that you would take some convincing. They chose you for reason Don and you have to be aware that this is not the end. They now know that you have the ability to recognise the signs and you will know when it's time to take action again."

Don and Karen listened attentively. Pope John Paul III then explained.

"Miss Jakobs is right, Don. There was a time when we thought that Gabriel had been chosen, we now know this was a decoy. Nothing is simple with God, nothing is simple with His message. God chose you because He knew He could work through you. He chose Karen for you too because He had already chose the place of the event, here in Idaho.

"He works in mysterious ways, Don, and He always gets what He wants. Look at the ones He took in this process. Katy, for example. She had plans to kill others, Don. The fact that she didn't add you to her list during her killing spree was because God intervened. Yes, you suffered heartache but it was nothing compared to what you may have suffered had He have not intervened."

"Katy? What has she got to do with all of this?" Don asked.

Pope John Paul III then handed Don a copy of *Dagens Nyheter*, a Swedish national newspaper. Don couldn't quite believe his eyes when he saw a photo of Katy on the front page.

The headline read, *Stockholm Kvinna ansvariga för de lokala slayings* (Stockholm Woman Responsible For Local Slayings). Don read how Katy had killed three men and how she, herself, had died in a fire in Birmingham. He read about the different identities she used and about the search of her apartment where police had found wigs, calling cards and surgical attire that had helped her cover her tracks and avoid detection for so long.

The motive, according to the *Dagens Nyheter*, was Katy's hatred of men. The newspaper was thorough and it delved into her background and the police's assumption that she had travelled to England to seek revenge on a former lover. He continued reading in disbelief.

"Johansson was born in Bergen in neighbouring Norway. She moved to Stockholm after her divorce from Norwegian businessman, Gunnar Pedersen, in 2009. Johansson used many aliases. Her employer, Swedish Healthcare, knew her as Novalie Gustafsson; her local gymnasium had her on record as Hilda Henriksson; and her library, where she had taken books on the subject of identity theft, had her name as Cornelia Lindholm."

Don could not believe what he was reading. This was about a different woman, surely? It certainly didn't seem like the Katy that he knew and once loved.

There was more.

"Johansson had been interviewed by the police regarding the death of her former boyfriend, Rikard Phillipson (26), who was allegedly stabbed to death multiple times by an intruder. At the time, Johansson had claimed that she had witnessed the murder and had fled the scene through fear of her own safety. It is now known that Johansson killed Phillipson after she had learned that he had wanted to end their relationship which had been described by neighbours as 'volatile'.

"A private journal found in Johansson's apartment showed evidence that she had meticulously planned the murder weeks in advance. Phillipson's next door neighbour and English tutor, Matthew Larkin, told the *Dagens Nyheter*, 'I'd hear them argue a lot. It was usually after they had returned home from a night out somewhere. Katy had some jealousy issues and Rikard had told me that he had planned to end things with her because of her behaviour'. Larkin was visiting relatives in England at the time of the murder."

Don was flabbergasted. He put down the newspaper and tried to stand. His legs, however, were too weak. He sat again.

Pope John Paul III then turned to Karen.

"And Lex Brampton. He too was out for revenge, Karen. He too was guided by God to your ranch. It was God's message to Archangel Michael that Angie would save the day."

"Why would God want to put me and Don in danger?" Karen asked.

"He knew that the bond between you and Angie was strong. There was no danger. Everything had been planned down to the last minute detail. It always is with God," Pope John Paul III told her.

Angie then took over the conversation.

"You see, Karen, us meeting all those years ago was planned. Brampton had served his time but he was not repentant. God gave him many chances but he chose to align himself with the Devil, the same way Katy did."

"But why go to all the trouble of bringing Don and I together. Surely, if God wanted somebody dead he could just involve them in some sort of accident or something?" Karen had a point, so Pope John III explained to her.

"It's a valid point, Karen, and one that I struggled with at first that was until I realised that everything that has happened to both you and Don is just part of the story. I believe that there is more to come and God needed to work through you both because the next chapter of this story will test your faith to such an extent that the reward in belief will save a lot of people's lives."

"But why us?" Don asked.

"Only God can answer that, Don. He gets blamed for many things, starvation, the murder of innocents, accidents that involve children, all those that are out of his control. He, with the help of those around you, the angels that watch over you, watch over every other single human. They often send signs but we, as humans, fail to recognise those signs.

"You, Don, have the ability to read those signs. You always have had but you chose to put them down to coincidence or use rationale to make them seem as if they meant nothing. The poem you wrote, Don, it was you reaching out; it was you wanting an answer to what was going on around you. What you wrote was prophetic, Don. Had your verse been found thousands of years ago, then I can say with certainty that it would have ended up in the Bible."

Pope John Paul III had read many scriptures both before and after alterations were made, and he really meant what he had just told Don; although equating Don's verse to a scripture was intended to keep him from the truth about the *Mankind documents*. He really wanted to tell them all that what they witnessed wasn't stars moving.

He wanted to tell them all about the visitations throughout history and the significance of Don writing a poem about the seven sisters, or Ursa Major as he preferred to call it. He knew he couldn't though. Many Popes before him had brought the *Mankind* knowledge to their graves; he had made the vow to do the same.

"So, if this is just part of the story, what else is there?" Karen asked.

"That I don't know but I do know that when it happens, you will both know. I can say this, however, the Devil has not finished his work and he will return. That will be your test of faith because no matter how old you will be upon his return, it will be your duty to seek him and banish him again. You will be doing God's work."

Cardinal Abandonato entered the room.

"Your Holiness, I'm sorry to interrupt but you need to come and see this."

Angie, Karen and Don had been invited over to the Vatican to meet with the Pope. 3 weeks had passed since the tunnel incident in Idaho.

"It may be a good idea if your guests see it too," Cardinal Abandonato added.

# Chapter Seventy-Six

The bombs had gone off within hours of one another. It was precision timing. The targets had all been Catholic churches. First to explode had been St Eugenia's Church in central Stockholm. It had been closed to the public for the past 3 weeks due to renovations. It was being reported on *CNN News* that there were some fatalities.

A couple of construction workers who had returned to the church after hours to collect some tools were missing. 20 minutes later, the second explosion, this time in Melbourne, Australia. St Francis' Church on Little Lonsdale Street was ripped apart, according to CNN, by a 'huge explosive device'. Mother Mary Catholic Church in Istanbul, Turkey, had been next in line. The news anchor reporting had claimed that three local children had been seen near the church at the time of the explosion.

Next in line, some 10 minutes after the explosion in Turkey, was the Cathedral Basilica of Our Lady of the Rosary, a Cathedral in Rosario, a province of Santa Fe, Argentina. It was unknown if there were any fatalities or injuries. Finally, 20 minutes after the blast in Argentina, St Olav's Catholic Church in Akersveien, Norway, exploded. There were at least two known fatalities.

No announcement had been made by any terrorist organisation. Nobody had made the obvious connection except for Pope John III and Angie Jakobs who, along with Karen, Don and Cardinal Abandonato, were watching the events unfold on the 52 inch plasma screen in the media room of the Vatican.

"It's started," Pope John III said.

"What has?" Don asked.

"The next chapter," Angie replied.

"How can you be so sure?" Don asked.

"Look at the countries where the explosions occurred. Look at the order in which they exploded," Pope John Paul III replied before adding, "Sweden, Australia, Turkey, Argentina, Norway."

Recognition formed on Don's face. "Satan," he said. Pope John Paul III looked at Angie, she seemed troubled.

He whispered in Cardinal Abandonato's ear, "Get me the Majestic-12 documents." Then told the room, "I'd like to speak with Angie alone."

# Chapter Seventy-Seven
## One Month Later
## Rhonda's Café — Geelong, Australia

"But it's impossible. Dan is going to crack the shits," Tayla Williamson told her best friend Collette Moore.

"Well, you have some explaining to do. Come on, Tay, you can level with me."

"How could you think such a thing, Collette? We've been friends for years, you know I would never do anything like that." Tayla started to cry.

"I'm trying to understand, Tay, I really am, but you have to face facts. What about Brett Austin, I know you've always had a thing for him and you two did meet up for coffee a few months back. How do I know if you haven't been meeting up once or twice since then?"

"Because I haven't and Brett just needed to talk." Tayla was still sobbing.

"Then why did you keep it from Dan. If your date with Brett was harmless, why not tell your husband?"

"It wasn't a fucking date. He just needed a shoulder to cry on."

"So, what are you going to tell Dan?" Collette asked.

"The truth. Okay, he may go mental at first but he will come around."

"We ain't living in Biblical times, Tay. In any event, give it a couple of more weeks before you say anything, it's probably nothing."

"Collette, I'm three weeks overdue, Dan is sterile. I hardly think this is nothing."

Tayla burst into tears and Collette moved to the seat next to her. They were sat outside a coffee shop in Geelong.

"We can work through this, Tay. I'm sorry I upset you. If you think I was suspicious then how do you think Dan will react?"

Tayla said nothing. She looked out to the ocean. Families were together on the beach, lovers were walking hand in hand. Everyone but her seemed to be blissfully happy. She was pregnant.

Seven pregnancy kits had shown her.

Neither Tayla nor Collette noticed the crow above them. It had been circling them for some time. Watching, listening.

The life inside Tayla Williamson was beginning its journey, its transition, its re-entry into the world. Once born *She* would be protected. Four fallen angels would be waiting for *Her*. The same fallen angels who helped conceive Her. Tommy McGinty, Clément Dubois, and Haskin Bruette.

News of *Her* pending arrival had been spread across the world during the past month or so.

As always, nothing was black and white. The past month three events had sent out a stark message to the world. Religious leaders from all denominations were already predicting the end of times. The five bombs planted and detonated at the Catholic churches across the world was the initial message. It was an announcement to the religious leaders, it was letting them know who was behind it all.

Next came the six fires across Salt Lake City, Utah that had seen six Latter Day Saints churches burned to the ground. Then the six Hollywood actors who had died on set whilst filming at a hangar in Burbank, California. They were filming a scene for a science fiction movie, *The Ariel Incident,* when a hydraulic door fell on them.

Crew members tried, in vain, to save them but all died instantly from massive head and internal injuries. Among the actors killed was Karen Crawford's ex-lover, Lincoln Lewis, he was just 57. He left behind a widow and three children. To date, nobody knew why the Treble Swing Hydraulic System malfunctioned.

And, finally, the six bullets that hit and killed Pope John Paul III as he waved to crowds from the balcony of the Vatican last week.

# Chapter Seventy-Eight

News of Pope John Paul's death shocked and saddened Karen and Don.

They'd watched the video footage that was broadcast over a week ago. The shooter was among the crowd. The security was lax and Riccardo Mancini had been able to fire off six rounds, each one accurate. The fifth entered Angelo Landro's right upper forehead, half an inch to the right of the anterior midline.

It was the moment that the lights went out for Angelo, despite Mancini managing to fire one last bullet into the chest of the Pope as he fell to the floor of the balcony.

Pope John Paul III was interned just 8 days after his death. Cardinal Abandonato removed the Pope's Ring of the Fisherman from his finger, then ceremonially crushed it with the ceremonial silver hammer in the presence of members of the College of Cardinals. It was a ritual that was centuries old. Leaders from around the world gathered and outside the Vatican, huge masses stood with heads bowed to pay their final respects.

A lone crow looked down upon the crowd of mourners from its perch on an adjacent rooftop. It bowed its head before flying off towards the south, just a dozen yards before it vanished into its vortex, making the trip to Kawarren, Australia in just under 7 minutes.

\*\*\*

They both woke to the sound of the phone ringing. Angie was on her way. She had been looking after Gabriel because she thought both Karen and Don needed some time alone after all of the recent events. She also wanted to tell them both that news of a newborn was on the horizon; that news had come to her in her sleep and she knew that it was some way connected with Don. She also knew that the newborn was somehow connected to recent events but couldn't quite figure out why.

Archangel Gabriel knew, as did the guardian angels that watched over Don, Karen and Gabe, as did the guardian angels that watched over Tayla and Dan Williamson.

***

Tayla's guardian angels were with her now, guiding her and sending out light and strength to her. She was going to wait one more week then tell Dan that she was pregnant. During that time, she was going to read up on couples who had managed to create life despite one, or both, of them being sterile. She would, if she had to, ask Dan to go back for more checks to determine the level of his sterility.

He'd been told many years ago that he was 100% sterile. His doctor had put it down to a random genetic abnormality. At first, Dan started to envy friends and relatives who announced their various pregnancies; this soon faded though, particularly when he met Tayla and learned that she didn't want children.

***

Angie arrived with Gabriel. Both Don and Karen met her as she came up the driveway, both itching to see their child again. It was only 24 hours since they had last seen him but it was the very first time that they had been separated since his birth. The journey from Angie's ranch, albeit short, had sent him to sleep.

Angie spoke of the dreams and her visions. There was a baby on the way, she told them, and they would be hearing the news soon. Karen sent an SMS to Bella, more out of curiosity, while Don sent a text message to Jake, more out of wanting to know how the football back in England was going. Nobody thought to send Dan or Tayla a message.

Why would they?

***

It circled the garden before landing next to an upstairs open window. Inside was Dan Williamson, his head in his hands, his shoulders bobbing up and down as tears flowed. Tayla was kneeling by his side, she too was crying.

Both angels looked at the crow and smiled. The crow returned a blink then rested in silence on the window ledge.

Tayla was, in fact, 7 weeks pregnant. She never made any connection to the dream she had just over 7 weeks ago. It had been in the mid-afternoon. Dan had been in Melbourne on business and Tayla had gone for an afternoon nap. She woke after around 2 hours.

Her dream was about her long-time friend, Brett Austin. He, in the dream, had held her down on the bed and had his way with her. If Tayla would have checked her arms underneath her bicep, she would have noticed the bruises. If Tayla would have woken during her dream, she would have noticed the dark mass on top of her body, pinning her arms to the bed and entering her.

If she had not have enjoyed the dream so much, she may have even attempted to push him off. Brett was hot though. She had desired him for some time but would never have slept with him. Marriage to Tayla was sacred and she could have never have cheated on Dan. Dreams didn't count though.

The hands and feet were developing on the embryo inside Tayla Williamson. It still had a small tail and had doubled in size over the past 7 days, it was now the size of a blueberry. Its hemispheres were growing in its brain while its liver was throwing out red blood cells, waiting until its bone marrow had formed so it could take over this role.

Tayla's guardian angels, Amelia and Lacey, would, over the coming months, send out signs in the hope that Tayla would see them and heed them. They could not interfere in the process of her pregnancy.

Archangel Gabriel pulled them back, all of them.

"And so it is," he told them, before adding, "We need to prepare for the months ahead. The end of times are upon us and only one person can carry out the act of sacrificing the child."

They all knew who had to carry out the sacrifice. It was Don. Archangel Gabriel told them all that Don would take some convincing.

He would have to kill the child, his niece, on New Year's Eve, 2019. The child, although human in appearance, was demonic and its time on earth heralded the beginning of the end for mankind.

They had just over 3 years to prepare themselves and Don.

***

As each day passed, the embryo grew in strength; all knowledgeable, all powerful. *She* knew *She* was safe in the womb of Tayla Williamson. *She* knew *She* would need help surviving once *She* was born, and *She* knew that Don Williamson was being prepared.

For now, *She* would grow.

For now, *She* would sleep. For now.

## THE END

# Epilogue

Before *she* was born, *she* knew.

*Her* mother, Tayla, was just a vessel. She'd kill her when the time was right.

*She'd* also kill Tayla's husband, Dan, the pathetic excuse of a man who, despite knowing he was not the biological father, stayed with her until the end. Don, and that cunt whore of a wife of his would be next, an uncle and step-aunt who had, in *her* previous life, left *her* to die on the 46th floor of the Hilton Hotel.

In time, *she* vowed, *she'd* go back to Sweden and continue where *she* left off.

It was December 2019 and *she* was in *her* third year on earth. Already *she* could think like an adult. Lindsey Williamson took her first steps when *she* was just an 8-month-old. *She* had great focus and exceptional problem-solving skills, was curious and always alert. At the age of 9-months, *she* was speaking clear, perfect sentences. *She* even preferred to be left alone, enjoying the company of *herself* more than other children *her* age.

*Her* high level of alertness made *her* aware of *her* environment. *She* quickly recognised and bonded with family members, always making eye contact with them very early on, and rewarding them with a smile and other signs of recognition, by cooing, or waving *her* fists. By the age of 14-months, *she* could feel both, positive and negative emotions quite strongly and had the ability to learn new languages, only *she* was unaware of this. *Her* brain was developing faster than normal, much faster.

The dark one had already set the wheels in motion, soon the earth would be *hers*.

*She* had recruited 57-year-old Wang Xiu Ying, a scientist who worked in the field of virology in Wuhan, China. Ying didn't feel the saliva enter his mouth as he slept. Lindsey Williamson had been visiting candidates in her sleep from the day she was born. *She* had this ability, *She* had passed it on to *Him*.

Wang Xiu Ying would carry it.

Wang Xiu Ying would spread it before dying of it. As would his wife.

As would their 33-year-old son. Then others would.

Millions of others.

Confusion would cause the people to revolt against the governments. As the death count would rise, the people would come together to overthrow their leaders, leaving the door wide open for *Her*.

Soon, *She* would be in control and the global governments would kneel before *her*.

Finally.

# A Message Within a Message

*And the great dragon was thrown down, that ancient serpent, who is called the devil and Satan, the deceiver of the whole world—he was thrown down to the earth, and his angels were thrown down with him.*

*And I heard a loud voice in heaven, saying, "Now the salvation and the power and the kingdom of our God and the authority of his Christ have come, for the accuser of our brothers has been thrown down, who accuses them day and night before our God. And they have conquered him by the blood of the Lamb and by the word of their testimony, for they loved not their lives even unto death. Therefore, rejoice, O heavens and you who dwell in them! But woe to you, O earth and sea, for the devil has come down to you in great wrath, because he knows that his time is short!"*

Revelation 12:9-12

\*\*\*

**What Angie Jacobs was shown**
**Section from the *Mankind Documents*, Original text for Revelation 12:9-12 Vatican City Papal Vault.**

*We came down in our own creature-like form, one of us rebelled and never returned with us, his human name shall be known as the Devil, Satan, the Dark One, the deceiver of the star system, Ursa Major—he absconded on one of our many visits down to the blue planet known as Earth. His location and place of dwelling is in the Unita Basin area of Utah in the United States. He resides there with his seed.*

*The indigenous people of the Unita Basin will describe the entity as a shape-shifter and a wolf-like figure. He will be capable of many feats. He can travel in and out and can cross oceans and other great distances in the blink of a human eye. He will send out vague messages to those who use technology in future years.*

*The leader of Ursa Major announced, "He has rebelled against us and shall remain on Earth, he will walk as a human and not as one of us. He will die as a human but will have the ability, like us, to be born again. Others will be born from his seed but will not have immortality. When death occurs they will roam out of sight until technology finds a way to make communication.*

*"His human-like figures shall be both male and female and will cause divide among humanity. His time will be short and we will intervene if the beings of planet Earth need our assistance. We will do this in stages as not to invoke fear into the Earthlings.*

*"In time, we will send down messengers to guide humankind, they shall be invisible to all but those few with a special ability, only those who can nurture the sounds and signs of the messengers. They will see them as we do, with wings. They will work for us and with us, only they will not know who we are until they are ready to know.*

*"The science of coincidence will keep most at bay, it will be our great ally, as will other stories put in place to hide our identity. Humanity is not ready for us but they will be soon. More of our vehicles will visit as we prepare to announce our existence to the planet, an existence that will be, over the years, drip fed to the people. We will always be watching over you and will reveal ourselves when you most need us. The Universe is listening to you."*

### Ursa Major Instruction for Mankind

\*\*\*

### \*\*\*COMING SOON\*\*\*
### NO OTHER MAN ~ THE SEQUEL

Don, Karen and Gabriel were flying Qantas Business Class. They'd land at Tullamarine Airport, Melbourne, then make the 2-hour journey in a rented car to Kawarren. Angie was flying in a day later, on New Year's Eve, 2019.

It was a journey neither of them wanted to make but they had been prepared well by the angels that followed them. Both Don and Karen now knew the signs. They were subtle signs but the past 3 years or so, they had learned how to read them, what was coincidence and what wasn't.

They were flying over Kazakhstan when Karen asked Don if he was ready.

"I'm ready," he told her.

Kazakhstan airspace had picked the object up on their radars, it was manoeuvring at speeds beyond anything that could have been man-made. They radioed the pilot of Qantas Q706 to ask if he could *make a visible* with the vehicle that was currently in a 9 o'clock position and defying the laws of gravity.

Flight Captain, Michael Lovesey, who had been flying commercial aircraft for 17 years, radioed them back, excitedly.

"I see it, it's a tic-tac shape," he told them.

Arun Kumar scribbled *Tic-tac* onto a notepad as he followed the object on his radar, all the time keeping in communication with Captain Lovesey.

It was 11.11 pm.

***

CPSIA information can be obtained
at www.ICGtesting.com
Printed in the USA
LVHW052226140723
752120LV00005B/78